SAM CRESCENT

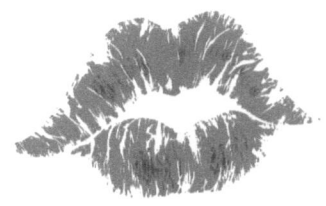

EVERNIGHT PUBLISHING ®

www.evernightpublishing.com

SAM CRESCENT

#

Crude Hill High, 3

Sam Crescent

Copyright © 2021

Chapter One
Ashley

I wasn't used to being important.

All my life, I'd been told how useless I was. How I'd destroyed my mother's figure. Stopped her from finding the perfect man. How men didn't want a woman with a kid. Before we moved to Crude Hill, I either hid out in my old bedroom when she had guests or left. I'd spent many nights camped out at a park, or down by one of the lakes while she pretended to be a single woman.

I did all of that out of love.

I loved my mother.

So much.

She was the worst and best person in my life. I loved her more than anything. Then *he* came along. A man with smooth words, and within a matter of months, we'd gone from living a life of struggle to luxury. He was a married man with a family. He didn't require me to leave. Knew all about the daughter, and for a short time, everything was perfect. Or as perfect as it could have been. He'd told me straight, I wasn't going to get anything out of the arrangement that he wasn't willing to give. While he had my mother eating out of the palm of his hand, he had a whole host of other plans for me.

Strange how life turned out.

The same man who held the threat of my life over my head was the same man whose daughter I befriended. I didn't do it on purpose. Emily was ... everything. She was the best friend I never had before. She didn't have to stick up for me, but she did.

She was the first and last person to put her life on the line for mine. It was because of her that I was alive.

Staring across my room, I couldn't tear my gaze away from the door. I had no choice but to focus on something. I would be sick if I didn't.

Earl Valentine.

Emily said she'd seen him. I'd hoped she'd been wrong, but now, for whatever reason, I'd been taken. I was locked away on a boat. Damn it. I hated this.

Why did people think it was so cool to go out in open water?

It was fucking scary.

Sickness swirled within my gut. All I wanted to do was throw myself overboard and vomit.

I didn't.

I couldn't.

The door was firmly locked from the outside.

Fucking fuckers.

I hadn't eaten in hours.

What was this game? More importantly, what was *his* game? I'd met Earl once, and I couldn't even be sure if it was the same man.

Seven years ago, at the party that had changed my

life, I'd danced with a man. He'd held me, stared at me, and for a short time, I'd felt like the only person who had existed in his world.

Was it the same man?

I'd thought about him often over the years.

This was what I'd turned into. A woman so desperate for attention and affection, she'd imagined a man into some kind of being.

I sucked.

Big time.

After running fingers through my hair, I glanced around the room while wrapping my arms back around my legs and keeping my body right. With how unstable everything was, I didn't want to let go of anything.

The water.

Why?

Ugh. I was going to be sick.

As if on cue, the door lock flicked open, and Earl Valentine stood in the doorway. Seven years was a long time, but I would recognize those shoulders and hands anywhere. The scar down his face wasn't scary or ugly, but sexy, showing how dangerous he actually was.

Neither of us spoke.

I watched him.

Waiting.

Terrified.

Curious.

I was a lot of things all mixed into one.

He was right here, in front of me, well, a few feet away.

"You're awake."

"I want to go home. This isn't funny."

Earl smiled, but it wasn't a nice one. Something sinister and dark lay behind his gaze, promising. I didn't want to know this man too intimately.

There was a lot more to this man than what met the eye. After years of seeing my mother move from dick to dick, I'd gotten a pretty good read on them. I recognized a keeper, a loser, an asshole, and the man you really shouldn't catch the eye of. Earl Valentine was one of those latter men.

"You think I'm doing this for your amusement?"

"What do you want?"

"A lot of things."

"Last time I heard, it was a cherry you wanted to pop." I hated speaking the words, but I wasn't going to cower from this man.

Seven years, Emily and I had formed a life together. She was sad most of the time, but there were always rare sparks of light in our darkness.

I loved her like a sister, and right now, being trapped on a boat with this man, it would leave Emily alone.

Earl tilted his head to the side, and I realized I'd surprised him.

Good. I'd grown up.

Since I'd been alone with Emily, we only had each other to count on. No men. No fathers. No mothers. Just the two of us, and we'd been doing quite well on our own.

Looking at Earl now, even though I didn't want to believe it, I just knew our time together had come to an end. I was stupid and naïve to have thought it would last a little longer. Happiness was always rare and short-lived.

Having a mother like mine taught me that.

There were times she'd feel guilty for the way she treated me, and for a week tops, she'd be the perfect mother, attentive until boredom hit her, or she believed she'd done what was needed.

Either way, she'd hated me by the end of it.

I was still alive. She was six feet under. Her thirst for a good life had caught up with her and nearly ended the both of us.

"Where's Emily?"

"I believe right about now she's back in Crude Hill."

This made me tense. "No."

"Yes."

"No, they can't take her back. She'll be killed if she goes back there." I knew all about the contract the four Monsters had made to keep Emily and me safe. Even though they were completely in love with her, they couldn't have her. Their fathers made sure of it.

It was why I'd gotten to live. They'd bargained her life and mine.

The thing about Crude Hill and the Monsters' Crew was that they had a rule. Once a man was a traitor or a rat, everyone in his family was taken down with them. No one was allowed to survive.

I was as good as dead because of my mother's connection to Emily's father. We both should be dead. Rotting away somewhere. Instead, we got seven years.

"This isn't funny," I said.

"I'm not laughing."

"Then you've got to stop Emily. I know you wanted her virginity once and all of that crap that went with it, but she's not the same person, okay? Please, do not let her get killed. She's my best friend." I hated to beg.

Staring at Earl, I despised feeling desperate enough to ask him to help her, to save her.

"Emily has her hands full, Curves. She doesn't need my help or my interference."

I wanted to hit him. The urge swept through me

like a sick and twisted wave of desire. I held on to it as I stared at him.

At that moment, my stomach decided to make its presence known by growling. It had been too long since I last ate.

"Follow me." He turned and started out the door.

Looking around the room, I tried to think of anything that could be used as a weapon. Nothing came to mind.

"Don't even try. There's nothing you can do, Ashley."

I clenched my hands into fists. This anger wasn't something I was used to.

Taking a deep breath, I followed him out of the cabin and to wherever he wanted to take me. I kept my gaze focused straight ahead.

I was sure the boat was rocking left and right. There were a few times I was convinced a sea monster was bumping the side, wanting to tip us over so he could have a snack.

Yeah, I had a thing for shark movies. Giant sea creatures, anything.

Emily didn't share my enjoyment. I went from the extreme of loving shark movies to being a lover of all things romance. I was a sucker for them. I wasn't a horror kind of girl, though. I couldn't stand them. There was nothing worse than being frightened out of your wits.

We headed out onto the top of said boat, and now I knew it was more of a yacht. The extravagance was clear. The crew didn't talk to me, but they nodded at Earl. He was the one in charge.

We moved to the back of the boat, or was it the front? Either way, it was a deck with a parasol to protect from the hot sun. I was sweating. I hadn't showered, and the clothes I was wearing were designed to take on dreary England. Not this kind of heat.

I was sure I stank. I could feel the sweat trace down my back.

Earl took a seat. I realized he was dressed all in white.

He rested his hands clasped together in front of himself. The power he exuded, even outside in the open air, shocked me. This man was used to getting what he wanted. I couldn't help but wonder if he was so used to getting what he wanted, why did he wait this long to exact revenge?

A virgin was what he wanted.

Emily didn't give herself to him, and he'd lost, big time. As I watched him now, I wondered what the hell he could want. Where did I come in? I was nothing. No one. I wasn't important. I didn't deal with powerful people. All I was good for was keeping an eye on Emily and cooking. I commanded a kitchen. I made those ingredients my bitch.

"Take a seat." He pointed at the chair opposite him.

The last thing I wanted to do was follow orders, but I found myself lowering into the seat provided.

A woman wearing a bikini approached, pouring him something out of a jug.

"A drink?"

"I don't drink."

"It's water, Ashley. You need it."

I nodded at the woman and hoped my nerves didn't show. Earl was the kind of man Emily was used to dealing with, not me. I wasn't used to any of this, and I feared it showed. I didn't want it to show.

He lifted up his drink and took a sip. Once mine was poured, I followed suit. The water was nice, cold, refreshing.

Quickly, I put the glass down. My hand shook, and I hated to show any kind of weakness. Hated this so much.

Earl was watching me again.

His hair had grown out some, I thought. He didn't have long hair, but thick. The length was enough to grab hold of and grip in place as he did … other things. I didn't even know why my thoughts went to sex.

I'd never been the kind of woman to be curious about the opposite sex. After all that my mother went through, I did everything in my power to avoid it.

At least I was still alive.

I hated the way he stared at me. He saw everything, and I didn't have the power to stop him from looking.

Tucking some hair behind my ear, I waited, knowing this wasn't going to go well if I spoke up. All I could think about was Emily. We hadn't been apart before. Seven years was a long time to get to know one another.

Time ticked on by. I couldn't keep looking at him. My gaze went around the boat, and seeing the ocean swirling around us didn't bring me any comfort. A storm. A giant sea monster. We were all as good as dead.

"I can play this game forever," Earl said.

I looked at him. "I'm not playing any game. I'm not here of my own free will. You got me, remember? I don't need to talk. This is all you." The desire to keep on rambling was strong, but I nipped it in the bud. I didn't want to completely irritate him, even though the very thought was fun.

Earl watched me and suddenly leaned forward. On instinct, I jerked back. It wasn't even an intention of doing that, but it happened quite quickly.

"I won't hurt you. You've got no reason to fear me."

I laughed. "No reason to fear you? You've taken me out in the middle of nowhere. I've got no family. All I've got is Emily. I've got every reason to be afraid."

Earl rubbed his hands together. "Then how about we agree I won't hurt you."

"You expect me to believe you?"

"I've never hurt you before."

"I've done nothing to deserve it."

"And you think you're going to end up with me hurting you?"

I licked my lips. My mouth was suddenly dry. I wanted the water but I didn't want to move. This man was dangerous. The last thing I wanted to do was incite his anger.

"I have no idea what you want from me. Why don't you tell me what you want?"

He snapped his fingers, and the people closest to him all started to leave, giving us space.

"I was offered a very precious reward for my compliance, and that was taken from me. Emily is not mine. Never has been. However, I still want my gift."

I stayed perfectly still. "I can't magically grow Emily a hymen."

Earl wrinkled his nose. "I'm not interested in Emily."

"I've never been gifted with genius, Mr. Valentine. You need to come out and tell me what exactly you want from me."

That smile again, only this time, it sent a shiver down my spine.

"Oh, Ashley, I'm very much aware of what I want from you, and if you really thought about it, you'd be as well."

I needed water.

"You're a virgin. Untouched. I've been watching you and Emily for years. Much longer than the Monsters would even begin to imagine. At first, I wanted to take Emily. To hurt her. To ruin her. I know the Monsters are to be feared, but they underestimate me. I earned a great deal of money doing business with them, but I have plenty of money. It's not an object for me." He waved his hand in the air as if it didn't matter. This was spoken by a man who clearly didn't know what it was like to have nothing. To go day to day, wondering when the next paycheck was going to come in. "I want my cherry. I want an untouched woman, and you, Ashley, you're that woman."

****

Earl

Ashley was even more stunning up close than in any of the pictures I'd seen, or videos that had been taken over the years. After I'd first been taken for a fool by the men's fathers, I'd had every intention of taking Emily, using her, putting her to work in one of the many brothels I owned, and getting my just reward. My virgin woman was gone, and I didn't like being offered something so precious for it to be taken away so swiftly. It pissed me off.

I wasn't a man to be messed with.

Over the years, I'd made sure to build a reputation that everyone feared. I killed without mercy. Crude Hill may be home to monsters and thugs. I was worse than all of them. I was a fucking beast.

I didn't need a reason to kill. I did it purely because I wanted to.

Without mercy.

For fun.

I traded in lives for cash, and I reveled in it.

Watching men and women fall for the first strip of human flesh. What I did made me sick. To many, I was probably the worst kind of person to ever live, but I didn't care.

Life was a game, and I loved to play it.

All I'd ever demanded was truth, loyalty, and the knowledge that when the time came for me to take a woman, she'd be untouched.

Ashley was that woman.

No man had even had the pleasure of kissing those full, plump lips.

I couldn't wait to tutor her. To have her kissing me. The idea of training her to accept my touch, to learn to fuck me exactly how I liked, well, it certainly made my dick rock-hard.

Sipping at my drink, I saw her glance at her own glass but refuse to actually take it.

Stubborn woman.

The position I was offering her was something most women would jump at. I'd had many women who worked for me beg to service me. They craved to be at my mercy. Of course, they'd experienced many a fat cock in their body, and I didn't have an interest in sharing.

I was a selfish, greedy bastard. A hypocrite. I was far from a virgin myself. All in the form of entertainment, I'd done some degrading stuff just to amuse myself with how far I could push a woman.

When it came to Ashley, she would never know a man's touch. Never feel another's cock inside her body. Every single part of her would belong to me. She would be my ultimate possession.

Mine.

"This is a joke." She stood up and swayed a little.

The clothing she wore wasn't designed to take

this level of heat. I reached for her, but she swatted my hand away.

"Don't touch me."

I gripped her shoulders. No one told me what to do. I forced her to take a seat and snapped my fingers at the woman holding a tray of fruit. After taking some pieces off the platter, I pressed them to Ashley's mouth.

"Open, or I force you to eat. Either way, I'm not having you die on my fucking watch. I've got too much shit to do, Ashley." The Monsters would cause me a great deal of problems if they found out Ashley had died. I had no interest in killing her.

She glared at me.

So sexy. So defiant. I loved it.

The last thing I wanted was a woman who was scared of me, practically shaking in the corner like a terrified little puppy. I needed the fire. The passion. Ashley was seething with it, and I relished it.

Give it to me.

She opened her lips, and I slid a piece of papaya into her mouth. The fruit was succulent, juicy. I only had the best. Her eyes closed and a little moan escaped. Another part of her I adored was her love of food. I'd watched her at supermarkets, farmer's markets, the way she appreciated good things.

We were more equally matched than she could realize.

After she'd eaten several pieces of fruit, I instructed one of my men to order her breakfast with my cook.

Once I snapped my fingers, they were gone, leaving me alone with her.

She wiped at her brow.

"Remove your clothes."

Her hands went to her neck.

"No."

"You're hot, tired, and hungry. We're not going to a cold climate for some considerable time. Remove your clothes."

She shook her head.

I pulled a blade from the back of my pants and flicked it open, the tip glinting in the sunlight. "Either you take them off, or I do."

She stood up, and her hands shook as she wriggled out of her pants. The items the restaurant had her wearing were pitiful. They did nothing for the curves she possessed. Full hips, a curved stomach, and juicy thighs that were meant to circle a man's waist. Her skin was pale from the lack of sun, and in a moment, she stood before me in her gray underwear, her hands trying to cover herself.

Her cheeks were a nice shade of red, and she kept chancing looks at the men who had turned their backs.

I noticed one of the women who stood waiting to serve us giving her the stink eye. I snapped my fingers and signaled it was time for her to leave. If she could not show respect to my woman, then she didn't have a right to be on my yacht. There were plenty of other jobs waiting for her, far less pleasurable.

"Sit."

Ashley did as she was told, and I couldn't help but feel a hum of pleasure rush through me at knowing she could take instructions.

It was good.

All I want to do was touch her, to feel her body next to mine, but instead, I sat back and watched her.

She was trying to hide her body.

"Sit back."

"Don't tell me what to do."

"You think there won't be a reward for your good

behavior?"

"I'm not a child. Don't treat me like one."

"Believe me, I don't see you as a child."

Seconds passed, and the heat in her cheeks built up. I loved that she was nervous about being naked in front of me.

Good.

I liked her virginal response.

She wiped at her brow.

Finally, the guard brought out a tray of food. Without waiting for my instruction, he set it up and placed it in front of Ashley without looking her way.

"Thank you," Ashley said as the man left.

No response.

Her shoulders drooped slightly.

"No one here will help you. No one will come to your aid. They work for me. I pay them."

"So they're used to you taking women without their consent."

I merely smiled at her. She had no idea.

She lifted up her fork and began to play with the food on her plate, wrinkling her nose.

"The food is not to your liking."

"I can't eat runny eggs." She picked up a piece of toast and nibbled on it.

I got up, tried the eggs, and found they were exactly to my liking. "They're good."

"I like overcooked scrambled eggs. It's fine. I enjoy toast." She took the second slice, leaning back and eating it.

This shouldn't bother me. She was eating, which was a good sign, but I didn't like the fact she didn't like the food I provided for her. It pissed me off.

Still, I sat back down and looked at her.

She finished off the second slice and went back to

trying to cover up her body. "What if I don't agree?"

"There's no room for negotiation."

"You can't kill anyone important to me. My mom's dead. The Monsters took care of that."

I tutted. "Oh, Ashley. You think your mother is the only person in the world you care about?"

"Emily is protected by the Monsters."

"True, but, I've been an ally to them for many years. I know their strengths and I know their weaknesses. Emily is theirs, and you see, weak people make mistakes. She's not protected."

I saw tears fill her eyes, and she turned away, trying to avoid looking at me.

"Emily doesn't deserve this. Leave her out of it."

"Then agree, Ashley."

She laughed. "You want me to agree. This is ridiculous. You kidnap me, tell me what you want, and you think I'm going to comply. This is my body. Mine. Not yours. Not her goddamn father's. Mine. I get to do whatever the hell I damn well chose with it." She got up and without even covering herself, she stormed away.

I didn't follow her.

There was only one place she was going to go.

My men tensed up, but I held up my hand. They were not to touch my woman.

I got to my feet and walked to the edge of my yacht, staring down into the water. I wasn't a huge fan of the ocean. It provided a means to an end. I was a lover of endless sunlight, and to always be one step ahead of my enemies.

The Monsters would interfere at Emily's insistence. I wanted time alone with Ashley. Making a deal to keep Emily safe so I could have Ashley was easy. My power reached far and wide. I was done waiting for what I wanted. The fact I'd taken seven years was a testament to the kind of patience I possessed. From the very beginning of dealing with Caleb, River, Gael, and Vadik, I intended to lie. I wasn't going to stay close so they could keep an eye on Ashley with me.

After counting to ten, I gained control, spun on my heel, and went back in search of her. I found her in the cabin, seated on the bed, arms wrapped around her legs. She rocked back and forth, her fear of the ocean plain to see.

"I want to go home."

"No."

She glared at me. "You can't keep me here."

"I'd be prepared to deal in that wager."

Ashley let go of her legs and sat up. "This is wrong and mean. You're ... this is ... you won't get away with this."

"No one will ever know you're gone. Like you said, you've got no other family, and if the Monsters know what is good for them, and I'm guessing they do, they're not going to allow Emily to go to the police. There is no one out there who cares."

I expected her to deflate. To give in.

Instead, she squared her shoulders. "You're so used to getting what you want."

Good. The fire was back.

"What I'm offering you, Ashley, is what most women would kill for. Do you have any idea how many women would love to have my attention? My devotion?"

"Then go to them. I don't want anything to do with you. If there are so many other women, take them. I'm not important."

I closed the distance between us, and she quickly shrank back against the wall, almost as if she hoped it could hide her.

So sweet.

I took one of her hands, then the other, pressing them against the wall, holding her in place.

"Let me go."

"No."

I moved my body against hers so she'd feel it. I was aroused. My rock-hard cock pressed against her stomach and she released a little moan. With the sounds she made, I already wanted to take her cherry, but I was a patient man. Today wasn't that day, no matter how hungry I was for it.

Pressing my face against her neck, I breathed her in. She needed a shower, but there was something hypnotic about Ashley. I craved her. From the first moment I saw her, and not just when she'd moved in with Emily, before then. Seven long years ago at a party. I'd gone to see Emily, but this brunette had captured my attention.

Emily was beautiful, no doubt about it.

Ashley was ravishing. Her dark-brown locks and tender eyes. An air of sweetness and innocence clung to her. She was the epitome of virginal. Emily was innocent by necessity. The first opportunity she'd bedded her men, and that had ended it. Ashley didn't care about other men. I'd seen how she treats them. They weren't important to her. Life, living, food, happiness, joy. Those were the kind of experiences Ashley searched for.

She went in and out of people's lives, but no one seemed to really see her or know her. To many, she wasn't important.

The only person to ever show any signs of giving a shit about her was Emily. It was why that woman still fucking breathed. She made Ashley smile. There was no way I could justify killing her and leaving Ashley with no one. Not until I was ready.

"Is this what you want? To take me by force?"

I smiled. "You know, a lot of men would have slapped you around. Put that mouth to good work."

She tilted her head back. "You're not like other men."

"No, I'm not. Keep testing me, Ashley. You'll push to the point you'll lose. You don't want to make an enemy out of me."

I let her feel my dick some more. Damn, all I really wanted to do was slide deep inside her cunt. To feel her cherry pop beneath my touch. The enjoyment came in the chase.

Stepping back from her took all of my control, but I did it, even though I wanted to do much more.

"Shower, Ashley. You stink." I stepped away out of the room and flicked the lock back into place.

My yacht was luxurious with beautiful en-suite bathrooms. Ashley was about to enter a world she'd only ever caught glimpses of.

Once I was back on deck, one of the women come toward me, carrying a fresh glass of water. I took the glass, sipping at the cold water and ignoring her stare which begged to be fucked.

The women who surrounded me were all loyal and subservient. They'd shown no wish to leave, nor did they want to go back to a life of misery.

Sipping at my drink, I hummed my approval.

The sun was hot. My dick was hard. My little virgin was below deck, taking a shower. Her curvy body beneath the spray, or did she decide to take a bath? Either way, the thought of her naked made me hot.

Pulling out my cell phone, I didn't have to use my imagination at all. I clicked into the security cameras, and sure enough, there was my ripe peach ready to be plucked. She was in the en-suite, her long brown hair finally down, and she even let out a little moan. Bubbles filled the tub, hiding her body from me, but that was okay.

Soon enough, Ashley would never hide from me. I was going to know all of her secrets, work her body until she was weak and desperate only for me.

I finished my drink and watched her as she bathed. This wasn't the first time I'd gotten this close, and it wouldn't be the last.

Chapter Two

I was bored.

I wasn't used to this feeling.

Working, experimenting, having girl time with Emily, it took up a lot of time, and I loved it like that.

Sitting in a cabin on a boat was the most boring thing of all.

I'd bathed twice. Slept for what felt like hours. Done nothing.

I was starving.

Time was just that. Going by.

At some point, I ended up at the bottom of the bed with my head hanging over the end, waiting. My thoughts went to Emily. If she was with the Monsters, then that meant she was happy. I'd seen how miserable she'd gotten without them. Four men, all of them completely devoted to her.

All my life, I couldn't even get my mother to truly love me. I wasn't jealous of Emily. I love her like a sister. I'd always wanted the best for her, but I did envy the number of people who actually loved her.

All four of her men.

I had one man who didn't even care about me. Nope, just a small, thin piece of flesh between my thighs. That was the most interesting thing about me, it seemed. I was a virgin and that gave me value. Nothing else. My mind didn't matter, or my love of romance. I was worthless.

The door unlocked, and I stayed hung upside down. The blood flowed to my head as I watched Earl enter my room. He leaned against the doorframe. The sane part of my brain told me to be nice. To play whatever game he wanted to play in order to make it out of here alive.

The other part of my brain, the one that seemed to have grown balls and talked right off to him, wanted to get under his skin. That part wanted to make him suffer, wanted to make everyone who treated me as less than suffer.

I'd never been a vindictive person, but at that moment, I could quite safely say it would be so easy to be one.

"What is the meaning of this?"

"No meaning." I stayed, staring up at him.

He was tall. Handsome. Even with his scar. Why couldn't he have been ugly? He was older than me. Perhaps in his forties. His age didn't bother me though. Strange.

"Are you hungry?"

"Will it be undercooked like the eggs?"

He smiled. I liked it. I really shouldn't, but it was nice.

"You've got a smart mouth."

"You've promised not to hurt me."

"And you believe me?"

"You'd have killed me already." I rolled over and fell to my knees before him. I was a virgin. I'd never kissed a guy or been felt up by one. Never had one give me an orgasm. The ones I'd given myself were pitiful. It didn't mean I was completely unaware of sex. I'd seen porn. I'd even heard my mom with some of the men. It was disgusting, and I knew kneeling on the floor, with my hair falling around me, I looked submissive. The clothes available in this room were not so sexy. Sweatpants and a large shirt, but I liked them. I felt like I could hide when I wore them. "Unless what is really going to get you off is the chance of me being dead. Is that what you want, Earl? A dead virgin?"

I watched him closely. He gave nothing so

25

obvious away. It was all in his eyes. The way they stared at me. I hit a nerve, but the truth was I didn't care.

I wasn't going to be at his or anyone else's mercy, not ever again. Even though my heart raced as I fought him, I took great pride in not giving in.

"If you want to eat, follow me."

My stomach chose that moment to answer for me. Traitorous hunger. Getting to my feet, I followed behind him. The boat was still swaying. Part of me wondered if a shark was circling. I could push him overboard and take over the crew. It would never happen. I had more chance of dying through drowning than taking over this boat.

I expected us to head above deck, but he led me to a sitting room. Along the curve of the room, I saw sofas. They looked so comfortable. A large television screen dominated a wall, and three large boxer dogs lifted up when Earl entered.

"Stay," he said. His voice commanding, deep, husky.

Another table was set for the two of us.

Earl held out a chair, and I went to it, sitting down, and he slid it beneath the table.

As I sat on my ass, his fingers traced along my arms, and I waited for him to touch me some more. It never came.

I placed the napkin into my lap and watched him sit. He'd changed out of the white trousers, and he now wore gray and white. I was a slob in comparison to him.

"Did you enjoy your bath?"

"Yes, thank you."

He snapped his fingers, and a man came out. I'd noticed none of the men even looked at me. I wondered if it was because of my ugliness or if he'd ordered them not to. Why would he do that? A small bowl with white-looking soup was placed in front of me. I waited for him to start before picking up my spoon.

I took a spoonful and closed my eyes. Cauliflower, herbs, I thought I detected some rosemary, one of my favorites. I knew not a lot of people liked it, but I did. It was especially good on roast potatoes. I couldn't believe that while I was seated opposite a man, I was thinking about food and ingredients. I was so fucking weird.

"Good?" he asked.

"It's delicious." I took another sip, and I wasn't lying. It was good soup. One of my favorites, in fact. I loved cauliflower. As an ingredient, it wasn't appreciated enough. Emily loved what I made out of cauliflower, from barbequing it up, to making it into a pizza, using it as rice. So many good things.

I finished the soup, wishing I had some bread to dip around the edges. There was perfectly good food, and I hated to waste anything because of the years of living with my mom when she'd worry about the next paycheck, or the wealthy boyfriend who would pay all of her bills.

Again, Earl snapped his fingers, and I sat through two more delicious courses before dessert finally came out. Chocolate mousse, yum. I used the tiny spoon provided to take small amounts to enjoy the taste. I did this in an attempt to know what ingredients were used. At that moment, I wished I had my notebook. Emily often teased me about carrying around it around, but I loved it. It was like a security blanket. Not that anyone could blame me after everything that had gone down.

"I love watching you eat," Earl said.

Now there was no food as a distraction, I had no choice but to face him. Holding my hands across my stomach, I stared at him and waited.

"Have you thought any more about my request?"

"You think you're giving me a choice?"

"Everyone has choices, Ashley."

This caused me to laugh. It wasn't a nice sound. All my life, I hadn't had choices. My mom took them away from me. Even the Monsters didn't give me a choice. I'd always been told what to do.

"I don't have a choice. You're not going to let me out of here until you get what you want."

"True."

I wanted to play with something. Fidgeting was a comfort to me, but the moment I was in his company, I seemed to freeze up, standing still. It was infuriating because I didn't want to give in to him. The last thing I wanted to ever do, was allow him to think he'd won. He hadn't won. Sure, the man made me nervous, but who wouldn't be.

He was handsome with a bit of a boy-next-door look, with blond hair that appeared to be swept back but was yet never out of place. Green eyes, striking, and they held me in place. He was muscular as well, with hints of ink displaying beneath his shirts. I'd never seen him naked, and the truth was the thought of it terrified me. He was all man in every way, but he was also scary as fuck.

This man was a beast.

The scar wasn't just the one indication.

It was the way he commanded. A simple nod. A flick of his fingers. All of it gave way to a man who was completely in control over everything.

I didn't know if I liked it.

Still holding on to my stomach, I waited for him to speak.

"Just because your choices are limited doesn't mean you can't negotiate."

I raised my brows at him. "Negotiate?"

"I'm happy to hear your terms and conditions."

This caused me to frown, and I sat up, trying to understand a little more clearly. "I'm not sure I follow."

"You're here for me. The end result is I will take your virginity and keep you as mine for as long as it amuses me. That's non-negotiable. That's the prize at the end. Getting to that point, during it, and of course, after it, all of which I'm willing to hear your requests and conditions."

Okay, this was new. "Why?" I asked.

"You think I don't understand the situation I've put you in? I do. I'm well aware of what I've done. Doesn't mean it has to be difficult for the two of us. I don't want some terrified woman in my company, Ashley. I happen to think we'd get along well if you gave me a chance."

I chuckled. "You're a monster."

"I like to think of myself as more a beast. We're not in Crude Hill anymore."

I hated that place. Just the very mention of it was enough to make me tense up.

With a hand on my knee, I looked at him, waiting for him to burst out laughing to show it was nothing more than a trick. He was the one who held everything. I couldn't leave.

"I need to think about it."

"Well, how about I tell you some of my conditions?"

I didn't think it would hurt, so I nodded. What was the point in ignoring what he had to say?

"You'll be by my side at all times. You cannot leave my company. I'm in control of every part of your life and your safety. You'll sleep in my bed, beside me. You have to be open to my touch. I want conversation, companionship, and above all, loyalty and trust. This is just to start."

"Wow," I said.

"Is there a problem?"

"Trust and loyalty? Companionship? What's wrong with just taking me to your bed and fucking the hymen right out of me? Let's not butter it up with sweet words like *virginity* and all that crap. What you want is my tiny piece of flesh that no other man has ever gotten the chance to pop. You can do it. I can't go to the cops. I can't expose myself or Emily. My hands are tied in every single direction. What's the point in trying to dress it up as anything else?" I wasn't going to pretend for him or for anyone.

Earl sighed. He fucking sighed. As if this was my problem. It pissed me off.

I stood up and stormed across the room, going toward the door. With a hand on the doorknob, I turned it, but it didn't budge. I kept trying to open the door.

"Damn it. Open the damn door," I said, spinning around to see him still sitting there, watching me.

"I figured this would happen. You're very volatile."

He was so calm.

I hated it.

"I'm not a robot barking out demands. I'm a human person who has feelings." After kicking the door, I stepped away from it, but rather than sit opposite him, I moved toward the comfortable-looking sofa.

Sitting down, I sank into the cushions. I wasn't wearing any socks or shoes, and I lifted my feet, enjoying the luxury.

I'd never allowed myself the opportunity to enjoy anything.

"This could make life a lot easier for you, Ashley. I understand that you're angry. You're right, I can drag you into my bedroom, chain you to my bed, spread your pretty thighs, and take what I want without a single thought to your well being. I'm the kind of man who can do it. But I'm choosing not to. I'm giving you a choice. You can either enjoy it, and think of something you want out of the prospect, or you can fight me every single step of the way."

His words lingered in the air. He'd pulled out his cell phone and was tapping away on it.

Grabbing one of the cushions, I held it in front of me. It wouldn't offer me any kind of protection, but it allowed me to calm down to a certain extent.

My brain was working so fast. I couldn't get it to stop.

I was infuriated, but also wondering what could be.

My thoughts wandered to Emily. I missed her. She'd be so angry at Earl right now. "Is Emily okay?" I asked.

Earl stopped tapping on his cell phone and looked up. "Of course. She has no reason not to be. She's with the men she wants."

"But you wanted her. Aren't you angry?" I asked.

He shook his head. "No reason to be angry. Emily's not mine. You are."

Was he hiding something? Resting my head back against the cushions, I closed my eyes, and once again, the boat was rocking. "You know, I hate being out on the open water."

"You do?"

"Aren't you afraid of sharks getting to you? Squids? Octopuses? Crocodiles? Snakes?" Even as I start to speak them aloud, I knew I sound so completely lame.

"You're a fan of those kinds of movies?"

"A fan, and it helps to make me very much aware

of the dangers around me."

"We're not going to get attacked by sharks."

"That's what you think."

He chuckled. "You're adorable."

"When your boat is sinking and you're being eaten by sharks, you'll be wondering why you didn't listen to me." I was smiling.

"This doesn't have to be an awful arrangement, Ashley."

"You've got to give me time to think. I didn't exactly plan to be taken and given the option of making this better than myself."

"Let's work on it then. What is the first thing that enters your head that you'd like me to consider as your terms and conditions?"

"Emily."

"What about her?"

"I don't want you to hurt her, and whatever agreement you've got with the Monsters to keep her safe, please do it."

He sighed. "You are a surprise."

****

Earl

That night, I allowed her to go to sleep in her own bed. She wasn't alone. I spent a great deal of time watching her toss and turn. Her gaze constantly looking at the door, waiting for me to enter. She didn't realize I could keep my word while also watching over her.

I'd spent a great deal of time researching this woman. Keeping an eye on her, observing her. I was the reason she got the job at the restaurant. No one would willingly hire her. I had no idea why people found her so annoying. I thought she was charming. Sweet. Adorable. She had an obsession with food that I could understand.

Sleep often eluded me. I'd never been a good

sleeper. For me, the night was always a chance to work. When normal people fell asleep, the true monsters and beasts of the world came out to play. I was used to getting one or two hours, never anything more.

I was enjoying breakfast on the deck when Ashley arrived. I'd gotten one of my servants to pick out a dress for her, as well as escort her to me.

Ignoring the woman, I focused on the true beauty in front of me. She was stunning.

Her long brown hair fell around her, curving her body. The dress I'd picked out molded to her curves to perfection. I liked the look and wanted to keep her to myself, so fucking badly.

She sat down, sliding out the chair and lowering herself into the seat opposite me. She'd lost the frown.

One of the women poured her a glass of water, and she thanked her.

I didn't thank anyone who worked for me. They were here to do a job. Ashley wasn't like me. She wasn't like anyone at Crude Hill either. She was an angel among demons.

Her eggs were of course overcooked. She took one scoopful, and I watched closely to see if she was testing me, but she moaned in delight. "Thank you."

"You really do like overcooked eggs."

"Sorry. I know I should be runny all the way, but these are so much better. I think it stems from my childhood. Mom never liked to cook, but she always made me eggs." She shrugged.

"Do you miss your mother?"

"Can we talk about something else?"

"Is your mother a sore subject?"

"More like a complicated one."

I was curious about this woman. It was why she was with me on my yacht, eating my food. I could have any woman I wanted. A snap of my fingers, a brief description, and she'd be right here for me to take.

Ashley was pure. Not just her virginity, but in the way she acted. Even seven years after everything that had gone down, she was so open. So loyal. I couldn't help but enjoy her.

"I can listen."

"You want to listen to me complain about my mom?"

"Why not?"

She looked down at her food. "It's not important. My mom was ... compared to many, a saint. I loved her. I still do love her."

"But."

"I love the thought of her being the best she can be, but she never gave me that, ever. She was always interested in what she wanted. Not what I wanted, or anyone else." She lifted a shoulder, then heavily dropped it. "I never wanted to go to Crude Hill. I came home from school one day to her packing everything up. Within forty-eight hours, we were in a nice house and I was enrolled into one of the meanest schools that ever existed." She swallowed. "I was so scared. I knew bad people existed. I just didn't realize they created a separate school and place for them all to live." She let out a breath.

"That doesn't tell me if you miss your mom."

"Yes and no. I miss the chance for her to be great. I don't miss the actual person she was."

She was sad.

"You're upset."

"I don't like spilling my past. I don't even like thinking about it. She died due to the choices she made. She was always so selfish. There are times I get angry because I never told her just how selfish I felt she was being, but does it really matter? It's not like she cared. She was always after a good thing. A sure thing." She put down her knife and fork. "I'm not hungry."

"I didn't mean for you to lose your appetite."

"The past is a sore subject for me. I imagine the same can be said for you. Were you born into this life?"

"Yes," I said.

"Oh."

"My father was a trafficker. You could say I was one of his many sons that showed great promise. He died due to a raid that went badly. I thought my father was the worst person in the world. Then I met my grandfather, and well, the rest is history."

"You have a grandfather?"

"Had." I put a bullet in his brain so long ago now. The moment I made a name for myself, I took over all of his businesses, made them bigger, better, and then I took everything from him, including his life. He'd broken me down, piece by piece, but I was the one who built myself back up. Not him.

"I'm sorry for your loss."

"Do not waste your sympathies on him. You would've been sold to the highest bidder. A virgin was a rare treasure indeed, but he didn't see you as such. You would've been nothing more than a business deal."

"You don't trade in virgins?"

I avoided virgins at all costs. The irony wasn't lost on me.

"Have you thought any more about our conversation last night?" I asked. As much as I enjoyed watching her through a camera, I'd rather have her at my side. I was a controlling man in all areas.

"I have thought about it."

"But?"

"I, er, I … I'm not very good at this." She took a

sip of her water.

I snapped my fingers for the contents of the table to be taken away. One by one, the women came, removed everything, and left us alone.

Ashley's gaze followed them. "You surround yourself with beautiful women."

"They have a good life."

"Do all of the women who work for you have a good life?"

"They do now," I said.

She rubbed at her temple.

Taking over from my father and grandfather had exposed a great many cruelties that I'd changed. She didn't need to know the true extent of the depravity I once inherited. Everything I owned and possessed, I was proud of. It could be a lot worse.

I sat back and watched her. "Relax, Ashley."

"I don't know how to do this. You've picked the wrong woman."

"For that reason alone, I've picked the right one. Let me guide you."

"You'll manipulate everything."

"True, but I can also offer you help. I know what I'm willing to give and as we talk, you'll be able to decide what you want."

She nibbled on her lip. With a nod of her head, I picked the easiest topic.

"Money."

This caused her to shake her head. "I'm not a whore. I don't … no." She went a little pale.

"Neither your mother, nor her lover, set you up to be taken care of. I'm not offering you money for your virginity, Ashely. As your friend and a guide, like a lawyer, I will make sure you are compensated for your time. For the days you're with me, I will pay you."

"You're going to pay me for sex. That makes me a whore."

"No, it doesn't. I'm paying you for your time. If I was paying you for sex, I'd negotiate a price for each. Your virginity being the highest, at say a hundred thousand, anal fifty thousand."

"Stop." She shook her head.

"So instead, I'm offering you a price for something far more valuable."

She laughed but it wasn't a good sound. "Far more valuable than my virginity? What could that be?"

"Simple, time. Time you can't get back."

"I can't get my virginity back. Once it's gone, that's it."

"I do believe there are surgeons who are happy to make it happen, but you're right, it doesn't grow back. However, you can have great sex, and you are rewarded with pleasure for that experience. Time, you can't make it stop. It cannot always be pleasurable. There is a great deal of pain, of loss. But even as we die, we all pray for more time."

Tears filled her eyes. "You've thought about this a lot?"

"No. I've seen a lot of people before death, Ashley. I know what a lot of people pray for. Time is a value people throw away." I reached into my jacket pocket. "So, I think you've been with me over twenty-four hours, but we'll take it day by day." I wrote out the check, peeled it off, and handed it to her.

"You can't be serious."

I just wrote her a check for a million dollars. To many, it was a fortune, to me, it was pure change.

"This can't be right."

"Why not?"

"I just, this is insane." She put the check down on

the table. "People don't pay that kind of money for me. For anyone. You're surrounded by beautiful women, Mr. Valentine."

"Call me Earl. Then we're in agreement. Every single day you're with me, that is what you will earn."

She shook her head. "I can't accept that."

"I'm not going to pay you any less."

"If I'm with you a month, that is an alarming … no."

I shrugged. "You've got to start valuing your worth."

"There's worth and then there's this."

"You think you're not worth that?"

She nibbled on her lip. "No, I don't."

"My grandfather, sick bastard that he was, he told me the first point of business was to understand your worth. If you don't believe what you're worth, no one will pay you for it. You'll be a laughingstock. Remember what you're worth, Ashley. Never forget it. Not for me, or for anyone."

She didn't pick up the million. The truth was, I'd already put plenty of money in a bank account for her. I would continue to pay into it for the rest of my life.

"So we've agreed on money. Next, sex."

"Wait." Ashley held her hand up. "I don't want to be harmed at all. I don't want you to do anything that will hurt or humiliate me. I can't be shared out. I don't want to be filmed. I … it's me and you."

"Those are your conditions?"

"Some of them. I want to be able to walk away. If I can trust you, when this is over, I want to be able to walk away without looking back. No memories, no nothing." She looked at me, her dark-brown eyes boring into mine. "I don't ever want to fall in love with you. This cannot be confused with feelings. It's mechanical.

Friendship at best. Sex. Nothing personal. I don't want anything else."

Now, this did surprise me and was an element I wasn't prepared for. "Fine. I don't do love. I'm not the kind of man who falls in love. I don't believe in it."

She rested her hands on the table.

"Now, sex, I want everything on the table. Your mouth, your ass, your pussy. It will all belong to me. I will not hurt you, or set out to cause you any kind of pain. I'm not into that. I've no desire to see you crying or hating me. I expect to be in charge. You'll do as I say, and you will submit to me."

"But it won't be anything awful?"

I smiled. "You've got a lot to learn."

"I'm not completely stupid about what can happen. I know sex can be … vigorous. Maybe we can explore it more greatly, but if I don't like anything, we stop."

"Then we stop."

"Do I need to have a … safeword?"

"I'm not a Dom and this is not a BDSM agreement." I thought it over. "Even though it could be seen that way. I'm in complete control. When we're around people, you will do as you're told. You will trust me in all things, and above all, you will not argue with me. Do you understand?"

"You're not going to lock me in a cage and throw away the key?"

I wrinkled my nose. "Some men may enjoy that, but not me."

"This is so weird," she said.

I couldn't stop my smile. "Why?"

"You've kidnapped me. You're going to take my virginity, so sex is happening. Er, and I'm being paid more than I'd ever thought possible. You're going to keep my friend safe, and I'm going to be taken care of." She let out a laugh. "My mom would be so jealous of me right now."

"And yet you look like you're going to throw up."

"Because this isn't what I had in mind. For my first boyfriend, I imagined kisses and hugs. Love. I saw a future planned out. He'd know I was his first and he wouldn't have to be a virgin. I get that." She covered her face with her hands. "I'm making this sound like a really bad romance movie."

"You're a young woman."

"It's a school girl's fantasy. I haven't been a young girl in a very long time. There's no way that's going to happen with me." She rubbed at her temple. "I feel a little sick."

"How about I take you out exploring?" I asked.

"Exploring?"

"It's time to get off this yacht. We're about to dock in a port. There's a quaint small town. We're restocking our supplies. If you promise to be a good girl, I'll take you with me."

"And if I'm not a good girl?"

"There will be consequences for your bad behavior, Ashley. I won't hurt you, providing you don't give me any cause. Do you understand?"

"So you'll hurt me?"

"Only if you give me cause."

She stared at me, but I couldn't figure out what she was thinking.

"I'd like to go with you."

"Good." I snapped my fingers and organized a small party for us to leave the yacht and go into town.

"We're not going alone."

I smiled at her. "You think Emily would stop the

Monsters from looking for you?"

"Wait? They're looking for me?" Ashley asked, standing as I did.

"Of course. Emily loves you and she doesn't like me."

"Do you wish it had been her?" Ashley asked.

I watched her as she brushed a wrinkle out of her dress. Did I wish Emily stood before me?

"No, I don't." I was glad it wasn't Emily. I was having way too much fun with Ashley.

Chapter Three
Ashley

I loved spending the past seven years with Emily. She was my sister. My best friend, and I'd die for her. But today had to have been one of the most amazing experiences of my life. I was totally blown away, shocked, and a little scared.

We left the boat at around eleven, and we'd only just gotten back.

Earl had made sure I was on the boat before he turned away from me and made his way in the opposite direction. No one stopped to see if I needed any help. I had a small bag hanging from my wrist. Rather than feel like a spare part, I made my way to my room, finding it completely barren.

The bed that had been made up was bare. The mattress had no bedding. After going to the wardrobe, I saw it was empty.

I sat on the edge of the mattress, not really sure what to do. I was alone.

With nothing around me, I recalled that first night Emily and I were alone in our brand-new apartment. How much she cried. I had let out a few tears too. At the time, Emily had thought I was crying because of my mom, and in a way, I was, but I was also so happy. The Monsters had given me freedom. Something I didn't think I was ever going to get, and just being in that apartment, even holding a sobbing Emily, it meant something to me.

I'd gotten out.

Holding the bag open, I pulled out the square box and lifted the lid. We'd passed several stalls and designer shops. While Earl had been taking a call, I'd stared into the window and I'd seen this watch. It was silver. The face had a few diamonds, or crystals, I wasn't sure which. Small. Delicate. I'd wanted it.

Earl had finished his call, joined me, and within ten minutes, it was boxed up. I took it out and slid it on my wrist.

I'd never been given anything so pretty. Of course, this came with a price. Everything Earl wanted from me had a price. I'd been with him two days, and my hatred of him had changed. Seven years ago, I despised the very sound of his name.

Emily was terrified of ending up with him, especially as she had four of her own men she wanted.

The man I'd spent time with, who was paying me for the pleasure of my company, was not the man I imagined. First, I did think of him as an old man with a sick, twisted mind. Earl was old, but he wasn't *old* old.

Resting my hands in my lap, I felt the weight of the watch on my wrist. *I can get through all of this. I can.*

Time ticked by, and still, I sat in the same place. What the hell was I doing?

Just as I was about to get up, Earl cleared his throat. He'd changed, and there was a frown on his face. "What are you doing in here?"

"This is my room."

He sighed. "No, Ashley, you agreed to share my room. All of your things have been moved to my room." He held out his hand. "Come and see."

I stared at his hand, worried at first that it would bite me. I had issues.

Standing up, I placed my hand within his and followed him out. Again, I didn't take in any of the views as we made our way past several doors. People moved out of our way, but I kept my gaze on the floor. The truth was I was so close to tears, and I didn't get it. I didn't have any reason to cry.

We stopped outside of a door, and he pushed it open, waiting for me to go inside.

See, a monster could be a perfect gentleman, and that was exactly what I was getting. I stepped into his bedroom, and the sheer scent of him assailed my senses. I liked how he smelled, how it was musky and sweet at the same time. Catching sight of the bed first, I stayed still and tense, not wanting to think about everything that was going to go down on that very bed. Ugh, the thought of losing my virginity out at sea was enough to make me feel sick. Knowing my luck, the moment it happened, we'd have world domination by sharks.

Weird.

I was about to turn toward him when something caught my attention out of the corner of my eye.

"Is that ... my notebook?" In fact, as I looked closely at the room, I noticed several of my things. On the vanity table were my makeup box and the clips I used to pull my hair back. Without waiting for permission, I went straight to my notebook, and there it was. My food notes. I didn't keep a journal. Talking about my feelings on the pages never appealed, but here, I had everything I'd ever cooked. Well, just a volume of part of what I'd been doing with my life. "How did you get this?"

"The same way I got you. Easily. I emptied yours and Emily's apartment."

"All of my stuff is here?"

"Some of your stuff is here. The rest I've had sent to one of my residences."

I looked at him, rubbing the back of my neck. "Your home?"

"I have several all around the world. My mood depends on where I go as to what I do."

I licked my lips. "You're not just going to be

done with me in a couple of days?"

Earl moved across the bedroom and picked up a picture frame. It was one of Emily and me, taken a few months ago. In a rare circumstance where I got Emily to smile. It had been hard to do, but she'd tried for me. "You two are really close?"

"Of course."

"One day, you'll get to talk to her."

"I will?"

"I'm not a complete beast."

"You never refer to yourself as a monster," I said.

"That title is claimed, and I'm nothing like the Crude Hill lot."

"You make them sound like children."

"They are."

"It's rather insulting, don't you think?"

"I'm not here to win any games with them. I'm not looking for a competition. Do you like your new room?"

"This is your room?"

"Yes." He leaned back on his hands.

My gaze fell to his crotch, to the obvious outline of his erection. He was hard and looking right at me.

"It's nice." I opened my book, seeing a cross through *fennel*. I was making some soup, and I clearly didn't like the addition of the vegetable. Beside it, I'd put *seed*, and again, this was crossed out.

"Put the book down and come here."

I looked up at him and found that he was still watching me. Slowly, I put the book down, but I didn't want to do that. I knew I didn't. With each step I took, I got closer to him until I stood right in front of him.

He took my hand and locked our fingers together. "You did really good today."

"Thank you."

"Always so polite."

He lifted my hand and pressed a kiss to my knuckles. I watched him close his eyes and then let go of me. The tips of his fingers brushed across my thigh, teasing along the edge of my dress.

His touch should have repulsed me.

It didn't.

I didn't understand why not.

Staring at him, I waited for the chills, the sick revulsion, but nothing came.

"Sit. Put your knees on either side of me."

"What?"

He sat back on the bed and tugged me close. I had no choice but to put my knee on either side of his waist, moving onto the bed. The angle put my pussy directly over his dick. I didn't sit down, but his hands went to the curve of my ass as he moved me into place.

The hard length of his cock touched me. He was still wearing pants, and I wore my underwear, but I felt him. Pure steel. I gripped his shoulders, trying to hold on. I was far from sickened. I liked it.

Staring into his green eyes, I waited for him to strike, to make me do something I really didn't want to do.

His hands went back to my ass, and he held me in place.

"You know, all day, there was something I've been wanting to do to you. Do you know what that is?"

"Fuck me?" The words spilled from my lips before I could stop them.

He chuckled. "I want to do that. It's a given, but no." He pressed his face against my neck and I gasped. He hadn't even kissed me yet. Just the tip of his nose brushing across my flesh. This shouldn't feel so good.

I was a horrible friend. The worst kind of person.

"I've wanted to kiss you from the moment I saw you this morning."

I jerked back, but I didn't get far as his hands were on my ass. "You do?"

"Yeah, I do."

I couldn't help but look at his lips. They looked tempting.

They belonged to my enemy. Earl Valentine was the enemy, wasn't he? I shouldn't want to kiss him. His cock between my thighs shouldn't arouse me. There were so many things wrong with this picture. The fact I was enjoying all of this made me a horrible friend. Emily deserved better than me.

Even as I screamed and cursed myself, demanded better, I put my hands on his cheeks.

No words formed on my lips. I moistened my own as I looked at him.

One hand glided from my ass to grip the back of my head, and then he pulled me down, just a little. Our mouths were so close, sharing our breath. Would it be so bad? One kiss. I'd never experienced this before.

I didn't know who moved first, him or me, but in the next second, our mouths met. Eyes closed, I didn't even imagine it was anyone else. There was no reason to. Earl consumed me. His lips danced across mine, and I knew I had to be awful at this. There was no way I was any good. I'd never taken the time to practice kissing. Not even on my hand. There was no point to it.

Men never held any appeal.

His fingers massaged the back of my head, and I gasped. This gave him an opening, and he deepened the kiss. When his tongue touched my lip, I jerked back, breaking the kiss. I hadn't been expecting it.

I covered my mouth with the back of my hand. "I'm so sorry."

He was smiling though. There wasn't a hint of anger in his gaze. "I'm trying to kiss you."

"I'm so horrible at this."

"You're a lot better than you realize." He rubbed my knee. "You've got to learn to relax. It will go much better."

"I am relaxed." The lie fell from my lips with ease. I wasn't. I was tense and angry and upset with myself.

Earl, as strange as everything was with him, hadn't done a single thing wrong. He hadn't taken. He'd asked. I was over him. He wasn't dominating me.

I had all the control, and I wasn't sure I was completely happy about that.

"Do you want to stop?" he asked.

"I don't know."

"Do you want to stop?" He grabbed the back of my neck and tugged me down. Any control I thought I once had was shattered out of the water as he consumed me, plunging his tongue into my mouth as he took my mouth. I was putty in his hands. He was the one who had the power here.

My nipples hardened and the heat between my thighs was nearly at a fever pitch.

I couldn't stop driving my pussy against his cock, wanting him to go deeper, desperate for him to not stop.

I was a hungry woman.

I'd never been touched, kissed, made love to, or fucked. All of this was new to me. With one single touch of his lips, he'd awakened me, and I hated and loved it with equal measure. It shouldn't have been this easy.

All too soon, it was over. Earl broke the kiss, and I wished he hadn't.

"You're amazing," he said.

Another gentle kiss brushed across my lips, and

then he eased me off him. As he got up, I sat a little dumbfounded on the bed.

"You might want to get dressed. We're having dinner in a few minutes."

What the hell happened?

****

Earl

I hadn't taken care of my orgasm like that in fucking years. I wasn't a horny teenage boy. I could have women at my disposal with the click of my fingers. They came to me. They always came to me and yet, within minutes of ending the kiss with Ashley, I was in my shower, dick in hand, beating one off. What the fuck was wrong with me? She was willing. I felt the way she pressed against my cock.

She was desperate for it, hungry. I could have had her. The truth was, yes, I wanted her to crave me and to beg me for it, but more than anything, when I finally took her, I didn't want her to be thinking of this arrangement.

Right now, Ashley believed there was an end in sight to our deal.

There wasn't.

Once was not going to be enough. She would belong to me. Her entire life was mine. I wanted it all with her. She wouldn't be able to deal with just how badly I wanted her. Everything would be revealed all in due time. Until then, I had to be happy with just enjoying the time I spent with her. I was trying to build up a relationship, and that shit was fucking hard.

We sat out on deck again. The sun had already set, but the lights from the yacht provided enough illumination for us to enjoy our meal. We were safe and sound. Every time Ashley was out with me, she was always clenching her hand into a fist, terrified. We weren't near any shark-infested waters. I found her nerves cute. As if I'd do anything to jeopardize her life. She was mine. I sat pondering this as she came toward me.

She was dressed in some shorts and a simple crop top. Her long hair was bound at the back in a ponytail. No makeup. If she was trying to be defiant, she was wrong. I loved her fresh-faced appearance. She looked even more innocent now than ever before.

She took a sip of the water and leaned back.

"You look tired."

"It has been a long couple of days." She rubbed at the back of her neck.

"What's wrong?"

"Nothing. Just a little tension."

Snapping my fingers, I instructed the nearest woman to give her a back massage.

"No, you really don't need to do that."

I ignored her, as did the woman, and she sat there tense, glaring at me.

"Could you please tell her to stop?" Ashley asked.

"Relax."

"I'm not going to relax."

"Why?"

"What's her name?" Ashley asked.

This made me pause. The truth was none of the women who worked for me had names.

"Do you even know?"

The connection we'd experienced back in my room was fading. By bringing the woman closer, it made Ashley even more aware of my dealings in the purchase and sale of women. I was pissed off now.

She leaned back. "What's your name?"

"I don't have a name."

Ashley's hands clenched. "Please, stop."

The woman continued.

"Please," Ashley said.

I clearly wasn't fast enough. She threw herself out of her chair, forcing the woman to stop. Ashley panted, and in truth, I was enthralled by the passion and lust shining within her gaze.

"You're fucking sick." She spun away and left.

Ignoring the woman, I followed after Ashley, who stopped within a few feet, whirled around, and glared at me.

"Stop following me. I don't want you near me." She walked backward.

"Ashley, stop this."

"No. You ... how could you?" She put a hand to her stomach. Tears filled her eyes. "There was a time she was someone. A daughter, a girlfriend even. Are all the women here purchased?"

I clenched my jaw.

"What a stupid question. That's what you do, right? Steal women, then send them off to their fate when they've done nothing to you." Ashley shook her head. Her lip quivered. "Is that what you would have done with Emily?"

"She was supposed to be my wife."

"Is that what you're going to do to me? All this niceness fooling me. At the end of it, why would you let me go?"

I took a step toward her, and she held out her hand. "Stop. Do not touch me."

I ignored her request. This was my fucking yacht. She belonged to me. I wasn't going to feel anything for her. She was my property. Not the other way around. She would do as she was told. I was so fucking angry, but not at her.

Ashley was ... different.

I went to search for her. She was the one who had been thrust into our world without a second thought.

The moment her back hit the deck railing, I held myself still. She could throw herself overboard if I wasn't careful.

"You're not being a good girl," I said.

"Fuck you."

Gritting my teeth, I could see some of my men were watching. Her insolence wasn't what I wanted to see.

"I suggest you come to me now or you will face consequences for your actions, Ashley."

"You promised not to harm me."

"I told you that being good will stop me from hurting you."

She gripped the railing tighter. Her entire body was shaking. I was so angry right now. She refused to come to me.

I knew the moment she was going to run. The tension in her body. I sprang into action, stopping her from going anywhere. Capturing her in my arms, I kept her still.

"Let me go." She let out a scream, but I couldn't let her go.

She'd forced my hand.

I was a beast. I thrived on my reputation. Worked to keep it that way, so as I grabbed her, I sat, positioning her across my lap and bringing my palm across her ass.

At first, Ashley was wild as I took control. I slapped her ass, bringing down my palm, hitting her gorgeous cheeks. I kept doing this until all the fight left her, and she was nothing but a submissive woman across my lap.

I wasn't a dominant man.

But I won't be insulted. Not in front of my men

or my staff.

She was so drained.

I didn't like it.

Picking her up in my arms, I realized she was heavier because her body was more of a dead weight. She didn't fight me, but I felt her entire body shake.

After carrying her to our room, I lay her on the bed and begin to remove her clothes. She didn't fight me.

I didn't like this.

She was a fighter by nature.

At times, Ashley didn't realize how strong she was, but I could see it. I knew it. She had so much power, she didn't even realize it. Once she was naked, I was tempted to leave her like that, but we'd already taken ten steps back.

For a while, Ashley won't trust me, and it pissed me off that I had to do what I did. The last thing I wanted to do was hurt her.

When a knock came on the door, I took the soup from the woman, thanking her. The moment I shut the door, I realized my mistake. I never thanked any of them.

Now, I was pissed off, but it wasn't Ashley's fault.

She sat on the bed, looking at me as if I was some kind of monster, and I was. I did this to her.

The truth was that I was saving her.

Sitting on the edge of the bed, I held the bowl of soup and tried to feed her. She turned away.

Not speaking.

"Ashley, stop this."

Silence.

After setting the spoon back into the bowl, I put it on the bedside table. She had to eat something. I wouldn't have her sick on my watch.

I stood up and threw back the covers. I sat again

and put a hand on the inside of her knee.

Silence still.

Slowly, I slid my hand up, staring into her eyes, waiting.

She jerked back, her hands going to the edge of the shirt I put on her. It was actually one of my shirts, and it completely dwarfed her. I loved seeing my clothes on her.

"Stop it."

"Then how about we make a deal? You let me feed you, or you give me something else."

"Why don't you just take it?"

I ran fingers through my hair. She was starting to piss me off, but I got it. She was young and defiant.

"Ashley, you enjoyed my kisses earlier."

"This isn't about your kisses. This isn't about anything to do with that. I can't even believe I allowed myself to think that you and I, that this could work. You're a ... no, I don't want to say it."

"I'm not a monster, Ashley. I told you that."

"You can dress it up how you want. That woman is supposed to be free."

"So? You think I don't understand how fucking shit life can be? You can judge me all you want to, Ashley. I'm not giving you her life, and truth be told, her life right now is fucking bliss. Some of the women have to spread their legs. She has to ride around on a yacht, serving. That's her job. She gets to eat, work out, even fucking date my men. That's my only request."

"You're trying to dress it up."

"No, Ashley. You're trying to make this more than what it needs to be."

She laughed. "This is my fault? Is that what you're saying?"

"Get your fucking head out of your ass. Your

mother landed you in a world where monsters and beasts exist. Yeah, that woman doesn't necessarily have the life she wanted, but I tell you right now, it's better than most. Belonging to me, being my property, that's something special. I happen to look after my women."

Ashley swiped at her tears. "You're so warped, you don't even see it. I'm not just talking about the women on your yacht. I imagine they've been brainwashed to believe this is a better life, and maybe you're right. They've got it good right now. But what if their life was destined to be better? What if that woman who was giving me a neck massage originally planned to go to college to study to become a doctor? She could have been the person to cure cancer. Someone who might have stopped a serial killer. Women are not a commodity. You treat us like one."

"Soup or being fucked?" I asked.

We glared at each other.

She could yell her shit at me all she wanted, it wasn't going to change the fact. Another shipment of girls had already landed, and that was the dock where we were headed. I had to check them over, make my selections. The others got sold on to lesser clients than me.

Gritting my teeth, I refused to think about her words, her scathing attack.

Ashley didn't know what the fuck she was talking about. In our world of pain and death, there was no time for heroes and rainbows. She would get everyone killed with her belief in everyone.

Look at what had happened with her mother. She'd been so desperate looking for love from her mother, she'd nearly gotten herself killed in the process.

I was so angry, but Ashley pulled the cover over her body and opened her mouth.

The soup it was.

I picked up the bowl and fed her.

The easiness from a few hours ago was gone. We were back to her hating me. I could bide my time.

Chapter Four
Ashley

I was being punished further.

My ass was completely bruised and sitting on it was so painful. I checked it out in the mirror, what felt like days ago.

Earl hadn't been back yet.

We docked, I knew that much. His bedroom door had been locked. Only opening for when food was brought in. I didn't get a woman. I got men.

Three different ones each day.

I'd seen nine men in total.

Three days.

And still, Earl hadn't come back.

I spent my time going through my notes, looking around the room, and just thinking. I didn't want to be alone with my thoughts. I hated it. All I could think about was Emily.

How was she?

Did she miss me?

I knew I'd miss our small apartment. I would do anything to be back there right now, enjoying my friend. I'd even talk about Crude Hill High. The school straight from nightmares. Or Emily's four men. I usually tried to avoid talking about them, but if that was what she wanted, I'd do it, for her.

I'd do anything for Emily.

By the fourth day, I was going out of my mind. If something were to happen to Earl, then what would become of me? I had no cell phone, no laptop. No way of alerting my best friend that I was in a foreign country, if I was even in one now. The boat had moved so much, the water a constant surrounding me.

Pacing the room was better than trying to sit on

my bottom. Because of the pain, I'd even gone without underwear, which was a strange feeling.

I liked wearing underwear. At least I still wore a bra.

I stood near a window, looking out across the ocean, thinking of all the ways I could die at sea, when the door opened.

This time, I didn't turn to see who it was. I didn't care.

I hadn't seen another woman for days. Was this my punishment as well? Had I ruined their lives?

When there was no sound of cutlery being put down, or the click of the door, I turned to see Earl stood in the room. The door was wide open, but that wasn't what had my attention.

Earl was covered in blood. His shirt was soaked with it, and it had dried.

My mouth fell open.

There was a man waiting at the door, and I still kept quiet as Earl stripped out of the shirt, his pants, even his boxer briefs, removing his watch as well. The man disappeared and Earl closed the door.

Not a word.

He went toward his en-suite, and I heard the shower run.

I stayed perfectly still.

After a few minutes, the shower turned off, and I heard the running of a bath.

Hands clenched into fists, I listened, and nothing. My curiosity got the better of me, and I went toward the bathroom.

Earl lay back in a bathtub filled with bubbles.

My gaze was on him.

"If you wish to keep me company, come and sit." He pointed at the toilet seat.

Glancing back at the bed, I was tempted to leave him, but after four days without any company, and I was going crazy.

I went toward the toilet, and lowered myself down, only to stop. Instead, I went toward the bathtub and kneeled beside it.

He glared.

"My ... er ... it's bruised." I glanced down at the floor.

"Let me see."

"It's fine."

"Ashley!"

I didn't know what he could do to me lying naked in a bathtub, but the way he said my name had me standing, turning toward him, and lifting the dress, showing him the curves of my ass.

Earl hadn't gone lightly on me.

I've never had my ass spanked before. Not that I thought it was erotic or anything. I didn't have daddy issues, or if I did, I wasn't aware of them. I wasn't aroused by his brand of punishment. At least he didn't starve me, throw me overboard, or cut me up.

Lowering my dress, I kneeled back on the floor and waited.

Silence.

I hated it.

Four days of feeling it, and I was tired of it.

I didn't want there to be any more quiet. Talking to him would admit defeat, wouldn't it? He'd have the power.

At that moment, I no longer cared. All I wanted was to talk to someone.

"None of the women served me," I said. Considering we hadn't spoken in so long, bringing up the very cause of our disagreement was so stupid. The moment the words left my mouth, I felt how thoughtless I'd been.

"It's not appropriate after your episode. You would get yourself or one of them killed."

Staring down at my hands, I felt the tears well up. I wasn't going to say sorry to him.

"Are you hurt?" I asked.

"Me?"

"You were covered in blood."

"It's not all my blood." He sat up and rubbed at his eyes, letting out a groan. "Just so you know, I get it."

I looked at him. "Get what?"

"You want to save everyone. You've got this ideal about the world, and guess what, I did once as well."

I frowned as I gave him my full attention. What was going on?

"I was born to a man who had trafficked a woman and kept her as a slave. I was the only son that lived, I believe. She didn't last long, from what I can gather. He got bored of her and sold her." Earl ran a hand down his face, looking like he wanted to be talking about anything but this. "When my dad died, I ended up living with my grandfather. If you think what I do now is awful, then know that I inherited a legacy I'm not proud of. I've gone out of my way to change. Give me your hand."

Slowly, I placed my hand within his.

He put his other hand on top of it.

"My grandfather believed everyone was for sale. All had a price. Men, women, children, pregnant women, babies. He was into it all. Not just sex. People want humans for all kinds of things." He let out a breath.

"You only deal in women?"

"I know it doesn't make it any easier or nice to bear, but yeah, I deal in women." Earl's gaze landed on me. His green eyes bored into mine. "I was once like you, Ashley. I didn't believe in the sale of flesh. I argued with my grandfather. Got many a scar on my back because I tried to set them free. When I succeeded in getting ten women free, he taught me a lesson. Took it out in my back, my thighs. He cut me up real bad, and then he went to teach me a lesson. If I thought he was bad, he showed me what truly awaited the women that were not selected by him."

I felt sick to my stomach. I didn't need to know any details. I could imagine.

"I embraced my legacy from that day forward, and when the time came for me to take over, I did. I removed some of his products, changed it up, became who I am today. I don't want you to stop having your ideals, Ashley. The world needs people like you, but you've also got to realize the world isn't full of fairytales. I can give up that business, but there are ten, fifty men who will take my place."

He let go of my hand, and I hated the loss of his touch. I felt so uneasy without it.

Putting my hand down, I covered it with my other, but my touch didn't relieve the emptiness. All it did was make it harder for me to bear.

"Take off your clothes. Get in the bath with me."

I quickly looked toward him. I had to have been mistaken, but he leaned back.

"Now, Ashley. I'm not in the mood to fight. It has been a really long day."

I didn't want to fight him, but getting naked in the bath with him, after the bruises he gave my ass, I didn't think I could.

"Do I need to give you another reminder of how I punish? Your ass is bruised. Imagine it taking another round."

I got to my feet, removed my dress and bra, and Earl helped me as I climbed into the water. I hoped to get as far away from him as possible, but he had other ideas, grabbing my hand and pulling me close so I had no choice but to sit on his thighs.

They were the perfect cushion compared to the bottom of the bath that would hurt my sore cheeks.

Earl wrapped his arms around my stomach. His face pressed against my neck. "Did you miss me?"

It was on the tip of my tongue to tell him no, but that would have been a lie. I wanted to fight him, but I also didn't want to piss him off. My ass was a testament to how much he was willing to take.

"Yes," I said.

"You don't have to lie."

"I'm not lying. I've been really bored. At least you provide me some source of entertainment."

"All you had to do was ask, and someone would have brought you something. A book. A movie. Anything."

I licked my lips. "I didn't think it was right to ask for anything after what happened."

"I warned you. It's over with now. You didn't have to be bored."

"It's easy for you to say it's over. Your ass isn't the one that's hurting." I pouted. I couldn't help it.

His hands rubbed at my stomach and his lips danced across my shoulder. "You know I can make it up to you?"

"You can go back in time and not hit me as hard?"

"No, but I can make you forget."

I felt his words were a trap. There was no way I was going to be able to forget the sheer force of his hand. Earl Valentine was a strong man who could do whatever the hell he liked. I got that. I wasn't going to be able to stop him if he really wanted to hurt me. He was the one with all the control, not me.

"Do you trust me?" he asked.

"No." I refused to lie.

For a long time, my life had been nothing but lies.

He chuckled, his lips brushing across my shoulder. "Then I guess I'm going to have to take what I want."

The hand at my stomach moved, and before I realized what was happening, he'd drawn his knees up between my thighs. He used his strength to keep mine pinned to either side of the bath.

He made me open and exposed.

I gasped as the warm water touched my most sensitive parts. What was he going to do?

Both of his hands went to my thighs.

"Relax."

That was next to impossible. I couldn't relax.

He slowly began to skim the tips of his fingers up the inside of my thighs, going toward my pussy.

I took a deep breath, not sure how to handle his touch, or whatever it was he wanted to do to me.

I licked my dry mouth. I couldn't think.

He cupped my pussy in his palm. No invasion or intrusion. Just his hand on top of my pussy.

His tongue glided across my neck, going to my pulse where he nipped at my flesh.

"I can feel you're warm, Ashley. It's okay to enjoy this. Even if you hate me. People can take pleasure from those they despise."

"Don't talk to me like I'm a child." I gasped as a single finger slid between my slit. He didn't touch my clit, but it was so close. I whimpered.

Earl knew what he was doing. He was a master

manipulator.

Closing my eyes, I tried to think of all the reasons I should hate this. Yet as his finger worked up my slit, none came to mind. I drew a blank, and it pissed me off. The moment he touched my clit, my thoughts were not my own. I lost all focus and gasped again.

"Believe me, Ashley. The last thing I think of when I touch you is that you're a child." His lips grazed my skin, and warmth rushed through my body. I was so turned on, I couldn't even think straight.

"Please." I didn't know what I was begging for, but I couldn't seem to stop myself.

"You see, I can make this easy for both of us. You want me. I can feel how your body responds to me, and you know how desperate I am to feel your virgin cunt wrapped around my dick. It's all I can think about most days. You're in my thoughts all the time. Your ass is red because you made me do that to you."

How dare he? "I didn't."

"I'm given a certain level of respect, and if my men think you're breaking them, I will lose theirs. I've built my empire through pain and fear. Don't make me have to make an example out of you again, Ashley. Now, come for me."

I wanted to deny him.

I wanted to tell him to go and fuck off and suck his own dick.

Instead, much to my shame, I came at his command. I was weak to him, and what was more, he knew it as well.

****

"What?" Ashley said, brow furrowed as she turned toward me.

I didn't want to repeat myself because as far as I was concerned, what I just told her was not happy news.

"Tomorrow night, we're going to Crude Hill. You'll get to see Emily."

This made her jump off the bed and rush toward me.

Ever since I'd given her an orgasm in the bathroom, I'd kept some distance between us. Her ass had stopped hurting her when she sat down. The truth was I'd had important business to deal with.

I broke my word when I took Ashley away, but I'd kept my promise to the Monsters in keeping Emily safe. I'd arranged for the bounty on her head to be removed. It had cost me a small fortune and a couple of favors, but I'd done it. Mainly because the bounty on Emily's head was also attached to Ashley.

The moment those assholes took Emily back to Crude Hill, it awakened the bounty and put my woman in danger. I couldn't have that.

"You heard me."

"We're really?" she asked.

"I don't lie." That lie fell easily enough.

Some lies needed to be told to help people. Staring at Ashley, I saw the sparkle in her eyes. A jealousy I'd never known before reared up inside me, threatening to consume my very soul.

She reached out and grabbed my arm. "But, does this mean you and I are over?"

I turned to her now, giving her my full attention. "I'm going to help protect your friend. Our arrangement, Ashley still stands. Your virginity, all of your firsts, they belong to me now. I'm not going to give them up."

Taking her to Crude Hill put her in the hands of the Monsters, of Emily. "Let me make one thing perfectly clear. You're leaving with me. If you give them any reason to try and keep you, or to fight me on this, I will make it my mission to ruin their lives. I will hurt Emily in every single way a man can hurt a woman. I won't do it myself, but I've got plenty of men who don't mind taking what isn't offered. She will be nothing more than a shell, and only when I've taken every single part of her soul, I'll kill her, and make you watch everything I do. Do I make myself clear?"

Tears welled in her eyes.

I was angry.

She was hurt.

Ashley licked her lips, her gaze going to my shirt as she gave her head a jerk in acknowledgment.

"Good. Think about that when Emily's asking you if you're okay. If you want her to get those bastards of her to stop me."

"I'll be good." Her voice was just above a whisper.

"Get ready."

I left her alone, slamming and locking the door of my bedroom. This wasn't part of my plan. With the Monsters on my case, as well as many enemies of my own, I always stayed one step ahead. I'd already gone over the logistics in my head, and the way to get Ashley off the ocean was to deal with the Monsters, keep Emily alive, and then I could take her to my private island, undisturbed.

The ocean normally felt freeing to me.

Since having Ashley with me, my life hadn't felt normal.

I watched her. Living on my yacht wasn't healthy for her. Of the food provided, she often only picked at it, and I'd noticed in the few days we'd been here, she was already starting to lose weight.

I didn't want a skinny bitch in my bed.

Heading back out on deck, I spent an hour

organizing the security detail and the necessary plans that would be in place while I was in Crude Hill. For a town, it was a piece of shit. Not a lot of beauty to be had.

The Monsters who had overruled their fathers had done so but not in a good way. If anything, they'd thrown a little temper tantrum, and the town had suffered for it. Not good. They were children doing men's work. Not that their fathers were any good. They were just as bad, but at least they had more control.

I'd earned a great deal of money from working with them. Swallowing down my pride to make money was easy. Especially as I'd already set my sights on Ashley.

When the time was right, I made my way back to my room where Ashley waited. She stood the moment I appeared.

Holding out my hand, I waited for her to take it. She slid hers into mine. I was aware of how right she felt next to me. Just another reason as far as I was concerned why I needed to keep her.

We walked out of the room, and I took her to where we were docked. My men were all ready, and a car sat waiting.

I helped Ashley inside first, sliding in beside her.

Her body shook a little.

"All you've got to do is behave, and it will go well."

She didn't speak to me.

My warning to her clearly struck a nerve. I was now pissed off at the quiet, but I didn't say anything.

Tonight needed to happen.

I didn't want any more bloodshed, but if she decided to push me, I would strike.

Arriving at the Monsters' house, I hated the garishness of the property. It was large and pointedly said they were the kings.

The car came to a stop, and Ashley looked nervous.

"Are you sure you can handle this?" I asked.

"Yes. I want to see Emily. I bet she's so happy."

I couldn't give two shits if that woman was happy or not.

Climbing out of the car, I held my hand out for Ashley to take. She did, and we approached the door, which opened.

There they were, Caleb, Gael, Vadik, and River. All four men, looking like they wanted to kill me.

Emily broke the tension as she rushed forward, hugging Ashley as if her life depended on it.

Before Emily could have a chance to fire off questions, Ashley started her accusations at the men. I was proud of her. She wasn't frightened. Emily kept glaring at me, but I ignored her.

All too soon, Ashley was taken away. One of my men was with her, and I was alone, dealing business with the main assholes who had put us all in this mess in the first place, in the library, of all places.

"You betrayed us, and now you think you can come into our domain and bark orders?" Caleb asked.

I should have known it would be him to start making demands. Pissy fucker. "The only part of our arrangement I didn't keep was staying too close to you. You think I didn't know there would be consequences of staying close? That woman has all four of you by the balls. One snap of her fingers, and I'd be dead and Ashley would be free. I'm not that desperate, and I'm certainly not an idiot."

"What about dealing with our fathers' prior arrangement to have Emily killed?" Gael asked. "What do you have to say about that?"

"I told you, I broke one part of our agreement. The other, I took care of. There wasn't a threat to Emily's life. All of the prior negotiations and bounty are over. I know how your fathers handled that mess, so I knew how to get rid of it." I didn't like any of this. It would be so much easier to kill them all, but I didn't want the Monsters' business. I was more than happy with my own.

"You knew how to erase it because you put it in place," Gael said.

This, I couldn't help but smile at. Gael was right. "Well, well, well, I had to wonder who would figure it out eventually. The fact it was you, I'm rather impressed." It was why I could make the bounty go away, and why I knew how to do it, the favors to call in, and how to make it stop. Taking a bounty contract away always had certain clauses attached. It was far easier to create a bounty than to take one away.

"Cut the crap. You did this to start with. Did you give them the ammo they needed to take Emily from us?" Caleb asked.

"I need a drink." I stepped toward the drinks table, pouring myself a large shot of brandy. "Do you want one?"

I got glares as a response.

"That's our booze, asshole," River said.

"I know." I smacked my lips together after taking a sip. "Your fathers, they came to me with so many ... options and concerns. They truly felt this girl, Emily, my intended, was a problem. Of course, she was supposed to be my sweet virgin, but we'll call that water under the bridge. So good. They first wanted to kill Emily. To get one of their MC contacts. Make it look like a complete accident."

"Let me guess, you decided against that out of the

goodness of your heart?"

I laughed. "I'm not that stupid. I'm a man who has built his empire from the ground up. I know you all have had this handed to you on a silver platter. It was so easy for you all, and you merely took it. But for those of us who came from nothing, we had to bleed. You know nothing about me, and anything you do find out, well, it's not exactly the truth." I inherited this from my grandfather, but the truth was, I had to bleed to get it. Nothing was given to me. I had to fight for everything I possessed. I played dirty. I'd stopped playing by the rules a long time ago.

"Why don't you cut the crap and get to the part where we don't want to kill you? Right now, I'm feeling mighty ready to kill you," Gael said.

"Patience. Your fathers are not going to take a hit out tonight. They've lost one of their own. Congratulations for taking care of him. Ace had been more for me killing Emily."

"You weren't down in that basement," River said. "You don't know what went on."

"I do know what they intended, and I was the one who played out what would happen if you guys ever found out what they did. With their own personal sense of loss, they saw my reasoning was sound. They weren't exactly the sanest people around now, were they?" I finished my shot. "So, I got them to make a deal. If you arrived, I would do as was negotiated. I'd put a hit out on Emily in the case of you following her. I was the one who set it up. Your fathers funded it. If you didn't arrive, they were going to handle Emily their own way."

"You think this is your helping your cause right now?" Caleb asked.

"Yes."

Vadik charged toward me, and I heard my guard

draw his gun. Gael pulled out a gun. Caleb and River did the same.

I chuckled. I would be a rich man now. I made a little gamble in my head just how long it would be before they started shooting, and I wasn't wrong. Assholes.

"Seven years. We've been in control for a lot longer than a couple of months. You had the power to bring us what we wanted. Why didn't you?" Vadik asked.

They really thought I would willingly give them what they want? Did they not live in the same world as me? Nothing was granted without a reason. "You think I'm just going to hand you what you want? I knew you were all time bombs waiting to go off. Your fathers believed with Emily out of the way, they could control you. Week after week, month after month, I heard the damage you all were responsible for. At first, I had to make sure you had taken real power. Your fathers have a lot of friends, which I'm sure you're more than aware of. Then, I had to go see Emily for myself, to see that she was still alive, and that she'd even work to fit into my plans."

"Where does Ashley fit into all of this?" River asked.

"She's my reward."

"Do you hurt her?" Caleb asked.

"You've seen her for yourself. Does she look hurt?" They haven't checked out her ass, which was a good thing.

"I know there are a great deal of bruises that don't show up."

"I don't hit my women." Lies were so easy. I didn't hit, I spanked.

"Don't treat us like fools. We know what you're capable of. The bodies that mount up from women you can't control," Gael said.

"Actually, that is business, and I have nothing to do with their deaths. To put your minds at rest, I can order Ashley in here to strip and you can see every single inch of her if you'd like, and while you're checking over my woman, I'll go to a room, and let's see what would happen if I was left alone with your woman for as long as you check mine."

Vadik charged forward, and I was done playing passive. I grabbed my blade and held it ready to strike. These boys didn't scare me.

"I take my protection seriously. You think I won't protect what is mine? Ashley is mine. Try to take her from me, and I will make you all suffer in ways you've only ever imagined."

They all stilled.

I waited to see who would test me first. I was almost desperate for it.

Finally, Caleb cleared his throat. "I think it's time we get down to business and allow our women to catch up."

It was a damn good choice because it meant we'd all get to live at the end of the day.

Chapter Five
Ashley

I was shown to another wing of the Monsters' house while I had to wait for Earl to arrive. Dinner had been awful. There was no other word to describe it. Tensions were running high. The men looked ready to kill one another. The fact Emily wanted to speak to him only made my nerves increase.

Earl's men stood outside of the room. I'd been surprised we weren't going back to the boat or to a different house. This wasn't like Earl to want to be in the same house as them. My nerves were now at an all-time high.

The moment the door opened, I stopped pacing and turned to see Earl standing in the doorway.

"You haven't had a bath?" he asked.

I glanced around the room then at him. "Are you okay?"

"Emily is not a problem, if that's what you were worried about." He closed the door and flicked the lock into place.

I watched him remove his jacket.

I didn't know how he could be so calm, so collected. It didn't make any sense. All I wanted to do was scream at him.

We were in Crude Hill. I lied to my best friend. Earl wasn't a gentleman. I didn't tell her about the money I was earning daily. I didn't know if I'd earn the same amount for getting punished. My life and my thoughts were all a mess, but it was so good to see Emily again. To be with her. I loved her like a sister.

"It's not just Emily. It's all of this. You knew what it was like at dinner. Doesn't that bother you?"

"We won't be staying in this house for much

longer. The sooner my deal with the Monsters is done, we're out of here. When that time comes, I suggest you be prepared not to see Emily for some time."

I wrapped my arms around myself.

Things had been tense between us since he spanked me. My ass no longer hurt. There were bruises still. If Emily had wanted to see me completely naked, she'd have seen them. It was so embarrassing.

I didn't want to think about it.

Earl moved toward me and cupped my face. His thumbs ran across my cheeks. "Did you have fun?"

I nodded. "Yeah, I did."

"Good. You're going to be here tomorrow to keep Emily company. I don't want you leaving. Do you understand? You're to stay here while I go and take care of business."

"You're trusting me to stay here all by myself?"

"Yes."

I nibbled on my lip, trying not to let my mind wander. "Do you think you can help her? Emily, I mean."

"I know I can help her." He removed his jacket, opening the buttons of his shirt.

I was struck by the sheer power he possessed. He kicked off his boots and looked at me. He caught me ogling his body. He had a very nice body, and I couldn't just look away. I totally should have.

"If you've been pacing since I went to talk with Emily, care to join me in the shower?"

See, this was what I was talking about. He was scary as fuck throwing out his threats, but when we were alone like this, he was sweet, almost like a gentleman. It was these moments I thought about when I talked to Emily. He was sweet and caring, and like a normal guy.

I loved it when he held his hand out, waiting for

me to take. Sliding mine within his, I followed him into the bathroom.

"You can't shower without getting naked."

The way he said it sent an ache through my body. It was strange that I'd rather go back in time with him, before I thought about what he did to all of those women. I wasn't one to judge. My mother had decided she couldn't stand having a difficult life, so she'd fucked a married man, all in the name of getting it easy.

With my gaze on his, I slowly peeled away my clothes, watching his reaction. He didn't give me anything. I didn't know if he liked what he saw or if he hated it.

I stood before him, naked. He still wore his pants, but once he looked his fill, he took them off and stepped beneath the shower.

He stood beneath the spray, taking the brunt of the cold water.

The moment I was under, I let out a gasp. It was nice and warm. Earl moved me under the main spray and reached for a bar of soap. He didn't grab a sponge and instead lathered his hands. I gritted my teeth as his hands touched my body, working the suds in, washing my body. The moment he grazed across my breasts, I couldn't help but close my eyes. The pleasure was instant. He didn't linger though.

He washed my pussy and my thighs. Once my body was taken care of, he got to work on my hair. I closed my eyes, loving his ministrations.

I was so turned on. I couldn't help but press my thighs together so I could feel something, anything.

He tilted my head back, and his lips brushed across mine, his tongue swiping along my bottom lip before plunging inside, and I moaned his name. Wrapping my arms around his neck, I gasped as his cock pressed against my stomach.

He was so hard, so thick. He made me ache.

Earl broke the kiss first, and I missed his touch, his warmth, his heat. I'd give anything to have him surround me again. All I wanted to feel was completely possessed by him. At that moment, I truly believed I'd give him my virginity. All he had to do was take it.

He put the block of soap in my hand.

I copied him. Soaping up my hands, getting them nice and slick, I placed them on his body. He was rock-hard.

The ink stood out, looking scary and sexy at the same time. This was a man used to getting what he wanted.

I liked touching him, tracing across his body. He stepped beneath the water, and I had no choice but to grab the soap and coat his skin again. When it came time to do his dick, he was rock-hard.

A part of me wanted to run away because I didn't know how to deal with a man like this.

I didn't run.

Wrapping my fingers around the length, I worked from the base up to the tip, then back down again.

He watched me as I did this. When he was thoroughly clean, I really wanted to explore his dick further, but I held myself back. I didn't give in to the demand. I simply worked his cock and enjoyed watching him squirm.

When I was done washing him, I expected it to be over, but he grabbed me, pressing me up against the wall. His hand went around my throat, tilting my head back with his thumb underneath my chin.

He took possession of my mouth.

I melted.

"Touch me," he said, biting down on my lips.

I didn't pretend. I went back to his cock and stroked him.

He groaned. "Yeah, that feels so fucking good."

Earl took possession of my mouth again, and I gave in. Kissing him back as he consumed me with the pleasure of his kiss. I couldn't get enough. I was hungry for more. He let out a moan, and I felt his cock getting harder. He started to rock within my grip.

His hand turned into a fist as he slammed it beside my head. I felt him come. The pulse of his spunk as it landed on my stomach. He pressed his face against my neck, breathing me in.

I did this.

I made him come.

I wasn't repulsed.

No, this was power. Earl wanted me. He came for me. I belonged to him in every single way, but that didn't mean I didn't hold any power. I held a great deal.

All I had to do was work it.

Earl washed his cum off my stomach, turned the shower off, and left the stall.

He didn't speak.

I watched him grab a towel and wrap it around his body. Then he turned to me. I went to climb out, but he lifted me up. I expected him to stop as soon as I was clear, but he carried me through to the bedroom. I had no choice but to wrap my arms around his neck to hold on. He didn't take me far. Just the bed, and as I went down, he came with me. I wasn't sure if I was ready to have sex right now, but as his cock pressed against my core, I wasn't entirely opposed to it.

Earl kissed me.

Even though his cock was now flaccid from already reaching an orgasm, he was big. I didn't exactly have many men to compare it to, but I knew he wasn't small. When he took me, it was going to hurt.

"Stop tensing," he said.

I wriggled beneath him, and his lips graced down my body, going toward my breasts. A gasp escaped as he took one nipple into his mouth, followed by the next as he sucked them hard. His teeth bit down, creating just enough pain to almost make it unbearable but not enough for me to not want it.

I was hungry for more.

For whatever he could give me.

"I'm not going to fuck you today," he said, surprising me.

"Why?" I wasn't disappointed, was I?

Glancing down at where he hovered above my pussy, I saw a smile on his lips.

"The first time I take you is not going to be at the Monsters' house. It'll be in one of mine, where I know I can enjoy you." He cupped my sex, opening the lips, and then his tongue pressed to my core.

I closed my eyes on instinct as his tongue swiped through, circling my clit, before going down to my hole. I couldn't help but tense as he teased me. He didn't penetrate. The promise was there like always, but he didn't follow it through.

His name slipped past my lips as I moaned. "Please, Earl."

"Do you want to come?"

"Yes."

"Then come for me, Curves. Come for me."

He sucked on my clit, his tongue gliding back and forth, and I couldn't stop it. The orgasm took me completely by surprise, and I released. It was amazing. For a few short seconds, I nearly saw stars, and at that moment, I realized why so many people had an obsession with sex. It was heady. It was amazing.

The comedown was just as good. Earl's arms wrapped around me, and I felt safe. He kissed the top of my head. "Now, get some sleep."

I didn't think it would be possible to fall asleep, but in his arms, in one of the softest beds in the world, I closed my eyes, content to just be at peace.

****

Earl

I'd been in Crude Hill too long. The desire to crush the four Monsters grew stronger with every passing second. They were good at what they did. They ran this town with a firm grip, but even still, they were children, nothing more than boys. Their fathers were proving to be a giant pain in the ass.

The truth was I'd expected them to come after me. What Caleb, River, Vadik, and Gael didn't know was that I was the one to put their fathers in a vulnerable position. It had helped for the four sons to take over the running of Crude Hill.

With time and patience, you could achieve anything, and with the distraction I put in place to lure their fathers away from watching the town too closely, it had given the boys the right opportunity to strike.

I wasn't going to point out the obvious to them.

Clearly, their fathers were on a warpath of pain and destruction themselves. I could understand that. Being locked away, drugged to remain completely submissive, was enough to make anyone cranky.

The only good thing to come after the past few days was the feel of Ashley in my arms at the end of each day. I hated being in the Monsters' territory, but seeing my woman's smile was worth it. Knowing she got the chance to be with Emily for this short time, I was glad to help.

Even though I spent most of my time wanting to

shoot the shit out of all of them, which was why I followed Caleb into the house. I was growing tired of all of these games. It was exhausting. Their fathers clearly knew the town better than they ever would, and any idea they had that they'd be able to control them was just plain fucking stupid. They should have killed them when they had the chance, not keep them on to torture and taunt them for their own personal pleasure.

The entire house was quiet, which was no different than any other day. Guards were still at the doors, and they acknowledged Caleb as we passed. I didn't stop following him until we got to his office. Caleb went straight to the drinks table. The little shit didn't even bother to offer me one.

"Are there any places you haven't looked?" I asked.

"Be quiet."

"Be careful how you speak to me, boy. A little respect goes a long way. Remember, I didn't have to come to you." I hadn't been spoken to like I was a piece of shit for decades. The last person to do it was six feet under, and I commanded his entire fucking empire—with a few alterations.

"I seem to recall threatening to blow your fucking boat up," Caleb said. "And you were in shark-infested waters. I don't think you would've lasted that long."

I laughed. The threat I'd gotten from Caleb had been cute. Yes, we'd entered shark-infested waters, much to my annoyance, and I'd killed the fucking captain, feeding his body to said sharks. I didn't want to put Ashley in danger. She hated the yacht so damn much. If she'd seen the sharks, she would've panicked. If Caleb thought I was scared by his little threat, he was so fucking mistaken. "Do you think that scares me? I know for a fact you wouldn't have done that."

"And why is that?"

"Ashley. You can hate me all you want, but I knew what she meant to Emily, and there was no way you were going to allow anyone to hurt her. Least of all yourself."

"Do you think I couldn't have covered it up?" Caleb asked.

"You could, but you see, that would have made you a liar. I've seen the way you look at that woman, and it's with stars in your eyes. Always." I laughed. I couldn't help it. All four men were so obvious with how they felt. "Be careful, people may start to see you as weak."

"What do you think they see you as?"

"Because of my need to have an innocent woman?" I asked. "The difference between me and you is I don't care. I take what I want, the consequences be damned."

"I wonder if you'll feel this way when you fall in love," he said.

This boy had a lot to learn, but I wasn't going to be the one to set him straight. Talking about Ashley with this man pissed me off. She was all mine, and I wasn't going to share her, not even a conversation about her.

"As thrilling as this is, I want to take Ashley back home." I was done hunting ghosts. All of this shit the Monsters had gotten was on them, not on me. They should have killed their parents when they had the chance, not kept them around like little trophies, rubbing it in their faces that they won. It was a sure way of getting everyone killed.

Until everyone was dealt with, I'd decided to take over a local hotel. Some of my men were already preparing it for my return with Ashley. The moment this shit was over and all four fathers were dead, we were leaving. I didn't want to be in Crude Hill a moment longer. There were potentially too many memories here for Ashley.

As if I summoned her, Ashley suddenly appeared. "When did you return?" she asked.

"Just now. Our final building was a bust. They'd burned it down to nothing. It's going to take a lot of money to do some rebuilds," Calen answered before I got a chance to, further pissing me off.

Ashley shook her head. "Wait, what?"

"What is it?" I went to her side. I saw the way she tensed, and I hated her response. There were times she accepted my touch, others where she seemed genuinely repulsed by me.

Ashley looked from Caleb to me. "Emily got a letter with a single white rose. It told her to meet you at the family graveyard." She looked between us. "She's been gone an hour. "Tell me you were there."

"Show me this letter," Caleb said.

Ashley rushed out of the room, and Caleb followed closely behind her. I pursued as I didn't want Caleb getting too close. She handed him a small, rectangular letter. From the look on his face, this letter didn't come from him, or any of the Monsters.

"Where's Drake?" he asked, already heading toward the door.

"He got a call before Emily saw this, from you."

"I didn't fucking call him."

Ashley gasped. "What?" Her gaze landed on me, and I saw the tears fill her eyes. She shook her head. "No. Please tell me I didn't let her go."

Damn it.

I cupped her face. "It's going to be okay."

She shook her head. "No. No. It's not going to be okay." She looked down at the letter Emily had gotten.

Caleb had dropped it to the floor. "Please, help them."

"I'm going to, but you've got to keep it together. Do you think you can do that for me?"

She nodded.

I kissed her lips. "Don't think. You did the right thing."

"What if they kill her?"

"I won't let that happen."

I wanted to stay with her, but instead, I was outside, chasing after Caleb. He was already heading toward the family graveyard.

"Fuck!" He glared at me. "I can't fucking get ahold of them."

"I'm right here."

Caleb stopped and looked right at me. "But can I trust you?"

"Have I given you any reason not to trust me?" I asked.

"Yeah, you've given me plenty of fucking reasons. You were once in bed with my fathers."

I put my hand on my hips. "Okay, clearly, your fathers have Emily right this second, but you're too busy licking your sore little wounds, so let's get this straight, I dealt business with your dads because it was good business sense. Do I have to keep repeating myself? It's just business. That's all it was. I have no special relationship with the bastards. Emily's in danger. I'm going to help for Ashley. That's it. That's all you need to know. Do I make myself clear?"

Caleb went to hit me, but I captured his fist.

"We don't have time for you to measure your dick right now. It could get her killed." I got it. I did. He was so tense because of what could happen to his woman. Emily could be dead right now, but here was what he needed to understand—it would be all his fault.

Not mine.

It seemed to kick him into action. Rather than beating on me, we were making our way to his family's graveyard. If it was me, personally, when it came to taking revenge on a parent, I would've buried them alive. I would've kept them down here for long enough, and then dug them up, taunted them, and then buried them. I would've done it for days, keeping them waiting for me until one day, I simply didn't turn up. That was how you properly mind-fucked a person.

Again, not something I'd be sharing with Ashley.

I heard the screams the moment we got to the graveyard edge. Caleb took off at a run, and I followed him. What I saw when I entered the place they were holding Emily had me springing into action.

For years, I watched my father then my grandfather beat on a woman. To me, they were never strong men. Taking on a woman wasn't hard, especially one who was so broken and frail. Emily was already passed out by the time we arrived, and while Caleb took on his dad, I took on the other shithead.

Chapter Six
Ashley

"You miss them," I said.

Emily stared into the candle. It was her first birthday away from Crude Hill, away from the monsters. Away from the life she'd always known.

"All the time. It never stops."

I'd never had that feeling about anyone. She sniffled, wiping under her nose.

"It will pass."

"Maybe make a wish," I said. "For the future. You never know, you might meet them again someday."

Emily shook her head. "Not possible. There's no way I'm ever going to be with them again. It's not safe to." The sadness in her eyes made me feel sick.

There was nothing I could do to make her happy.

Unlike Emily, I was happy. Yes, my mother had been killed, and there were times guilt did hit me at being okay with that. Mom never once cared about what I wanted or what was the best for me. The first day I was bullied at Crude Hill High, she told me I had to learn to fit in. Life wasn't going to come easy for me.

"Make a wish," I repeated.

Emily took a breath and as she did, I made a wish also. One day, I hoped she was in love and back with her Monsters.

****

Pulling out of the memory, I felt the tears start to pool again. I didn't want to cry. I was so sick and tired of crying. Ever since Earl and Caleb left, I'd been pacing the library. I did this. I was running fingers through my hair, scared. Emily had looked so happy when she got that letter, and now, I felt so stupid.

I didn't advise her to wait.

There was no reason to stop her. She was so happy. It was all I could think about as I left Caleb's office and made my way to the front door. No one stopped me as I stepped outside. I needed to make sure Emily was okay.

I made my way toward the end of the drive, then came to a complete stop.

Caleb was running toward me. Vadik, Gale, and River weren't too far behind with Earl coming as well.

The moment I saw Emily, tears filled my eyes. She was passed out in Caleb's arms. I couldn't believe the sight of her. She was beaten so badly.

They didn't stop, and I tied to follow them, but Earl grabbed hold of me.

"There's nothing you can do right now. They're taking her to the hospital."

"Emily." I screamed her name.

Earl continued to hold me back, and I couldn't stop screaming. I was the one who was supposed to look out for her. We shared so much together. So many memories.

****

"Make a wish," I said. This was now her second birthday with me.

"Ashley, you always say this."

When we were in our apartment, we never used our brand-new names. Dangerous, I knew, but that was how we kept a hold on our reality. It was a reminder of all that we lost.

"Because you rarely get a chance to make a wish. I haven't seen any falling stars lately, and it's your birthday. Come on, please, just do this for me." I always tried to make her birthdays special. She was a hard woman to please.

We never made friends with anyone else. I'd tried to

make connections, to really start this new life, but I'd never been good at it. Once people began asking questions and were curious about my life before we moved to England, I had no choice but to cancel or break up any potential new friendships. Emily was content to just have me, I thought. There were times I was sure she wished I'd been killed right along with my mother, like today, when I wanted her to make a wish.

"It's stupid," Emily said.

"Come on, there is nothing stupid about it." I smiled at her, trying to encourage her. "Come on, please, please."

"Ash, enough, okay." She stepped back from the cupcake and started to pace our small living room.

I'd taken the time to decorate, purchasing some streamers and balloons. All of them calling out to the birthday girl.

Two years and still, she mourned.

The decision the Monsters had made had destroyed what little hope and happiness Emily had.

"I know it's stupid. There's no chance of wishes ever coming true." I took a deep breath. "Do you know what I wish for?"

Emily looked toward me, bored. That was all on me.

"For someone to one day look at me like I'm the only person in the world." Tears filled my eyes as I looked at my best friend. "I hope just once I get to experience what you got for a couple of months."

"I only got it for a couple of months, Ash."

"Yeah, and there are women out there who go through life and don't get it with a single guy. You had it with four. Do you know how amazing that is?" I held out the cupcake. "Stop seeing all that you lost, and start realizing all that you gained."

****

The memory struck me hard, and I felt myself

hyperventilating, screaming. I had to protect Emily. She needed me.

Something sharp hit my arm, and slowly, the world began to slow until I felt my whole body fall.

****

Earl

I didn't take Ashley to the hospital. After the doctor had given her the sedation, I'd carried her up to the room we'd been sharing inside the Monsters' house. She was still out of it, and I sat by her bedside, waiting. I'd already received word from the men that Emily was fine, or she would be.

The damage their fathers had inflicted had been quite severe, but that pain was over now. All of them were dead. The contracts on their heads were gone. I'd taken care of everything, and now, my reward lay before me on the bed. I didn't want to be here anymore. The thought of staying in Crude Hill even one more night was enough to enrage me. Ashley wouldn't be good until she saw Emily.

My time here was extended, and it pissed me off.

Seated in the chair, I couldn't believe I was actually watching this woman, guarding her. There was a perfectly good hotel room waiting for us, but I was here, watching and waiting. If my grandfather could see me now, I'd get a beating. He'd have Ashley spread eagled and demand that I fuck her raw. That I take her virginity from every single hole, that I force her to take me in her pussy, her ass, her mouth.

Running a hand down my face, I gave thanks that I'd killed my grandfather.

Ashley let out a little moan, and I watched as the sedative slowly wore off. She'd been so lost in her pain, it had startled me.

This woman was supposed to be easy. She was a

sweet woman. Compliant. Submissive. Yet, every single step I'd taken with her, I'd come to see there was a lot more to Ashley than I realized.

Her eyes opened and she lifted her hand with a groan. "What's going on?"

"The doctor gave you a sedative. You weren't handling Emily's attack very well," I said.

She lifted up in bed, her gaze coming to me. Tears were already falling down her cheeks. "Is she okay? Is she awake? She hasn't died, has she?" The panic started to rise within her.

Getting to my feet, I moved close to her and sat on the edge of the bed. "The doctor is close by, Ashley. If I need to give you another sedative, I will."

"Please, don't. I just ... I promised her. Emily and I, we would protect each other." I had to wonder what Emily had done to protect this woman from me. She swiped at her tears. "I shouldn't have let her go, Earl. She got hurt because of me."

"Why should you have stopped her?"

"Because the letter, the vagueness of it. I know these men. They wouldn't have sent her a letter. They would have come and taken her." Ashley covered her face and began to sob. "This is all my fault."

I could let her stew in her own pain, but this was far from her fault.

Cupping her face, I forced her to look at me. "Stop!" My voice was sterner than it needed to be, but the noises she made stopped. "This has nothing to do with you. Emily's attack was not about you. It was about power and revenge. What you got caught up in, and even what Emily got caught up in, is a family fucking dispute. The change of reign. Those boys took over, and they made mistakes. That has nothing to do with you. You've been out of the loop for seven fucking years. You have no right to take this on. Do I make myself perfectly clear?"

"But—"

"No! No buts. No nothing. What went down today has nothing to do with you. Fucking nothing. Do not give me a reason to start a war with these little pricks."

She frowned. "What?"

"You heard me. If you keep trying to take the blame, I will make them pay. You're not the one at fault. They are." I was tired of Caleb, Gael, Vadik, and River being a topic of conversation. They had invaded my precious time with Ashley for too long. "Whose fault is it?" I asked.

She tried to pull away from my grip, but I wouldn't let her. She wasn't getting away with this. I wouldn't let her. Plain and fucking simple.

"Earl, please."

"Answer me."

She closed her eyes, counted to ten, and then opened them, looking right at me. "It's not mine."

"Exactly, so who do you have to blame?"

"The Monsters."

"Good." I pressed a kiss to her lips. "If I think you're going to take any blame in this, I will hunt them down."

I didn't move away.

"You can't keep doing that," Ashley said.

"What?"

"Threatening to hurt the people I love."

I paused and looked at her. "You love the Monsters?"

She wrinkled her nose. "No. Eww. I love Emily. She's like a sister to me. She's who I care about. Not anyone else." She blew out a breath. "If anything was to happen to them, I know Emily would never be the same again."

"Then stop taking the blame for shit that's not yours."

She touched her head and groaned. "I feel a little sick."

The doctor had warned me this might happen. After climbing off the bed, I helped her to her feet, and we made our way down to the kitchen. There were guards everywhere, but I ignored them. I put Ashley into a seat and went to the fridge.

"Do you know how to cook?" she asked.

I pulled out some eggs and glared at her. She held her hands up. "You've never cooked for me before."

"Ashley, you like things overcooked and burnt."

"No, I don't. I like my eggs overcooked, according to chefs. To me, they are perfection."

I didn't cook.

I hadn't cooked in a very long time. In fact, I didn't think I'd ever had a reason to cook for myself. When I was a young boy, food was a reward. My father would toss me some bread, or a snack, or something. Real food came when I went to my grandfather, and again, there were times that was held over my head as some kind of reward. I didn't get the chance to learn to cook. In the world I was raised, women cooked, not men.

With her gaze on me, I tried to think of how to cook.

She tutted at me.

"You're doing it wrong."

"Then tell me." I'd rather have her distracted by helping me cook her food.

"I can do it." She went to stand up, but I put out a hand to stop her.

"No. I can cook. Instruct me."

She hesitated, almost like she didn't believe me. I waited.

"You really want to cook?"

"Does anyone truly love cooking?"

"You must think I'm very weird then. I happen to love it."

I smiled. "Doesn't make you weird." I'd always found her passion for food endearing. There were so many other things that could take away her time. This at least made her happy, and it was easy for me to accept.

She instructed me on how to make her food. I listened, and she taught me. I ended up smashing shells into the bowl, but she was there to guide me. Telling me how to remove it, and then whisking it up.

I burned the toast, and the eggs had some dark brown bits on it.

After plating it up, I put it in front of her and waited with bated breath. She took a bite and smiled. "It's really good."

"You're lying to me."

She wrinkled her nose but laughed at the same time. "Maybe a little."

"You don't have to eat it."

"I want to. It's nice that you cooked for me."

After serving myself some, I had to say, they were downright awful. Ashley though, she didn't complain. She ate the food, and I watched her, tentatively eating my own. They weren't great. In fact, on the last mouthful, I was close to vomiting.

Ashley finished all of it.

I made her stay seated while I made us both a cup of coffee. This wasn't so hard to do.

"Is it all really over?" Ashley asked as I put a cup of coffee down in front of her. I sipped at mine and nodded.

"It's all over."

"That means we're going to be leaving soon, doesn't it?"

"There's no reason for us to stay here, Ashley. You know that."

She nodded and pushed some hair off her face. "Being here, does it make you wish you'd gotten to Emily first?"

Her question took me by surprise. Being back here didn't make me yearn for anything other than to get the fuck away from it all. I'd never been attracted to Emily. How did I tell this woman that Emily was just business? They were friends.

"No. I don't want Emily." I finished my coffee, relishing the burn of it.

"Really?"

"Yes, really."

"It doesn't seem right," she said.

"Now that you've seen Emily, do you want to back out of our deal?"

"No. I don't."

Silence settled between us. This pissed me off. I didn't want Emily getting between us. "You need to be prepared for us leaving. At the first opportunity, we're going to leave."

Chapter Seven
Ashley

"I don't think you should be going," Emily said.

We both sat out in the yard. Guards were all around. Earl was with Emily's four guys, making arrangements for us to leave.

"There's nothing here for me right now, Em."

"There's me. I'm here."

I pushed some hair off my face. I still hadn't cut it even though I'd been tempted. There were times when I was around Earl when he seemed like the nicest man in the world. Then the reality of who he was and what he did set in, making me realize I was naïve.

"You know I will always love you. You're more than just my best friend, you're the sister I never had." I reached for her, holding her close. I wasn't going to tell Emily about the threat Earl still had over her.

The danger of the Monsters' fathers was all gone, but he was still there. He hadn't changed his tune, and I would never forget that.

"Ash, I don't like this. You're hugging me as if it's goodbye." Emily pulled me away from her and cupped my face. "Tell me what the fuck is going on. What is going on with Earl? I can talk to my guys. If you really don't want to go, I can make it stop. He's got no power here."

I couldn't help but rest my hand on her stomach. "You've got a little angel growing here."

"I can't believe I'm pregnant."

"I can. You're going to be an amazing mom."

Emily snorted. "You think I'm going to be amazing. I don't even know how to take care of a kid. I'm going to be a disaster. Look how I was raised."

"Do you think I'd make a bad mom?" I asked.

Emily frowned. "No, not at all. You're going to be amazing. I see you baking pies and treating boo-boos."

I couldn't help but smile. "Thank you."

"I'm being honest."

"And it means a lot, but the fact is, my mom wasn't great, Em. She left me to my own devices. She would tell me how much of a pain in the ass I was because she wanted to be with her boyfriend and I was a drag to her. You're not like that. You're never going to treat your kid like that. I like to think we know the best ways now to treat our kids. No one is perfect."

Emily threw her arms around me, and I rubbed her back. "I'm here."

"I don't want you to leave, Ash. I know we're back home now, but we're supposed to get through life together."

"I'll be a phone call away." I made the promise before I could think about it. I really shouldn't be making suggestions that Earl could take from me. He was the one who held all the power.

We stayed outside for a long time. Emily wasn't happy about being locked up in the big house. She liked to have some space, and right now, after the days spent on Earl's boat, which he kept reminding me was a yacht, I was enjoying the ground not moving around me.

The sun had started to set when we were called in to dinner.

There was still tension at the table. Earl and the men would never get along and I didn't mind that.

By the time the meal ended, I'd had enough and made my escape to our room. Earl had wanted to go back to the hotel he'd arranged, but with us leaving in a few days, I figured it was the best time to be with Emily.

I wasn't alone for long before Earl was in the

room. He locked the door, and I ignored him, going to the bathroom. After removing my clothes, I ran the bath. It was still running when he entered the room.

"Are you going to tell me why you're giving me the silent treatment?"

"No reason." I stepped into the water, wincing at the heat, but I didn't get out. "I've got nothing to say."

His arms were folded as he leaned against the doorframe. "Do I need to be worried about you leaving me?"

"No. I told you, I'm coming with you."

"Then what's the problem?" he asked. "I don't see what the fuck is the problem."

"I'm going to miss my best friend, okay? Is that such a problem for you? A mystery? You know I care about her, and I don't know how long I'm going to be gone. I don't know anything about how my life is going to be. Can't you give me some time for that?" I couldn't help but tense.

"You can still talk to Emily on the phone. How about that?"

It was on the tip of mine to tell him that I'd already negotiated that, but I had a feeling he was going to be pissed.

"Thank you."

The smirk he gave me had me clenching my hands into fists.

"You don't think I know you already made that agreement with her?"

"I'm sorry."

"No need to be. I had every intention of letting you stay in touch." He stepped into the room, dropping down to his knees beside me.

I couldn't help but tense up, but all he did was grab the sponge and the soap. Unable to take my eyes away from him, I watched, mesmerized as he started to work the sponge, lathering it up. Why did him washing me feel so intimate? Shouldn't I feel like he was treating me like a child?

When his hands were on my body, they made me melt. I loved the way he touched me. Each time his fingers grazed across my flesh, I came alive. My nipples felt tight, and he didn't take his time. He washed me almost mechanically.

He stood when he did my hair, and once I was all done, he grabbed a towel. It was time for me to get out.

I stood, and he helped me out. Wrapping the towel around my body, I stepped into the bedroom, expecting him to take me to bed.

He didn't.

"I'll be back," he said.

Before I could ask him where he was going, he was gone.

I was all alone in the room.

After quickly drying my body, I changed into some pajamas and sat on the edge of the bed. I stared at my hands.

He didn't order me to stay in the bedroom or tell me to go to sleep. I wouldn't be breaking any rules.

Without talking myself out of this, I left the bedroom. There was a guard outside, and I lingered, expecting him to tell me to get back inside.

He didn't.

I made my way downstairs, and ignoring the conversation coming from the library, I went to the kitchen. It didn't matter whose kitchen it was, it was the one room in the house that made me happy.

The moment I entered, I paused.

Caleb sat at the kitchen counter, nursing a beer.

He looked up at me but didn't say anything.

"I can leave."

"Why? I'm not stopping you."

I stepped further into the room, going to the fridge. I'd gotten accustomed to the kitchen quite quickly. With the milk in my hand, I grabbed a saucepan and poured a mugful into the pan.

Caleb hadn't left and he wasn't talking.

I tried to ignore him, but his presence made it impossible. He had always been scary to me.

"Are you okay?" I asked.

He drank his beer while looking at me. This was so hard.

"I'm fine. Why are you out of your room?"

My cheeks heated. I felt them start to warm under his gaze.

"I … I can walk around and do what I want." *Within reason*, but I didn't add that.

"You think I don't know the kind of man he is?" Caleb asked.

"If I couldn't leave my room, the guard posted outside would have told me." I turned my back on him, looking at the milk. It was so easy to overheat milk, and it would just boil over.

"Ashley, do you want to go away with him?" Caleb asked.

Time. That was what I needed.

The milk was nice and warm, and the chocolate chips were in a small container, which I grabbed and measured out a couple of tablespoons. After dropping them into the milk, I did the finishing touches to my hot chocolate, pouring it back into my mug before returning my attention to Caleb.

His gaze was still on me, waiting.

"Tell me," he said.

"I don't think this is appropriate."

He laughed. "You don't think it's appropriate?"

"I'm going with Earl."

"But you didn't pick him. He's taken the choice right out of your hands."

"It's not like that." I stared into my mug. It was totally like that. I was taken from a job I loved, and the next thing I knew, I'd woken up on a boat with all of my choices taken away.

"Then tell me what it is like because I'm coming up with nothing."

Rather than answer him straight away, I took a long sip of my hot chocolate, not even caring anymore if it burned me. Caleb and his friends didn't care about me when they made this bargain, so why would they care now? Because of Emily? I meant nothing to them.

"This is none of your business."

"I'm making it my business."

I couldn't help but laugh. It wasn't a pretty sound either. "Really? The same business it was that got me captured in the first place? How you bargained my life for Emily's? All you and the rest of your friends wanted was her. I didn't matter."

"You were safe."

"You don't know that. For all you knew, he was going to take what he wanted and throw me out to the ocean."

Caleb's fist hit the counter. "No! He's the one who betrayed our trust, Ashley. Him, not us. We organized for him to be close. He wasn't supposed to take you out on his yacht, traveling all over the world. You were meant to stay close by for Emily."

"Well, whatever you bargained, you sold the one thing that was mine. You want to yell at me, to try to make this better, go ahead. I'm not stopping you. It still doesn't give you the right to demand answers from me when you sold what was mine so easily."

"Ashley—"

"Can you look in the mirror?"

"What?" he asked.

"It's a simple question."

"Of course, I can."

"What do you see?"

The frown on his face was priceless. I would've been laughing long and hard if I found it funny, which I didn't. Nothing about this was funny to me. I found it irritating. I was tired of him trying to pretend to be the bigger man, the brave man, when the truth was he was neither.

"I really don't see the point of this."

Tilting my head to the side, I stared at him. He didn't flinch or squirm. There was no guilt or remorse.

"Well, I see your father and Emily's dad."

"For fuck's sake."

"Yeah, go ahead, curse me out. Be angry. Hell, be so fucking infuriated with me. I don't care. They all at some point make a deal or a bargain with a woman's innocence. They chose who gets it. Not her. That's the exact deal you made." The hot chocolate I'd been enjoying suddenly lost its appeal. "Good night."

I put the mug on the counter. Maybe someone would come and pick it up, and then I wouldn't feel like I wasted food.

"I'm sorry," Caleb said.

"No, you're not. You got what you wanted."

I didn't linger to talk to him more, there was no point. I wasn't going to pretend any of this was okay. They made their deal. I was part of it, even though I didn't want to be. Just because Earl hadn't raped me, or taken what he wanted and tossed me aside, didn't make any of this right. I was so angry all of a sudden. Earl acted like a gentleman now, but what if he got bored? Once he'd had his fill of me, taken everything he could, and tossed me aside, what was I supposed to do then? I didn't have the first clue what to do. If he was being honest, then I was going to be rich for the time I'd spent with him, but no matter how he dressed it up, I'd still feel like a whore if I would get rich off my virginity.

Walking out of the kitchen, I made my way back to the bedroom. I didn't want to talk to anyone. All I wanted was to be alone in my bedroom, or the guest bedroom. It wasn't mine. I wasn't staying here. It didn't belong to me.

The moment I entered, I saw Earl sitting on the bed, fingertips pressed together.

"Where were you?" he asked.

I was surprised he didn't have all of my moves monitored. "In the kitchen."

"You're pissed off."

I didn't answer him. I slipped off my shoes because I didn't like walking around barefoot, and moved toward the head of the bed. Earl captured my hand before I could stop him, pulling me toward his body. The moment he touched me, I felt the swirling, intense need spiral within my body. This was what scared me.

This man wasn't mine.

He was a beast, not a monster, and he was used to getting what he wanted. He traded in human flesh, while I had no choice but to deal with him now. I didn't just give in to him. I fought him, tugging on my wrist like my life depended on it. To a point, my heart did. I was angry when I should have been happy.

Emily was safe. So long as I kept with the bargain I made with this bastard, she and all of her men will be safe. I couldn't tell her this. I had to keep it to myself.

Earl wasn't happy with my fighting. Before long, he was up on his feet, and he was so much taller than me. All it took was a few moves, and he had me pinned to the bed, my arms spread out above me. I tried to buck him off, bite him, anything. I wasn't screaming though. Even as I appeared to be losing my mind, I continued to have a sane part that told me to keep quiet. The moment I made a sound, they could all come running.

Did I want Earl dead?

I didn't know.

Releasing a huff, I tried again to throw him off me, but I somehow managed to get his cock flush against me. I felt how hard he was. Part of me wanted to fight, to tell him to fuck off, to scream, and to bring all kinds of hell down on his ass, but instead, I just lay there. Taking a deep breath, I ignored the woman inside me begging for me to fight more. Tears filled my eyes.

"What's going on?" he asked.

"Nothing."

"This is not nothing, Ashley. Tell me."

"No! We're not in the company of others. I don't have to be on my best behavior. I won't tell you just because you demand it. Or are you going to grab a guard and force him to come in here so I don't have a choice? Spank me again. Tell me, Earl, what exactly are you going to do?"

He slammed his lips down on mine, kissing me. This wasn't a gentle kiss. He wasn't being nice or kind. This was a ravishment. He was punishing and rewarding me at the same time. Our teeth clashed together and caused a slight pain, but I didn't care. This wasn't supposed to be beautiful. He wasn't my lover. He was my owner. I was nothing more than his property. No, a piece of flesh between my legs belonged to him. I was the one who was attached to it. There was nothing loving about this. No happiness. We weren't in love.

His fingers sank into my hair, and I couldn't contain my gasp as he gripped the length and tugged it back, exposing my neck. The feel of his lips brushing across my skin was almost too much for me to bear, but when he got to the curve of my breast, a moan escaped my lips. Especially as he released the strap of my shirt. I didn't stop him as he dragged it down my arm, exposing my breast to him. He kissed down to my nipple, his tongue circling the bud, and waves of pleasure rushed through my body.

Closing my eyes, I released a little moan. The tips of his fingers worked from my knee and up the inside of my thigh until he cupped my pussy.

"This is all mine," he said.

I knew. The instant he said the words, I felt like a bucket of ice water had been thrown over my head, and I tensed up.

Before he got a chance to speak, his cell phone went off, and whatever had been happening between us stopped.

****

Earl

Business always came first.

Ever since Ashley froze up on me, I hadn't been able to get her alone. I'd finished all of my dealings with the Monsters, we'd done what was needed, and then we left. I had no choice but to leave her on the yacht while I took care of some problems with several shipments.

I came back to the yacht to find Ashley had spent most of her time in the bedroom. She rarely ate. My men were ordered to keep an eye on her, and the women who worked for me had also reported her complete lack of interest.

Arriving at my private island, I expected her to be

happy. That was two days ago. Staring out at the ocean, I knew she was watching me. The first few nights, I'd been locked away, completing much-needed work, but now, I was only needed for necessities. Ashley had me all to herself.

I swiped my hand across my face, wondering what the hell happened back in Crude Hill. I didn't like how cold Ashley had become.

My men were stationed on the island, and several of the women came with me so they could clean any mess we made. They weren't to be seen unless I demanded it.

I rarely came to this island. This was a tranquil place, full of peace and quiet I rarely felt. My life didn't allow me to disconnect from the world. My enemies were many, and more often than not, they tried to take what belonged to me. Turning on my heel, I found Ashley in the doorway, staring at me. She wore a pure-white dress. The straps were thin, but I saw she wore a bra. The light spilled across the sand, and she tilted her head back to look at it.

My island was beautiful.

Most women would be on their knees begging for me to do whatever the hell I wanted to them. Not Ashley. She didn't even seem impressed.

Watching her, I saw the sadness in her eyes until finally, she turned away from me and walked back into the house, pissing me the fuck off.

I didn't linger at the beach.

I stormed toward the house, slamming the door open, and I found her in the kitchen. She was pouring herself a cup of coffee, and that action alone was enough to send my anger over the edge.

Grabbing the cup from her, I threw it with much-needed force across the room. "What the fuck is going on?"

I caught the flinch before she stepped away. There was no way I was going to let her get far. I was angry, yes, and I knew what I wanted. I grabbed her arm and pulled her close to me.

"Get off me," she said.

Unlike on the bed, she didn't fight me. She glared. I felt the weight of her look right down to my fucking toes.

"I get that you're pissed off and you're doing your little spoiled brat routine. Enough. I don't care for it."

"Yes, sir, or should it be yes, beast? What do you want me to say? Do you want me to be meek? Submissive? Are you going to threaten my friends again? What more do you want from me? It's not enough that you want what's mine, but what more can I possibly give you?"

She batted her eyelids, trying not to cry.

Her hands were curved into her body. She was tense in my grip. Seeing her like this, I didn't know, it made me sick to my stomach, and I slowly let her go. She stepped back from me, and I gave her time to compose herself.

"We have an agreement."

"I know."

"Then tell me what happened."

"It's nothing."

I slammed my palm on the counter. I was tired of being lied to. "Now!" She knew what I wanted.

"Stop it."

"No. I'm not going to stop it. You're going to tell me what the hell happened."

"Nothing happened."

I gripped the back of her neck and hauled her

close to me. "Do I need to make you tell me?"

"You're going to hit me again?"

"No, I can think of a lot of other satisfying ways of making you tell me."

"Rape?"

"It's not rape if you want it." I didn't know why I was getting so angry, but the rage consumed me.

Ashley licked her lips, her gaze looking deep into mine. I got the sense she wanted to say something. Nothing good could come between us right now.

She was breathing deeply, and the truth was I was ready to take her right there and then.

"Do you want to hurt me?" she asked.

"No."

"Then let me go."

She didn't have the power here. I kept hold of her neck, keeping her in place so she knew what was good for her. I wasn't going to let her go, not even for a moment. "No. You seem to be under the impression you've got power here. Do you want your friends to suffer?" She tried to pull away, but I wasn't having that. I didn't want her to go anywhere. The growl that emitted from her lips was full of frustration, anger, and pain.

I moved us both so she was pressed against my body and the kitchen counter. There was nowhere else for her to go. Her hands gripped the edge of the counter, holding on to it, likely thinking it would stop me from doing whatever the hell I wanted to.

It wouldn't.

Nothing was going to stop me.

"You want to know what my problem is?" She paused, and I waited. "You. You and men like you. Caleb, Gael, Vadik, River, you, their fathers, Emily's dad. All of you men who can play around with women's lives. With their bodies. I'm angry at all of you, and then you think you can ask me if I'm happy, or if I want to go, and it's like everything is okay, when it's really not. Nothing is okay." She pressed her lips together.

I didn't know what to do or say. My body liked being pressed up against her. She had all the curves I craved.

Slowly, I let go of her neck and took a step back.

She didn't move. Her hands kept a grip on the counter.

"I want you to take your clothes off and go and lie down on the sofa."

She swiped at the tears she'd tried so hard to repress. There was anger and disappointment in them. I really didn't give a fuck.

Following behind her, I watched as she removed her dress, dropping it to the floor. I bent, picked it up, and pressed it against my nose, breathing in the scent of her.

"And your panties and bra. Completely naked," I said as she went to sit down.

With her back to me, she took care of her underwear, sliding it off and throwing it to the floor. This time with a lot more force.

I waited.

She sat on the sofa, trying to maintain her modesty.

My cock was aching to get out of the tight confines of my pants. I focused on her. "Lean back. Relax."

"Like I can relax."

I sat opposite her. "I won't move from this spot."

"Earl, I don't want to do this."

"Tough. Do as you're told or I will come and do it for you."

She sank her teeth into her top lip, and I waited.

I could do this all day, stare at a beautiful woman.

She finally did as I requested.

"Now, spread your legs."

"You've got to be kidding me."

"I don't joke around." I was horny as fuck.

Again, I expected to wait, but this time, she spread her legs. There was a great deal of attitude in the way she moved, but I got what I wanted.

With my gaze still on hers, it took every single ounce of control not to blow just from looking at her. And I wasn't even looking anywhere else than at her eyes.

"Lick your fingers."

She wasn't testing my patience anymore.

"Touch your pussy."

This time, I followed the action of her hand as she slid it down her body, touching her pretty pink pussy.

She wasn't as wet as I would have liked her to be, but I was a patient man. Most men would have torn through her virginity and taken what they want, discarding her. I wasn't one to take this gift and discard it. There was pleasure in the buildup. In making her wait for it.

Ashley intrigued me.

Her sweetness. Her resolve. Even her loyalty to Emily. Determined to keep her friend safe when everyone else had her on the chopping block.

Then of course there was her virgin state, her body. She made me feel alive in ways I'd never felt.

Women were often a passing fancy. There were so many at my disposal, and I didn't take the time to enjoy them.

She reached her pussy, her fingers grazing across the small nub of her clit. That one touch, and she arched up just a little. A single jolt of a reaction, but it was enough for me to want more.

Quickly, she pulled her hand away as if she had been scolded, and that simply wouldn't do. Not for me.

"Touch your pussy. Stroke your clit."

"I don't know what your game is."

"Have you ever thought, Ashley, that you just need to come?" I chuckled at the death glare she gave me. "You can hate me all you want, but it's not going to stop the fact you're going to be playing with your pussy until you come. The moment you stop, I'll get my cock out, and I'll find more ways to enjoy myself."

She stroked her clit.

The inexperience of her touch was clear to see.

I wanted to taste her. To slide my tongue through her pussy and taste her exploding on my tongue. Instead, I held myself back, allowing her to become accustomed to her own touch. Waiting for the pleasure to take over.

Ashley kept closing her eyes. Only for a few seconds, but it was enough for me to know she felt the tension build. The desire curling within her gut. The deep-seated need to take what she wanted.

She was angry. Alone. Helpless. There was power inside her, and I wanted her to learn to tap into that, to be able to take what she wanted without thinking.

Seconds passed.

Minutes.

Finally, she sank against the sofa. Her head flung back, eyes closed as she rocked against her hand.

I allowed myself the pleasure of watching her. The way her cunt went slick. She was soaking wet as she released a moan. I wanted to hear my name on her lips, but I waited. This was about her.

Her tits shook with every thrust and indrawn breath.

My cock pulsed in my pants. The urge was even

stronger to take myself out and stroke to completion, but I held back. I wasn't going to spoil this.

Ashley came, and as she did, my name spilled from her lips. It sounded almost like a promise of what was to come. I was going to be the one driving her orgasms.

The release ebbed away and she lay back, gasping, happy, and I watched, smiling.

She opened her eyes, and the reality sank back in.

"Whenever you're angry or pissed off with your circumstances, I want you to play with your pussy until you come, screaming my name." Getting up from my position on the sofa, I didn't hide my obvious erection.

I closed the distance between us, took hold of her wrist, and licked her fingers, tasting her cum.

Delicious. Just like I knew she would be.

Chapter Eight
Ashley

The anger faded.

I didn't like the idea of bringing myself to orgasm to help calm me down. After Earl demanded I strip naked and play with myself, I hadn't seen him. He'd left. I didn't want to face him.

Not with how easy it was for me to fold to his whim.

I could pretend it was because of the threat he held to my friend, but the truth was there was a tone that made me ache. I didn't like it.

He wasn't a good man.

I knew this.

I knew that if I didn't do as he said, he'd hurt her.

Stepping outside of the house, I moved toward the edge of the beach. The lapping waves danced at my ankles. The water was so cold, and it was late. The sun was setting, and I was so tired. Resting my hands on my shoulders, I stared up at the sun, wondering what the hell I was supposed to do.

Earl Valentine was such a confusing man. One moment, I couldn't stand him. The next, I couldn't get enough of him.

I hated him and wanted him with equal measure, and that wasn't good.

Gritting my teeth, I closed my eyes, tilting my face up to the setting sun, trying to get as much vitamin D as I could. The island was beautiful. I hadn't said anything to Earl because I didn't want him to think I liked this.

Ever since my conversation with Caleb, I'd been pissed off.

I didn't even understand it myself.

This, in part, was my choice. I could have asked the Monsters to take care of this. To stop me from being at the mercy of him, but again, I didn't. I kept my thoughts and feelings to myself.

They didn't need to know the deal I'd made with him. The money that waited for me.

The very thought of the wealth made me sick to my stomach. Was I turning into the same person my mom once was?

"You're out here all alone," Earl said, coming to stand behind me.

I didn't need to open my eyes to know how close he was. He was an impenetrable force.

"I'm not alone. We both know you have men guarding this place. You wouldn't allow it to be any other way." I wasn't under any illusions about my freedom.

I could attempt to walk as far away from his home as possible, but someone would be there to stop me. Earl hadn't gotten where he was in the world by sloppy antics.

His hands on my hips made me jump. I couldn't help but open my eyes when his chin rested on my shoulder.

This was too intimate.

I was his captive.

He was my captor.

"It's a beautiful night."

"Please stop this."

"Stop what? Treating you normally?"

"Treating me like I've got a choice."

"You can make this easy or hard, Ashley. The decision is yours." His lips brushed across my neck.

It felt good.

My stomach chose that moment to rumble.

I tried to pull out of his arms, but he held me still.

"Enjoy the sunset."

I was enjoying it. Being back in Crude Hill, it reminded me that all of this was a lie. He wanted something from me. All he cared about was popping my cherry. If he didn't get to do that, he was going to kill my best friend. There was no romanticizing this. I was a business deal. One piece of my flesh was the cost.

On the boat, I'd started to think it was more.

I couldn't allow myself to sink into the fantasy of love, of something more.

This was sex.

Fucking.

Pure and simple.

I had something Earl wished to claim.

I wasn't a keeper. He didn't see me as being the mother of his child. I was a product. I was like the women he purchased and sold as if they were cattle.

The sun set, and with it, reality was back full-blown.

Earl didn't leave me alone. He held me tightly, and I couldn't help but feel like there was a threat within his action. He wasn't going to let me go.

"Give me the woman on the yacht back."

"I can't." It was almost impossible for me to go back.

"Ashely, I don't want this person."

I didn't turn, holding myself perfectly still within his grip. "What do you want?"

"You."

"You've got me."

"No, I don't. I've got the martyr. I want a woman." His hands unwound. It was slow, but as he took a step back, I felt the loss right down to my core. "Look at me."

This was a trap. I knew it was.

I turned to look at him, wishing I had some magical power or some kind of ability to stop myself from being drawn to him. There was nothing.

"Tell me what is going on," he said.

There was nothing I could say to help this. He was immune to true human feelings. He didn't get how this felt.

"Have you ever been bought because of one simple thing?" I asked. There was no use in beating around the subject.

My virginity was on the line.

"No."

"Then you can't help me, which means there's no point in talking to you about it. No point at all." I tried to step back, but he held my arm.

"Do you think after everything I'm just going to toss you aside when I'm done?"

I couldn't stop the laughter from bubbling up in my chest. "That's exactly what you're going to do."

"And you believe it?"

"Why would I have reason to not believe it? You've made it completely plain to me all you want from me is sex. No, not even sex, just my virginity. That's all." I shrugged. "What more could you possibly want from me?"

Now it was his turn to smile, and I started to realize why they called him a beast. It looked sinister. Almost like a promise of what pain would be coming.

"Ashley, you're a young woman. I gave a potential end in sight to help you, but at no point did I say you were going to go." He invaded my space.

His hands came up to capture my face, holding me in place. At first, I was a little scared, but he was gentle, caressing. Sweet. I couldn't get enough of him when he was like this. I was addicted to his touch. Desperate and hungry with equal measure. All I could see was my need for him. How desperate I was to have more.

He was so close, but he didn't kiss. The only part of him touching me was his hands. Nothing more.

I waited.

"Do you really think I'm going to let the one woman I've been searching for, for a lifetime, go? No, that shit's not happening. Not to me. You're mine, Ashley, and it's going to stay that way." His lips brushed against mine.

So soft.

I couldn't hold back the moan trapped within my chest, and I let it go. In the back of my mind, part of me believed this was total bullshit. He was saying what he needed to in order to get laid, but at that moment, I didn't care.

The truth was, I hated feeling this way. It was consuming, exhausting, and I just wanted to be happy. I'd spent seven years hunting for happiness, never to truly grasp it.

The kiss went from soft, to hard, to almost brutal. He gripped the back of my head as he deepened the kiss.

His tongue slid across my lips, waiting for me to open to me, and I didn't fight him. I let him inside and moaned as I stroked my tongue across his.

For a reward, he released a growl that I felt deep in my core, an answering pulse deep in my pussy. My nipples hardened, wanting him to touch me.

The hand on the back of my head stayed there. The other traveled down, going toward my ass to grip it, drawing me closer.

The instant our bodies touch, I came alive. This was why I wanted to keep my distance. I couldn't stay mad at him when my body was aglow with need, and it had his name all over it.

His teeth sank into my bottom lip, and I gasped. There was pain but so much pleasure. I couldn't get enough.

The waves lapped at our feet. We stood in total darkness, the only light coming from his house. I didn't want him to stop. The moment he did, I feared reality would set in.

He broke from the kiss, holding me close.

"You're not going anywhere, Ashley. You're mine. I don't let go of what I want, not ever."

"Until the next virgin comes along?"

His chuckle vibrated between us. "Did I say I was on the lookout for multiple virgins? There's only one cherry I crave to pop, and she's standing in my arms." He kissed me again. This wasn't gentle but pure ownership.

I gasped.

He swallowed it down.

Consumed.

Taken.

That was how he made me feel.

Finally, he let me go long enough to take my hand, and then I followed him as I walked into the house behind him. My stomach chose that moment to growl.

"I'm starving as well."

The spark was still there, bubbling beneath, but whatever he was going to do, had faded. I didn't know if I could take him waiting. I knew it was all about the anticipation, but I was desperate, hungry, and consumed. I needed to have him, but I wouldn't push this.

I wasn't … ready.

Did he know that?

Was that why he was waiting?

Was he being … considerate?

No, there wasn't a single chance of that. He was a beast, and they didn't wait, they took without mercy.

This was all part of some plan of his. He was the one in control and only when he said so, would he take.

****

Earl

I didn't have time to spend sitting around, getting to know this woman. I stared at her sleeping face. Ashley looked so peaceful. The thought of waking her, well, it didn't bode well. When she did, I wouldn't be able to resist her.

Reaching out, I stroked a stray curl out of the way so I could stare at her. When she was asleep, she looked even more innocent than when she was awake.

Last night, I hoped I got through to her. I'd given a deadline but that didn't mean I was going to stick with it.

The money in her bank was compensation for her time here, but I'd also stopped that. I could always transfer a lump sum when our time was over, if it was ever going to be over.

She released a little moan and tensed just slightly.

I watched, expecting her to wake, to do something else.

She just let out another tiny sound and stilled.

The blanket had worked its way down her body, exposing the negligee she'd decided to wear last night.

It was red with a lace trim.

Without waking her, I peeled down the blanket, exposing her body to my view. She was really stunning.

I loved her curves. The fullness of her tits, thighs, hips, and ass. I couldn't get enough of touching her, not that I'd spent nearly enough time these past few days.

One of the straps at her shoulder had fallen down, giving a hint of a full tit. I helped it along, moving it down past her tit to see her red nipple.

The action made her stir, and I watched as she opened her eyes. There was no panic. The sleep cleared from her gaze almost instantly.

This was what I'd come to know about Ashley. She didn't sleep for long, and the moment she woke, she was alert.

"Morning," I said.

"Morning." Her answer was throaty.

I was already thinking about sex, but now, it was so much more. I stroked a finger across the curve of her nipple. She didn't pull away.

Cupping the entire tit with my palm, I rubbed her nipple, and she moved slightly, giving me much better access to her body.

I let go of her breast and worked the negligee up over her head, then threw it across the room to land on the floor.

My cock was rock-hard.

Her tits were so big. All it would take was for me to push them together to create a valley, to fuck her until I spunked all over those mounds. The thought alone had pre-cum leaking out of the tip of my dick.

Her hands stayed above her head, holding herself still.

A pair of loose-fitting shorts, red silk, with lace along the edges, covered her pussy. I moved over the bed, gripping her hips, pulling them down, and tossing them to the side. She released a moan. Her legs bent at the knees, and I put my hands on her knees. She didn't fight me as I spread them open, revealing her pussy.

With my gaze still on her, I slowly traced my fingers down the inside of her thighs. Her breath caught just slightly.

When I touched her pussy, she let out a moan and

tried to shut her legs on me, but I was far stronger, keeping them spread open.

"Please," she said.

"Shut up." The command fell from my lips with ease.

Closing the distance to her pussy, I spread the lips wide. Staring up the length of her body, I stroked my tongue through her slit, circling her clit.

She cried out, arching up. I kept her in place with the width of my body and my hands holding her down, refusing to let her go.

"Earl."

"I'm going to lick this pussy until you come all over my face, and then, you're going to take care of me."

In response, she moaned. I loved the sounds she made. It was like she couldn't hold back.

Holding her down, I took her pussy. Licking, sucking, even biting. Her clit was so swollen, and she was even wetter than I could have dreamed.

I wanted to slide my tongue inside her, to fuck her, to give her the merest hint of pleasure of how my dick would feel, but I wouldn't do anything that would jeopardize her purity. When I took her, it was going to be with my cock, and I was going to relish every single thrust and pulse.

I'd waited too long to waste a moment.

I'd feel that cherry pop beneath the pressure of my cock.

Ashley was going to learn everything about pleasuring me. Being at my beck and call. I craved it. Seeing her fall.

It was what I lived for.

I was going to have everything she had to offer. All of it.

As I slid my tongue back and forth across her clit,

she shook on the bed, her body tensing up.

Her hands clenched at her sides, and still, I held her in place and sucked at her clit, not wanting to give up. She was all mine. I'd waited too long to have her. I wasn't going to wait another moment.

"Please," she said.

I wasn't going to let her go until she came for me. It was what I wanted. After releasing her thighs, I moved my hands behind her ass, squeezing the cheeks, eating her pussy. She was so fucking tasty, and what I loved more was that no other man had touched her.

She was all mine.

Every single part of her.

I was hungry for more.

The moment Ashley exploded, I felt an answering flood of pleasure in my body. This wasn't fake. Being in the trade of human flesh, I was used to a degree of falseness. The lies that were whispered within the darkness to make the payment go a lot smoother. The women I'd paid to fuck, they'd done the same.

They lied.

With Ashley, I didn't want the lies.

Only the pleasure.

The peace she could offer me.

I didn't ease up, making her take every single minuscule pleasure from my touch. My name spilled from her lips, echoing around the room. I was the fucking king in her world. The only man she could ever be with.

I was holding myself back with her, I knew it.

Ashely wasn't ready for the kind of man I was, and certainly not for what she inspired within me on a daily basis.

I'd never been this possessive about anyone.

I'd never been consumed with a rage that verged

on need.

I was desperate to spear my dick into her cunt to make her bleed, to have her as mine, but I held back, letting her enjoy the aftershocks of her release until she couldn't stand it. Only when she couldn't take another stroke of my tongue did I allow myself to ease back. Climbing from the bed, I removed my boxer briefs. I normally slept naked, but with Ashley in my bed, I'd made a few concessions. A lot of them actually.

There was no fear in her eyes.

Wrapping my fingers around my length, I watched her. She sat up from the bed and swung her legs around.

She didn't make any move to hide her nakedness, and I loved that. I wanted her to own her body, to be proud of it. I was addicted.

Without waiting for my instruction, she stepped toward me then lowered herself to her knees.

With her head directly facing my cock, it took every ounce of control not to fuck her face. It was what I wanted to do.

Another time.

I let go of my length, reached out, and circled her hair around my fist. The way she looked at me, I felt like a fucking king.

"Open your mouth," I said.

She opened her lips, and with my spare hand, I fed my cock to her.

I groaned the minute I slid across her tongue, hitting the back of her throat. I didn't make her gag on it, pulling all the way out before sliding back inside. Her eyes closed.

"No, look at me. I want you to see me when I fuck your mouth." I was possessed, and she did as I asked, opening those pretty brown eyes. I couldn't get enough. I didn't allow her to choke on me.

Sliding in and out, across her tongue and leaving my pre-cum as I went, she swallowed me down, my length covered in saliva as she did. Her hands went to my thighs and with each moan, I felt an answering pulse in my balls.

I was so close to coming.

I didn't know if I wanted to come in her mouth, or on her tits, marking her untouched flesh.

At the last thought, I made my decision, taking my cock in my hand. With the grip in her hair, I moved her to the position and then worked my cum all over her chest, coating her tits. Some of the white droplets captured her nipples.

I stepped back from her after I spilled every last drop and looked at my artwork.

She was beautiful.

She licked her lips and held her hands down at her sides.

After going to my knees, I didn't care that I rubbed myself in my own release. Gripping her hair, I held her in place and kissed her hard.

It was the best fucking wake-up call I'd had in a long time.

Chapter Nine
Ashley

"You're alive. That has to mean something," Emily said.

I tucked some of my hair behind my ears. The slight wind was sending my hair off in all directions.

"Of course, I'm alive. Why wouldn't I be?"

"Don't be so naïve, Ash. You know what he's like."

I didn't roll my eyes, but I wanted to. "You don't hear me making comments like that about your men."

Emily's smile didn't quite reach her eyes. I knew she was worried about me. I'd been cooking breakfast that morning when Earl came in, and he'd been on a call. He told me he was sick and tired of his phone blowing up with Monsters. I was to talk to Emily.

I hadn't seen him since.

Hot and cold.

That was how Earl was.

"Exactly, that's the biggest difference, Ash."

Emily pulled me out of my memory. "What is?"

"They're mine. Earl's not yours."

I didn't like the reminder. It wasn't exactly fair.

"Can we talk about something else?" I asked.

"No. How are you? Are you being fed? Are you happy?"

"Yes, I'm fine. I'm being fed." I left out the part of happiness.

"Ashley, talk to me."

"Look, I don't know what you want me to say to you, Emily. All of this arrangement is a little confusing, okay? No, Earl's not mine, but I belong to him. Does that seem fair, no, I don't imagine it does. Again, complicated."

"No, there's nothing complicated about it. You always wanted the dream. The white picket fence. The one guy who came home to you."

I groaned. "Will you stop? At no point did I make myself sound like a housewife. I intended to work, okay. Yes, I originally wanted the ideal. The kids, the husband who loved me, the normal, everyday kind of stuff. In our lives, we don't get to have that."

"Do you have any idea how much I want to hug you right now and tell you it's all going to be okay?"

"You can't protect me, Em. You haven't been able to for a very long time." I wasn't stupid. I had ideals. I'd tried to be the positive, preppy person Emily had needed for seven years.

Emily didn't know the full extent of my pain.

I didn't talk about it.

The years of being yelled at, treated like I was no good. Emily was under the illusion my mother was good. I didn't have it in my heart to tell her the truth, that my mother failed so many times in life.

Yes, growing up, I'd spent hours thinking about a life away from her. About meeting a man who loved me and who I could love, but it never happened. Earl. I didn't know what to make of him.

I loved it when he touched me. The way he seemed to give me orders without speaking a word. Watching him was a highly addictive sport of late.

Of course, when I could find him.

The house he owned on this private island was huge. I could go hours without seeing him.

Right now, I sat looking over the ocean, enjoying the waves. I wasn't too close.

I also had a pair of binoculars, which I kept randomly using. I was weird, all right, I kept trying to find a shark fin, or an octopus's tentacle.

Way too many giant sea creature movies for me. Some were so lame, they were good.

"I don't like the thought of you not living your dream. You've been taking care of me for a long time. Don't think I don't know it, either. I do. I know you've been by my side, protecting me, helping me."

Seven years of helping her get through her heartache.

Leaving her men had really done a number on her.

"You know I love you, Em. Can we not talk about future plans and what we're not going to get out of life? Tell me about your pregnancy."

She was terrified of being a shit mother. There was no way she could be. Emily was a huge softy at heart. The Monsters gave her the chance to be herself, to embrace her softer side.

The girl I once knew back in Crude Hill High, that had been the survivor. That school didn't allow for people to be soft. It was a glorified war zone.

Fucking terrifying if truth be told.

The first day had been a nightmare for me. I was nothing more than a whore's kid, and I'd been easy pickings. If it hadn't been for Emily, they may have killed me and disposed of my body.

I owed Emily so much.

"I don't like changing the subject," Emily said, complaining.

"Tough. It's what we're going to talk about. Come on. Tell me." I held the laptop as Emily stood.

"Can you even see a bump?" The camera was at her waistline.

"Can't see anything, but you do need to eat more. You're way too skinny."

"Then you need to come back home. Cook for

me. The guys would love you back."

Emily got comfortable.

Crude Hill wasn't my home.

I didn't say as such. I refused to upset her.

"Do you have morning sickness? Strange smells? Aching nipples?"

Emily burst out laughing. This wasn't fake. She was truly happy and seeing her this way filled me with so much joy. My best friend had finally found her peace. There was no way I couldn't be happy for her.

"I see you changing the subject. Yes, the morning sickness has started and it's gross. Thankfully, I have my pick of four guys willing to hold my hair and rub my back. Drake helps as well. Coffee makes me feel sick. My nipples are sore. That's pretty much it. Oh, I have this need to make sure the nursery is ready."

"How is Drake doing?" We could come back to safer topics. I never liked Drake in school. He was far too volatile, and I did believe he still was. He hid it well. Either that or his loyalty to the Monsters kept him in check. Again, not my business.

"He's much better, actually. I keep asking him if he's dating his nurse but he's being very tight-lipped on his love life. I tried to get some info from Gael, but they don't talk about Drake's sex life. I think he's into some kinky kind of shit. Kind of scary stuff. Oh, I totally forgot to tell you, Amelia came back to Crude Hill. She's living with us and will be enrolling at Crude Hill High."

I couldn't remember Amelia. "Who?"

"Oh, right. It's kind of not a secret but he's never really made it well known. River's sister. He takes full care of her now. His mother refused to come back, and she pretty much sent her daughter packing. Kind of sad. Amelia seems sweet though, quiet. Like a mouse."

"Please tell me you're being nice to her."

"Ash, I am nice. Besides, she's family." Emily stifled a yawn. "Enough about me. Tell me about you."

I turned the laptop around so she could get a good view of the ocean.

"Holy shit," Emily said.

"Yep, that's my view. It's beautiful."

"Ash, I'm not stupid, okay. I know you. What does Earl have to offer you?"

Resting the laptop on my knees, I stared out at the ocean as I thought about it.

"Ash?" Emily asked after several seconds.

"I know you don't like this arrangement, and you don't see what I could possibly have to gain. The truth is, I don't know. When I'm with him, I don't feel the need to leave. I like being around him. He can be fun."

"You know what he's capable of. What his entire empire is made up?"

I returned my gaze to the screen. "Emily, think about the Monsters, and what they've been involved with. What's to say they haven't benefited off of the women that have been taken and sold?" I hated that part of him.

The world was a horrible place. I got that.

"You're defending him?" I heard the shock in her voice and don't like it.

"I'm not ... damn it, Emily, stop it, okay. I've got to go." I didn't want to carry on a conversation that made me feel so guilty and mad at the same time.

Without waiting for her to stop me, I turned off the chat, signed out, and closed the laptop down. I didn't move, staring out at the ocean.

Earl wasn't too far away.

I could feel him.

I didn't turn around.

"How long have you been there?" I asked.

"Long enough."

"She's my friend and she's worried about me."

"Your friends are safe, Ashley, so long as you stick to the deal and they don't meddle in my business."

He sat down beside me. His warmth surrounded me, even though I wanted to be angry.

He had women on the island. The house was always clean. Not a speck of dust anywhere. The dishes, when we were in the dining room, were always cleaned away.

They moved around without being seen.

"The women you keep close. Do you fuck them?" I asked. The words spilled from my mouth before I had a chance to hold them back.

"No."

"Have you ever ... fucked them?"

"Ashley, be careful."

Tears filled my eyes. It was times like this that I realized our dynamic was captive and captor. I wasn't a girlfriend. I was a piece of flesh.

I felt stupid for thinking it could be otherwise. I gripped the laptop, about to stand, but his voice held me still.

"Yes, I've fucked them. I've had no choice. You can believe me or not, I don't give a fuck. This life, I've fought my way to the top. You don't know how I came to be, Ashley. You don't know what I've sacrificed, what I've fought to claim."

Turning toward him, I saw him staring out across the ocean.

There was no guilt. No remorse.

"I fucked them because it was a requirement. You're aware this used to be owned by my grandfather," he said.

"That's not building it from the ground up. That's

not fighting for your life, for this, every single day. You got it handed to you on a silver platter."

The laugh that erupted from him sent a chill down my spine.

"You think because I was the only living son that I could have all this? The wealth, the power, just because of my last name. Just because his son fathered me." Earl's laughter was dark, sinister, full of hate.

I felt sick, but I didn't get up and leave.

The beast lurked beneath, ready to pounce.

He'd told me vague parts of his life with his grandfather and his father, but I hadn't gotten a lot to build up a picture.

"My father hadn't even earned the right to take over from him. He was learning the ropes. Dealing every single night in pussy. It's what he was doing when he died." Earl's hands were tight, the threat in them clear.

Fear traveled through my body at what he could do.

"You want to go around thinking the world is black and white. That it's either good or bad. You're wrong, Ashley."

He didn't tell me anything more. Earl got to his feet, turned on his heel, and walked away.

I came to realize the reason I was allowed to be alone. I couldn't get the fuck off this island. His men were there. And there was no way out other than with his express permission.

I was trapped here until he was ready to get rid of me.

****

Earl

A young teenager.
"What?"
"You heard me, boy. You get in that room and you fuck

her. If you don't, I'm going to make one of my men, and believe me, they're going to leave her broken and bloody."

I looked into the room.

It was a dirty place where my grandfather kept the girls. It was all designed to make them feel like animals. Their human rights were gone. They were property. They were marked. A single brand burned into their skin at their hip. Each one letting his customers know who she belonged to.

Staring into the room, I saw the property was young. Couldn't be any more than sixteen. I'd seen her arrive. The men had already tasted her virgin state. Blood covered the pants at the apex of her thighs. They'd raped her virginity and made her keep the evidence on her for their own sick games.

My grandfather had been pissed.

A virgin was worth so much more. He'd played along, found out who'd done the deed, and right there, in front of all the women, he'd put a bullet in the man's head.

Now, the girl who'd been torn, she was here, for me.

I hated this.

He commanded his men.

They all did as he told them.

My grandfather had a sick, twisted way of keeping himself entertained.

I didn't know what to say.

My dick wasn't hard.

It was never hard.

Not around the women.

I'd seen what the men do. This was what my father did. I heard them beg. Sometimes at night, I woke up to their screams, begging to go home. Some didn't. Some accepted their fates and they stayed still. They were the good ones, my grandfather said, but they were also the cheapest.

Men didn't always want the ones who weren't broken.

The ones with spirit took the highest price. They went up for auction. Their screams, their promises of retribution, each word, each fight, it all brought in more money. The broken went to the brothels, where night after night, they were taken.

The blow to the head pulled me out of my thoughts, and I realized I'd been staring into the room for a long time. My grandfather's patience had faded.

Hands wrapped around my neck, cutting off my air supply.

"Listen to me, you piece of shit, you go in there, and you fuck her, every single hole, or I will have my men use you."

The door was opened, and I was thrust into the room.

Past experience told me to keep my balance, and not to show that I was taking deep breaths.

My heart raced.

The girl sat on the bed, the dirty clothes still on her body. She didn't look up. Tears fell onto her hand, but she still doesn't make a sound.

I didn't say a word.

The thought of touching her made me feel sick. My grandfather and all of his men were watching.

It wasn't that I'd never been mean or hurt a woman before, this was different. This woman should have been special. The more I got involved with his business, the more I hated it. My mom was part of this world. I never got to see her for who she truly was. I'd only ever known her for a whore.

This girl, and that was exactly what she was, a girl, was already broken. The silent tears, the blood, the drooped shoulders. Taking her would just be shattering another wall of whatever sanity she had left, and I couldn't bring myself to do it.

I hesitated too long.

Within seconds, my grandfather was there, drawing the cane he carried with him down across the back of my head. The blow sent me to the floor. Three men followed in.

My grandfather placed his cane across my throat. The more I struggled, the less oxygen I could get inside. Panic started to cease, but he held me still.

There were times he still shocked me with the strength he possessed for an old man. He played on his age, allowing people to think he was weak. He wasn't. He was one of the strongest and sickest men I knew.

I thought my father was bad. Compared to this man, my father was a saint.

"You're going to watch. She could have enjoyed the experience. I gave you the chance to have a sweet, newly broken-in cunt. Now you get to see how a real man takes her."

He made me watch as they tore the clothes from her body. The three men, two held her down while the other defiled her. One by one, they took turns, using every single hole of her body, and when they were done, she was dead. The last man had strangled the life out of her.

Rage coursed through my veins. A desire to kill filled my core.

It should have been over.

It wasn't.

My grandfather, to prove how big and powerful he was, threw me to the ground, and one by one, the men finished what they had started with her.

Pulling out of the memory, my hands clenched into fists. It was a long time ago. Almost as if it had happened to someone else. My grandfather had watched, bored as they raped me. Later that night, I had no choice but to clean myself up, and my grandfather had warned me. He had no time for pussies. I followed orders, or I was going to be nothing more than a toy for his men to amuse themselves with.

I learned.

I stayed alert.

I followed instructions, even the ones I couldn't stand. Each day, my rage and thirst for revenge had grown until the day had come when I finally killed my grandfather and all the men who had been in that room that day.

Ashley didn't need to know any of that.

My burden. My baggage. No one knew.

Not a soul.

I didn't think of that time. There was no point. It was a waste of time and energy.

I wasn't going to apologize for what I did or why. I left Ashley on the ground without saying another word.

There was no use in talking.

She had her judgments, and to be honest, I didn't give a crap. She could hate me all she wanted. The life I intended to give her was full of luxury. If she needed something to help ease her guilt, she could donate everything she earned to some kind of a woman's shelter.

I walked into the house, and I was surprised when she joined me in my office a few seconds later. I was already pouring myself a large glass of brandy.

"I know the world isn't black and white." She opened, closed her mouth. "This is useless."

"Ashley, you're not going to change who I am. You're going to have to get used to it."

"And if I don't?"

"You're going to have to figure out how to deal with it." I wasn't changing. This world I'd created was all mine. I didn't care how she saw it.

"You really don't care, do you?"

"You're a young woman, Ashley. You have ideals about the world, and most of the time, I appreciate it. Doesn't mean it fits with what everyone wants. It doesn't. You can hate me all you want, but you know I'm right. Are we going to keep going around in circles about this?"

"Tell me about your grandfather," she said after a few seconds had passed.

"No." That was one topic I would never discuss.

"Why not?"

"There are stories you don't need to hear. You think I'm bad, he was worse. The stuff he did. It would turn your stomach, and I don't want to wake up from you screaming because he gave you nightmares."

"And he helped to raise you."

I saluted her with my drink. "Want one?"

She shook her head. "No."

Staring at her, I recalled the nightclub she'd been in with Emily when I approached them recently. Ashley had looked so sexy. She'd captured my attention, but she had seven years ago as well.

"Maybe if you had a drink, it would loosen you up."

"Is that how you want to take my virginity? When I'm not in my right mind to say no?"

I smiled. I couldn't help it. I happened to love her bratty behavior. The spine. The fire. It meant she wasn't broken, and there was nothing appealing to me.

"Ashley, you and I both know if I wanted to fuck you and take what is mine, I could have done it already. I don't even need to try." Sipping at my brandy, I glanced down the length of her body.

The dress she wore molded to every curve. It was made for her. She was so fucking pretty, and my balls ached. I needed to come. Even though I'd come all over those full tits hours ago, I felt the need for a brand-new release.

"Have a drink." I moved toward my sound system. Without asking for her preference, I put on an upbeat dance song. It was one of the tunes that had been playing that night when they celebrated Emily's birthday.

After going back to my drinks table, I poured another glass of brandy. No pressure. If she wanted to drink, she could. If not, then I respected her for it.

"What are you trying to do?" she asked.

"Have fun. Do you know how to do that? Or do you want to keep jumping down my throat about how useless I am as a male?"

I finished my glass and poured myself another.

"I don't think you're useless."

"You hate what I do." I finished off the second glass, the pale liquid helping me to relax. The music finally permeating through the fog. I needed to relax.

I needed to fuck.

There were so many women who'd come to me with just a phone call. I could make Ashley watch while I took them.

I didn't.

I did what I'd never done in my fucking life. I allowed the music to seep into my mind, permitting it to take over. Dancing to the beat as I watched Ashley.

She had the drink in her hand. Her gaze on me. I would have done anything to have her naked and ready for me.

Her gaze stayed on me.

She tipped the glass to her lips and drank. I watched her throat work.

My need for sex was so strong that watching her throat work, I imagined my cock sinking into her mouth, choking her as she took me.

I'd come all over her tits, but now I wanted to fill that sweet mouth.

Seconds turned to minutes, and Ashley finished off one glass while I went on to my fourth.

The music changed through multiple songs, and Ashley's hips began to move. She swayed left and right. I watched her.

Eyes closed, head tilted back to the side. Her hair fell around her in waves, shaping her body.

Slowly, her arms went up, and it was like she got lost in the beat as she danced with free abandon. She looked like a nymph, calling to me.

Finishing off my drink, I answered the call, banding my arm around her waist. She didn't fight me.

I kept one hand on her ass, and with the other, I cupped her face.

She opened her eyes, staring into mine.

I was sure she could see every single part of me. The hard, the soft, the broken, the impenetrable. Ashley didn't know it yet, but she'd stripped me, layer by layer until there was nothing left.

Open.

Exposed.

Vulnerable.

I wasn't a weak man.

This woman had power over me.

I couldn't allow that to happen.

Sliding my hand down from her cheek, I cupped her breast. The music continued to play, and I went to the zipper at the back of her dress, working it down.

She didn't fight, not as I pulled the dress down.

I was completely dressed, and she was naked as I pulled her close to me. I took care of the bra, but the brandy had gone to my head. I grabbed my blade from my back pocket, flicked it up, slid it between her hip and the fabric, and sliced up, removing it.

Clothes on her body offended me. She shouldn't be wearing anything in my presence.

Walking her back to the desk, I swiped my arm across the contents and lifted her up, putting her on the edge.

"Earl."

"Shut the fuck up."

The last thing I wanted to hear was her voice. The accusations. The judgment.

I pushed her so she had no choice but to lay back.

Her body was open for me.

Splaying my palm out across her pussy, I tested her clit, sliding my thumb between her folds and finding her soaking wet.

She could fight me all she wanted, but it wasn't going to take away the fact she wanted this. Her body craved mine.

It would be so easy to grip my cock, press the tip at her core, and slam balls deep inside her cunt.

Taking her cherry wouldn't come to that. She'd be on a bed, and there would be time to enjoy. I was ready to fucking explode.

Working my thumb through her clit, I watched her as she pressed her thighs open. Her body asking what her mouth couldn't.

With my spare hand, I unzipped my pants and gripped my cock. I wasn't wearing any boxer briefs. I was so big, but I was able to work my length out between the gap left by my zipper.

Up and down, I worked the length, preparing myself. The tip was already slick with pre-cum.

When it came to Ashley, I didn't intend to ever wear a condom.

With the tip of my cock at her pussy, I moved between her slit so the head would work against her clit as I thrust forward.

She tensed up, clearly expecting me to fuck her.

Not yet.

All in good time.

I thrust forward, making sure she was wet enough to take this, to work my cock. The moment I was satisfied, I went to her hips, held her in place, and began to fuck her pussy. Each bump against her clit had her moaning my name, arching up, and calling out *yes*.

I couldn't get enough of her.

Ashley didn't know it, but her body, her very fucking self was made for me and me alone.

Up and down, I worked my cock, knowing it wasn't enough. I wanted to plunge balls deep inside her cunt, but I held myself back. I played the good little boy, allowing her to get used to me, to fall for me.

My balls tightened at the sweet sounds she made.

She was so close to orgasm just from my cock alone. I didn't stop, though. This was about me tonight, not her.

Thrusting forward and back, I groaned as with one final thrust, I came, spilling my release onto her waiting stomach.

I stared down into her startled eyes, and the one thing I knew was that Ashley was all fucking mine.

Chapter Ten
Ashley

We were surrounded by ocean, but Earl still had the foresight to install a pool at his private island house.

It seemed rather silly to even have a pool with all that water.

I'd changed into the bikini I found. It was way too revealing. I'd never worn anything like it. The bikini bottoms were small, only just covering my ass and pussy. The bra, pretty much the same. A single piece of string between each cup. More string tied it in the back and around the neck.

My breasts were heavy, and it didn't offer much in the way of support. Back home, I'd have opted for a one-piece. Much more fabric to be able to hide behind.

I didn't mind my body.

With the food I like to eat, I'd accepted I'd never be thin again. I used to be. In high school, eating had been a comfort, but also, with the way my mom was, I'd often be filled with anxiety that it made it difficult to eat.

There was no one around.

Earl had shut himself away in his office.

After last night's dance, followed by semi-fucking, we'd gone to bed. I'd woken up in the middle of the night to find him wrapped around me. The feel of his arms hadn't upset me. I'd found comfort in his touch, and I hadn't wanted him to stop.

I'd fallen back to sleep easily, which was a relief. Usually when I woke up, that was it for me, up for the rest of the night and the day.

Sleeping had always been hard for me.

In the early days of moving to England, the new sounds had made it difficult to relax. I was always having to get used to places to have a good night's sleep.

With no one around, Earl occupied with whatever it was he did while he was here, I snuck out to the pool.

Paddling in the big ocean wasn't going to happen. The very thought of it made me absolutely terrified. Sea-creature fear.

I sat on the edge of the pool, paddling my feet in the water, getting accustomed to the feel and heat.

It was nice.

I gripped the edge and lowered myself into the water. Wadding through the water, I went up and down, then took on the breaststroke, doing the full length of the pool and back again.

Then I floated on my back, staring up at the blaring sun. I'd never been one for summer, or at least I wasn't back in England. I was a comfort girl, sweaters and jeans to keep me warm.

Now though, with the warmth beating down on my skin, I felt lighter than I had in a long time.

I wasn't going to get comfortable with it.

Anything could happen.

On Earl's island, time seemed to stand still.

There was no fear. No pain. I spent a great deal of time confused, especially about Earl's illegal activities. I wasn't going to change him. He was a man who was set in his ways.

An arm clamped around my waist, pulling me down into the water.

A scream fell from my lips, but water filled my mouth as I was taken beneath the surface. The arm holding me down let go, and I quickly broke the water to see Earl standing there, watching me, a smile on his face.

When he smiled, the scar on the side of his face seemed less severe than usual.

My heart raced as I looked at him. "Are you crazy?"

"You looked really peaceful."

"For a reason. I can't believe you did that."

Earl swam toward me, cupping my face. I expected him to kiss me.

I didn't realize how much I wanted his kisses until he got close enough to be a temptation.

I licked my suddenly dry lips. Would it be so bad to kiss him? I knew how good his lips felt against mine. There was no harm in that.

He was going to be doing a lot more than kissing my body.

I waited.

Earl slipped the strings of my bikini open.

"What are you doing?"

"No one is around. You don't need to be modest."

Staring into the pool, I caught sight of his obvious erection. He took care of the bikini in no time. Loosening the strings and letting them fall to the pool floor beneath.

He did the same with the bottoms.

They were gone within seconds, and like him, I stood in the pool naked.

"What about cleaning the pool?" I asked. I went to cross my arms over my breasts, but he stopped me.

"Nothing you need to worry about. It's why I pay people to do it." He dropped a quick, almost playful kiss to my shoulder and stepped back.

I watched transfixed as he slid to his back. The length of his cock, hard, standing tall.

Squeezing my thighs together, I felt an answering pull he created just from looking at him.

No man should have that kind of power, and yet, he emitted it.

I was naked. He was naked.

He was aroused, and so was I.

Ignore it, Ash. You can do this.

I started with the breaststroke, and once I calmed my racing nerves, I flipped over and continued with a backstroke, going the length of the pool as I did.

It was easy. I felt in my depth and comfortable.

Earl faded to the back of my mind where he belonged.

I didn't know what he was doing, and I wasn't going to look for him.

Time passed.

My thirst built, and I moved to the edge of the pool, about to jump out when Earl wrapped an arm around my waist.

"What are you doing?"

"Where do you think you're going?" he asked.

"I'm thirsty."

"So am I," he said. His lips brushed across my neck. A shiver of heat raced down my spine.

He had me pressed flush against the edge of the pool. His hands on my hips, going to my ass, and then he slid his palm between my cheeks, cupping my pussy.

I sank my teeth into my lip, trying to contain the cries that threatened to spill out.

"You make it so hard for me to concentrate. Do you know that, Ashley? I watched you walk out of the house, come to the pool. That bikini should be illegal."

"You packed it."

"I know, which is why I was the one to get to remove it from you."

Two fingers stroked across my clit, and an ache started to build. I didn't know how he knew what to do with my body. I was putty in his hands. Gripping the edge of the counter, I tried to control my reaction to him.

He chuckled.

"You think it's going to be that easy?" he asked. "I know what you want, Ashley. You're ready for me.

We're going to be fire together. You and me. We both know it." His tongue flicked across my pulse before his teeth sank into the flesh.

I cried out at the sudden pressure. It felt good, even though I didn't want it to. His hands moved to my tits, cupping them, kneading the mounds. He pinched a nipple, and I arched against him, trying to get closer.

"I bet you love knowing how crazy you drive me. How much I think about fucking you. You distract me from my work, Ashley. It makes you a very dangerous woman. My enemies, if they ever knew how much you mean to me, they'd try to take you to manipulate me."

They were words that called to me, but I didn't know if I should believe him.

As he worked my clit, they were all the right words I needed to hear. Pleasure rushed through my body, and I couldn't deny it. I didn't want to.

His rough kisses sent me over the edge, and I came hard, calling his name.

Earl worked my pussy until I had nothing more to give. Then he spun me around, keeping me trapped beside the pool.

He took my hand, placing it over his erection.

I knew what he wanted.

I was tempted to deny him.

The heat in his gaze sent another bolt of pleasure rushing through my core.

He knew I couldn't deny him, wouldn't even dream of doing it.

Up and down his length, I worked him, and all the while, he looked at me as if I was the very thing that could save him. That aroused him.

It didn't take long before he grunted, coming into the water.

I let go of his cock, and he grabbed the back of

my neck and slammed his lips down on mine, consuming me.

****

Earl

We'd eaten dinner, and rather than go upstairs, we hung out in the library. Ashley had a cookbook spread out in her lap. Her feet curled beneath her. She was wearing a pair of shorts and a t-shirt. The sheerness of the fabric showed off her braless state. Her nipples were rock-hard.

I noticed she kept pressing her thighs together, and her gaze continued to find mine.

I knew what she wanted.

Her body was hungry.

I'd awakened the need this woman wants, and now I'd left it up to her to pursue.

Sipping at my brandy, I thought about the night I had her spread across my desk. It felt good fucking between the lips of her pussy. I knew it would be even better to be inside her.

She ran fingers through her hair, looking like she was ready to explode.

The emails I was answering were boring. I'd already dealt with the ones sent in code. The kind that couldn't be easily decrypted and of course sent through a secure server. Whenever I dealt with the drugs, women, and guns of my business, I took the time to do so in private so Ashley never got the chance to see what I was dealing with.

Right now, it was my legal business.

She flicked the page with so much force she tore the page.

"Shit, I'm sorry."

Closing my laptop, I placed it down on the table and turned my full attention toward her. "Do you want to play a game?"

"I'm not a child anymore. You don't need to amuse yourself with me."

"I was thinking a game of truth or dare," he said.

This made her eyes roll. "Seriously?"

"We can play a game and make it interesting, or you can continue to squeeze your thighs together, hoping to give yourself some minuscule pleasure just by that touch alone. What will it be?" I asked.

Her cheeks were flushed. She thought I didn't know what she was doing. At times, Ashley was so naïve.

"Truth or dare?" she asked.

"Yes."

"What's to stop you or me from constantly going for a truth?"

"This's what will make it interesting. We have a truth and then a dare, and we must complete it," I said.

"And it can be anything?" she asked.

"Yes."

Ashley licked her lips, glancing all around the room before her gaze came back to mine.

"Do we have a deal?" I asked.

She nodded.

"You may go first." I sat back, watching her.

"Have you ever been in love?" she asked and frowned.

"No. My turn." I decided to go easy on her. "Have you ever been in love?"

She relaxed at my question. "No, I don't think so. I'd have to get to know a person to know how I truly felt about them. Okay, so it's a dare?"

I nodded.

Ashley tapped her fingers on her thigh, closing her book, her focus now on me. "I dare you to … remove your pants."

Again, she frowned and put her face in her hands. This was childish and somewhat entertaining.

I removed my pants and sat.

For the first time since we got here, I opted for boxer briefs with my pants. This game had only just come to me. "I dare you to come over here and kiss me."

She uncurled her legs and walked toward me. I watched her, wondering if she'd cowardly back out.

Ashley cupped my face and her lips brushed across mine. Soft. Sweet.

As quickly as the kiss started, she took a step back. It was now her turn to ask a truth question.

"Do you ever regret what you do?" she asked.

"No."

"Not even once?"

"That's two questions. I will answer it, but you have to give me two dares from you."

"But I'm asking you a truth."

"Rules are rules."

Her teeth appeared on her lip again and she nodded.

"I have experienced regret during my time."

She wanted to ask me more, but I beat her to it.

"Have you thought about being fucked by me?" I asked.

Her cheeks were bright red. "Yes."

"Good. I've got two dares to play," I said. "Do you want to take them both now?"

She nodded and said, "Yes," at the same time.

Running my finger across my lip, I looked at her, wondering what I could have her do. "I dare you … to remove all of your clothes, sit back, spread your thighs, and finger your pussy while we play. That will deal for two of the dares."

"You can't be serious."

"I'm not laughing. I'm totally serious."

I expected her to deny me.

Ashley was full of surprises. She got to her feet and removed her clothes, getting naked for me.

I watched. My cock was already thickening in my boxer briefs.

"Do you want me to get a towel for the sofa?"

I liked that she knew she was going to be aroused.

"No. I've got people who clean it."

She sat back down, spread her thighs, and I watched her hand move between her thighs. A single finger touching herself.

"It's my turn," she said, somewhat breathlessly. With the way she touched her pussy, I was so close to calling the game to an end.

"Did you want to do this with Emily?" she asked.

I wasn't expecting that kind of question. At first, I wasn't sure I'd heard it properly.

"What?"

"You heard me." She paused in touching herself. Her fingers held on her pussy.

"Keep playing, and no. I didn't want to do this with Emily." Was she jealous? "Do you want me to do this with Emily?"

"No."

I smirked. I couldn't help it.

"It's a dare," I said. "Ask me."

"I dare you … to let the next bunch of women who have been captured go back to their families, safe."

I tensed up. "This is not part of the game," I said, annoyance taking over.

"You didn't put any boundaries on the dare. You either play or you forfeit. What's it going to be?"

"It's just a game."

She removed her hand. "Then I can stop at any moment and bring this to an end."

I watched her.

Just as she was about to get to her feet, I stopped her.

"Deal," I said.

"How do I know you'll see it through?" she asked.

"I will make sure it is done. You have my word," I said. Now I was somewhat pissed. The next shipment was coming in tomorrow. Allowing them to be set free went against every single part of me.

I could lie.

This game was supposed to be fun, but she'd made it serious.

It was my turn. "I dare you, Ashley, to let me fuck your tight little ass, right here, right now."

She went even redder at my words.

This wasn't supposed to escalate.

"Don't you ... isn't there..."

"Yes, or no."

She stopped touching her pussy.

I tutted. "You should have known that when you up the stakes, there are consequences."

"Don't you have to get some lubricant?"

I smiled as I reached into the secret compartment of the sofa, retrieving what I needed. I was a man prepared for everything. "Yes, or no. If it's a no, we go back, and the dare you've given me is forfeit as well."

I wasn't a man who would give a woman an out.

Ashley pushed me. Tested me.

"Yes," she said, surprising the fucking shit out of me. Especially when she moved, sinking her knees into the cushion, presenting me with her back. Her head rested on the edge of the sofa, her gaze on me as she reached around, grabbed her ass, and spread the cheeks wide, showing off her anus. "I'm all yours."

My cock was rock-hard.

Getting to my feet, I slid my boxers down, exposing my rock-hard cock. I had the lubrication in my hand, and I moved behind her. Opening the lube, I squeezed some on my fingers and pressed them against her asshole, getting her nice and wet.

She let out a little gasp, and if it was possible, her body got even tighter at my touch.

"You can end this at any time."

I had every intention of fucking her ass, but I planned to enjoy her pussy first, getting her used to taking cock before I brought her to the more intense side of fucking. She'd made her choice by the last dare she'd given me.

"No, I want this."

I wasn't sure if that was a lie or not. Either way, I pressed the tip of my finger against her ass.

Tension mounted in her body as I worked my finger over her puckered hole.

Pressing the tip against her tight muscles, it was near impossible to penetrate her ass. In and out, I worked my finger inside her.

She was so tight.

I put down the tube of lubrication and reached between her thighs to cup her pussy. Spreading her lips, I stroked across her clit, feeling the moisture begin to gather. I stroked and teased her clit, driving her wild with need. I wanted her to be completely into it. Taking her ass, if I wasn't careful, was going to hurt. I didn't want to hurt her. All I wanted to do was get her to the point of pleasure that she couldn't handle it.

In and out, I worked my finger in her ass while teasing her pussy, drawing her closer to the peak, driving her higher and higher.

She was so tight.

Adding a second finger, I continued to work her pussy, feeling her tighten all around me with each flick across her pussy.

She was getting wetter.

My dick was so fucking hard.

When I could stretch her ass to a third finger, her hands gripped the edge of the sofa. Her knuckles were pure white, but she also let out a moan, and her cunt was dripping. She pressed her palm against me, but she wasn't trying to push away from me.

Letting her go, I swiped my palm across my dick, covering it with her arousal before grabbing the lube.

She was nice and slick, but I didn't want to hurt her, and the only way to guarantee that was to be prepared.

I coated my entire length and tossed the tube to the side. I wasn't going to be needing it.

With her in position, I angled her just right so I could have the perfect access to her body. She tensed up again.

"Fucking relax," I said.

I gripped her hip as I pressed the tip of my cock to her anus.

She tightened up.

Moving from her hip, I cupped her pussy again while at the same time I worked my dick into her ass.

I pushed past the tight ring of muscles, and she released a cry. It wasn't one of pain, but I held myself within her, stroking her pussy, building her orgasm back up, until she was the one pushing against my cock, trying to take me.

Inch by glorious fucking inch, I pressed into her tight little asshole.

Ashley took me balls deep, and as I sat at the hilt, the hand I'd been holding my dick to guide into her slid up, wrapping around her neck, pulling her back against me.

I was still teasing her clit, not wanting to let go. Giving her every single kind of pleasure I could think of.

My name fell from her lips.

A promise?

Hunger?

Slowly, I began to work my dick out of her tight ass until only the tip of me remained. I did shallow thrusts, not pushing all the way in, working her pussy as I took her ass.

She was so fucking tight. I knew her pussy was going to be as well. No man had possessed her ass or her pussy.

I was going to be claiming all of it.

Ashley's firsts all belonged to me.

Biting her neck, I sucked on her pulse, desperate to mark her. To secure her as mine for the rest of my fucking life. I couldn't get enough.

I felt the change within her ass. The flutters telling me she was about to come. I didn't make her wait.

As I got her off, her moans filled the room, echoing off the walls. Ashley came with abandon, never holding back. She didn't fake it. Every single part of her was real. As she came, she became mindless. Her body jerking against me, begging for more, riding my cock as I fucked her ass.

I gritted my teeth, trying to stop myself from coming, but it was no use. I wanted to fuck her so hard.

Holding myself back wasn't a practice I was used to.

The instant her release was over with, I grabbed her hips and fucked her ass, going deeply, using her body to satisfy my own needs.

My fingers tightened, and I knew I was going to leave marks tomorrow, but I didn't care. I slammed deep inside her and flooded her asshole with my cum.

We were both panting.

I didn't pull away, not immediately.

Moving her hair out of my way, I kissed her neck. "Be careful how you play with me, Ashley."

It wasn't supposed to sound like a threat, but even to my own ears, it did.

Chapter Eleven
Ashley

I hadn't seen Earl since last night.

He didn't come to bed.

At least, I didn't think he did. There was no mark on the bed to show he'd been there. I lay for an hour after I woke, touching his pillow, wondering why he didn't join me.

It wasn't like him.

In the short time I'd known him and we'd been sleeping together in the same bed, I'd gotten used to his arms holding me.

One night, and I already missed him.

Even after what happened last night, I still wanted him to hold me.

The game shouldn't have gone the way it did.

I couldn't take the dare back, and once it left my mouth, and I wanted to see if he'd actually see it through. Of course, he may not, and my submission to him was fruitful. Only … I'd enjoyed it.

The way he'd taken me.

His gruff demand.

His hands on my body.

The touch of his cock.

His fingers.

All of it created a hunger I didn't understand.

How could I feel anything for him? And yet, I had.

By the time he'd worked my ass and my pussy, I'd wanted it. I didn't mind what he had to do to get it.

I was sore this morning. After he'd completed inside my ass, he hadn't wasted any time. He'd used tissues to cover my anus, wiping the drops of his cum that spilled out. Then he'd picked me up and carried me upstairs even though I told him not to. He'd run me a bath and stayed with me as I washed.

The salts had helped to ease the tension that had built within my body.

I couldn't believe I was still a virgin but had experienced anal sex.

After flinging off the blanket, I walked to the bathroom. Once I'd used the toilet, I flushed and went to the sink. I washed my hands, reached for my toothbrush, and went through the motions of my morning routine.

Breath fresh, face washed, hair in some kind of order, I walked back into the bedroom.

Without thinking, I made the bed before finding something to wear. I settled on a summer dress. This time, I wore a bra and panties.

I'd been a little more adventurous on the island and opted for no underwear, but today, it felt like an extra layer of protection.

When my stomach's growls got too loud to ignore, I left the bedroom in search of the kitchen.

Stale bread lay on the counter beneath a towel, getting ready for the French toast I intended to make.

Gathering my ingredients from the fridge, I started to prepare, aware I couldn't hear a sound.

Silence wasn't usual.

Earl sometimes came and found me when I was making breakfast.

Still nothing.

I wanted to call out.

I was tempted to stop making breakfast, to go and find him. As I dipped the bread into the bowl, letting it soak up the mixture, I headed toward the kitchen door but stopped myself.

If Earl wanted me, he'd have come and found me.

Maybe he needed space.

Last night had been intense.

I knew because even as I tried not to think about it, I couldn't seem to stop. Each action seemed to remind me of last night.

My body ached in places I didn't know were capable. Drawing my focus back to breakfast, I pre-heated a skillet, added a tiny bit of butter, and then layered the two drenched slices of toast, turning the heat down. I wanted it to be lovely and crisp on the outside.

I stood at the stove and couldn't help but sense someone was watching me.

Glancing over my shoulder, I looked left, then turned to look right. Nothing. I got the same sense wherever I went. When I didn't allow myself to think and to just feel.

It was an odd sensation to have. One I knew that meant I must be going crazy. No one was around.

There was no way anyone was watching me. I checked to see if one side of the bread was lovely and golden. It was, so I did a nice little flip to toast the other side.

Cooking was my therapy.

I loved being in the kitchen and had often fantasized about having my own cooking show. Crazy, I knew, but it was what helped me get through when Emily had her really bad days.

With my toast done, I slid it onto a plate, grabbed a knife and fork, poured myself a cup of coffee, and dug in.

I ate alone. Still with the lingering sensation of someone watching.

The hairs on the back of my neck seemed to rise. I finished my breakfast and rather than linger indoors as the house made me a little nervous, I headed out to the garden. I passed the pool and kept on moving until I found a shaded area with lots of trees providing shelter. I stood beneath them. I hadn't gone too far because I could still see the house.

Crossing my arms beneath my breasts, I stood and waited, wondering what the hell I was doing.

It was stupid to be afraid of a house.

Earl wasn't too far.

Annoyed with myself, I went back, but I didn't enter.

Lowering into one of the chaise lounges, I sat back and tried to relax.

Boredom hit me hard. My need to go into the kitchen built with every passing second.

The fear hit me hard, and I hated myself for being so afraid.

There was no way Earl would allow anything to happen to me.

I stood up.

Sat down.

Stood up.

Sat down.

Angry, I released a groan and stood the fuck up. I wasn't going to be beaten by a *feeling*. A *feeling* had no meaning to it. My imagination was running wild.

I walked slowly back to the house.

I hadn't cleaned the breakfast dishes this morning, but entering the kitchen, I see they were already gone. This made me pause. Maybe those were the eyes on me? The people who worked here, they needed to know when to come and go, right?

I had yet to see anyone else besides Earl.

He'd told me they were around, knowing how to do their job. They had to be the ones I'd felt watching me.

Feeling stupid, I turned the stove on. Just the

sound of the oven firing up brought me a sense of calm.

With that on, I was ready. I pulled out some ingredients from the fridge that were necessary for baking, and then checked to make sure I had the relevant pans.

There weren't many, but I had enough.

I even spotted some yeast in the fridge. I checked the date and was happy to notice it hadn't been opened.

Some cinnamon rolls were in my future, providing I actually had the key ingredient to make them all work.

Going to the pantry, of course, I found it.

I didn't know how Earl knew this was what I'd want to make.

I got to work.

Pouring out some milk, sprinkling in some sugar, then the yeast to allow it to bloom.

I hummed to myself as I worked.

No knowable tune, just a sound.

I was happy.

Even with the feel of someone watching me. I tuned it out and focused on baking. I measured out the flour, then some salt as the yeast started to work. I included some more sugar, melted some butter, and then some vanilla.

Again, I was shocked by how many ingredients he had that I could use.

I loved baking almost as much as I loved cooking.

With the yeast ready, I poured the mixture into the bowl and started to knead it with my hand. I couldn't find a mixer, but a little handwork was no problem.

Once it was all mixed, I poured it out onto the counter and got to work, kneading the living daylights out of it. Pushing my palms in, drawing the dough back.

The moment it was springy, and I'd built up a bit of a sweat, I swiped my arm across my brow and then oiled the bowl. Dumping the dough inside, I covered it with some plastic wrap and left it to rise.

Cleaning up my mess didn't take any time at all.

The oven was still on. While I waited, I made a batch of sweet scones. Everyone liked a scone with a cup of tea.

They were in the oven, and the dough was nearly ready after just an hour. I got back to work, making the cinnamon filling.

I'd finished assembling them and allowed them to proof for a second time when Earl arrived.

I put the tin in the oven and gave him my full attention.

He was in a suit.

In his hand was a piece of paper.

I'd already cleaned all the mess.

He slid the paper across the counter to me.

"What is this?" I asked.

"Look at it."

I didn't know if I want to.

My heart had already started to pound. Lifting it up, I saw they were a list of names, followed by locations. Turning it over, I counted fifteen female names on the list, and then looked over at Earl.

The sickness swirled in my gut.

"I didn't back out of my dare."

"You had them waiting?" I asked.

When it came to his life, I shouldn't question it. This was his work, not mine. Had I saved these women? Put them in more danger?

"Yes."

Earl turned back to face me. "An auction was scheduled in three days. It gives the men enough time to get them in line."

"You mean beat and rape them?" I didn't miss the tic in his jaw.

He was pissed off. I made him that way.

"I've told you to not ask me questions you don't want answers to."

"I'm not asking you anything I don't want answers to. Your men beat and rape the women into fear. So they don't fight. So they stand obediently for others to pick over them like cattle."

"This is the end of this discussion," he said.

"I will pay you back all the money that you're saving for me for *company*."

He'd turned away, heading toward the door. My words made him stop.

His hand reached out, touching the doorframe as he turned toward me. "You're serious?"

"Yes. Every single penny. I don't want it. In return, you never take women again."

"You're a fool, Ashley." He left the kitchen, and I rushed to catch up with him.

I wouldn't forget about the cinnamon rolls, but they were the last thing on my mind right now. All I wanted was to know if I could save more women.

"Don't walk away." I reached out for his arm.

He grabbed me roughly and pressed me against the wall. "No."

"Please. The money you're paying me. There's no way you would be getting that much in a shipment of girls."

"In one shipment, no, but you're meddling in shit you have no right to."

"Please."

"No."

"Earl."

"No!" The word was final, the sound echoing around the walls. I couldn't help but feel the tears flood my eyes because I knew it was useless in fighting.

"You need to stop trying to save everyone and think about yourself every once in a while."

"What is so wrong with me wanting to help people?" I asked. I didn't get it.

Where he held me hurt, but I didn't ask him to stop.

"Do you think they'd give a shit if the roles were reversed? That they'd even lose sleep knowing someone was hurt and they could do something about it?" he asked.

"I don't care if they would do the same or not. I'm not doing this for any other reason than because I want to. If I can help, then I will. What is so wrong with that?"

He moved so fast, his lips right next to my ear. His body pressed against mine, and it wasn't erotic. It was a threat.

"You're a naïve fool, Ashley. This world is full of monsters and beasts. We don't pander to you. Left out in the world, someone would come and hurt you. They'd eat you alive and spit out your carcass."

"Do you think you're scaring me?" I asked. He was, but I hoped he didn't know that. Emily had said many the same things in the past seven years. She told me I was too trusting. Too open. Too vulnerable. I cared too much.

If all of that was true, and I guessed it really was, why did it have to be such a bad thing? I cared about people. In a cold, hard world, I tried to offer some kind of hope, and yet, according to Earl and Emily, it made me a fool.

At that moment, I was angry.

"You're terrified. You're shaking."

"Don't mistake my anger with fear. I'm not afraid of you." I pushed against him.

"I haven't given you any true reason to fear me, sweetheart. You want to push those buttons, last night was a walk in the fucking park. I can make you do things that will have you on the edge of your fucking seat. Now, that money is yours. The women are saved, and don't ever fucking test me again. You won't like it."

He let me go. His grip had been holding me up. Now I sank to the floor.

He was right. I was terrified.

I wanted to help people.

I was tired of those closest to me seeing that as a weakness rather than a strength.

****

Earl

"Women are a tool. They're there to be used and taken. It's why they're the weaker sex. They're not strong. Our cocks are hard. We're designed to take."

Running a hand down my face, I poured myself a large brandy. One of my grandfather's many little speeches, pertaining to the differences between men and women, ran through my head. At the time, I had no choice but to listen. To my grandfather, women were put on this earth to be taken by men. To be used by them. They didn't have a mind. They had no right to think for themselves. The only uses they had were their mouths, assholes, and pussies. Everything else about them was useless.

Even with all that teaching and attempt of brainwashing, I didn't believe it.

I'd learned to close myself off.

Business was exactly that, business.

It couldn't be changed.

I adapted what needed to be done.

Now, as I drink the brandy, a luxury in life, I knew the fifteen women from the shipment that would have brought in a pretty penny were all back with their families. I'd kept my word. Followed through with my agreement, and I couldn't stand the tightness within my gut.

I'd lost count of the number of women I'd sold. They were nothing more than numbers. Tallies on a piece of paper, numbers in the bank.

They weren't supposed to matter. I'd resigned myself to them being lonely, runaways, lost. Women who'd been easily led astray, who had a shit life to begin with.

I didn't have to see Ashley's dare through, but for some fucked-up reason, it was important to me to show her that I kept my word. I had. Apart from the renegotiation I'd done with the Monsters, I'd never lied. I'd manipulated the truth.

The women had been waiting in the usual location. A warehouse with each room locked and bolted. A single mattress with a bucket in the corner for them to use for the toilet, giving them nothing. The lives they were purchased for, some were good. I knew that. Some of the men even fell for their products. Others, I didn't imagine the life was as good.

As I poured myself another shot of brandy, my hand shook, and I ignored it, swallowing down the amber liquid.

None of it should have mattered.

Nothing.

Yet, as I'd given the order, my men had been arguing. Telling me that I was making a mistake.

The women didn't see me, but I made sure they knew they had been protected by a fucking angel, and if they talked, I would hunt them down and kill them. Once I discovered that each young woman had a family. The cop on my payroll, whom I paid greatly for information, had found out there was a missing person report on all of them.

They weren't lost.

They were fucking wanted.

I only questioned once, but I was clearly fucking lied to about how they were taken. I truly thought they were lost, not actually taken.

My grandfather had once hinted at what they did and where they found them. Now, I was sick.

The brandy didn't help. Nor did the smell of the cinnamon rolls.

So many fucking women.

They were nothing more than a job. I shouldn't fucking care.

Ashley was my problem. She had made me see them.

With the brandy no longer helping, I loosened my tie and threw it across the room.

I felt out of my mind. Ashley was the problem. She could fucking fix it.

After leaving the office, I found her in the kitchen.

She'd removed her oven glove. Her eyes were a little red.

Going to her, I grabbed her arm, pressed her up against the fridge, and sank my fingers into her long brown locks. After tilting her head back, I slammed my lips down on hers, silencing any protest, ravishing her mouth.

Each touch of this sweet angel soothed my soul.

No one else had cared about her, not really.

Not the Monsters. Not Emily. Just me. She'd

been used and discarded. Her mother had been a piece of shit.

I'd assembled pieces of her life and knew there was a part of Ashley's heart that was shattered.

It fed her need to help others. To make sure they didn't ever feel like she did.

I got it, but I didn't like it.

She was the treasure in life. No one else.

It pissed me off.

Her hands went to my waist. She wasn't pushing me away.

Breaking from the kiss, I grabbed her hand and pulled her upstairs. She didn't tug back, nor did she fight me. There was no one to stop us. No one to hold me back.

Ashley was mine. Fucking mine.

I entered our bedroom and removed my jacket. The clothes were too restrictive. Grabbing my shirt, I pulled it apart. Buttons sprayed left and right.

Before I got to my pants, I was on Ashley, tearing her dress. The fabric gave way beneath my grip.

It was a pretty dress, but it looked even better in pieces on the floor. The moment it was off her, I felt a sense of achievement. The bra was next, followed by her panties.

I quickly took care of my pants and boxers, kicking off my shoes too. I moved Ashley to the bed, getting her to lie down.

Gripping her knees, I spread them open, not giving her a chance to argue with me as I slid my hands down toward her pussy. The lips were already slightly open.

I moved my fingers between her slit to find she was a little dry. I held her thighs open and leaned down, pressing my face against her inner thigh, laying kisses on the tender flesh. There was so much more I wanted to do, but I merely bit down. Once again, I was holding myself back.

When it came to Ashley, I had to. I didn't want her to fear me. I wanted her to crave me as I did her. To become addicted.

Leaving her was a fucking chore and I hated it.

I hated this woman with a fiery passion for how she made me feel. I was a bastard beast. I didn't have feelings. The women I bought were a product. They were a means to an end.

Angry at Ashley, I held the lips of her sex open and took her clit into my mouth, sucking on it hard.

Her cries filled the air, and that was exactly what I wanted, what I needed to replace whatever the fuck was going on in my head.

Ashley caused this. She could help to take it all away.

I used my teeth, scoring around her bud. She arched up, her tits shaking.

Flicking my tongue back and forth, I watched her, hypnotized as she ground herself on my face, enjoying the pleasure I could give her.

I wanted her to come hard. I didn't stop, making her take all the pleasure I had to offer. She was mine. All mine, and I didn't share. I wasn't letting her go.

I brought Ashley to orgasm, but as far as I was concerned, it wasn't enough. I wanted more. I drew a second orgasm out of her, and by the time she was on her third, she was screaming my name. She wanted me to stop but not stop at the same time.

She couldn't take anymore.

Kissing my way up her body, I glided my tongue toward her nipples, circling each bud as I took one then the other into my mouth. I pressed them together, flicking my tongue between each moan, hearing her moans.

I let her go and wrapped my fingers around my dick, working from the base up to the tip, then back down again.

The desire to fuck her cunt was so strong.

Her virginity would be mine.

She was slick enough. Ready for me.

I placed the tip of my dick at her entrance. I couldn't turn away. Staring at where she'd take me. Her thighs quivered.

I wanted this.

To fuck her.

To break her in.

To make her mine.

I didn't penetrate.

I was angry. This wasn't the time to savor.

Pulling away from her pussy, I stood up and worked my dick. Ashley sat up, and I wrapped my fingers in her hair, taking her to the floor.

"Open for me."

She opened her mouth, and I placed the tip of my cock there. Then I started to fuck her lips, sliding across her tongue, going to the back of her throat.

This time, I didn't go easy.

I made her choke on my dick, swallowing me down.

Ashley's hands sank into the flesh of my thighs, holding me still, but I had a firm grip on her hair and stroked myself to completion.

"Don't swallow until I fucking tell you to."

My cum flooded her mouth, and I eased from between her lips, tilting her head back. Some of my release was already on her pink lips.

"Show me."

She opened her mouth, and it was full of my spunk.

"Now swallow it."

She closed her mouth, and I watched her throat move.

"Show me."

Ashley swallowed all of my cum.

"Good girl."

Letting go of her hair, I should have felt satisfied, but I wasn't. The orgasm had taken away my anger and my tension. I was so close to fucking her for the first time, and that wouldn't do.

When I claimed her pussy, I'd enjoy every single second, and it wouldn't be in anger.

Chapter Twelve
Ashley

I never saw the piece of paper again.

It was like it didn't exist.

The women were no more.

They'd gone home to their families, and I didn't know if I'd done the right thing or not. Earl kept his distance.

I didn't know how much time passed.

Days and nights passed. I lost count of how many.

Only when I talked to Emily did I have any indication of how long I'd been on the island. We were approaching five months now. Five months since he'd brought me here. Still, I was a virgin.

I really thought he was going to take me that day.

Earl came and went off the island.

I didn't know how he left. Each morning he was gone, and he'd return. I didn't hear a helicopter or see a boat.

I could go exploring, but each time I tried, I actually saw one of his guards. It was the only time I saw someone else.

The silence. The loneliness was starting to wear on my nerves.

So much so that I stood at the edge of the ocean, the waves lapping at my feet. The sun was setting once again. The island was so beautiful, as it always was. The beauty was fake. All of this, it meant nothing.

There was no truth in it.

There was no happiness here.

Just the sense there could be.

Tears filled my eyes as I took another step into the ocean. I hated the water.

I liked swimming in a pool, but the ocean contained so many other living things. It terrified me.

My heart raced as I took another step.

I didn't want to be on this island anymore.

It was so lonely. So quiet. I missed the hustle and bustle of London. The rudeness of people. The laughter. The anger. I missed the rawness of humanity.

Here, it was like I was set apart from it all.

I'd landed in some dystopian world, and I couldn't handle it. Not anymore. I needed to be surrounded by something more.

Tears spilled down my cheeks as I took another step, then another. I was waist-deep in the ocean, with the sun setting. With sharks, and so many other beasts that would kill me.

The one on the island, he wouldn't touch me or hurt me. He'd spanked me, yelled at me, sometimes grabbed me roughly, but he hadn't truly hurt me.

There was no chance of him killing me, and at that moment, so lost and alone, it was all I could think about to be peaceful.

Emily once told me she thought of dying, of taking her own life, and it made me wonder if I had it in me to kill myself. Could I keep on going? The water scared me the most, but this not knowing was the worst.

He kept me here like an object, waiting for him.

Ever since our dare, he'd been distant. He was unhappy with me.

Did I finally make him feel something? Anything? I clenched my hands at my side. Every part of my body screamed for me to turn back, but I took a step further, and another until the water lapped at my chin.

If there was a shark or a sea beast, they could take me now. I was deep enough. I thought.

My heart was pounding. The urge to swim

consumed me. If I started swimming, I could keep on going until death claimed me.

I lifted up and began to float, staring up at the night's sky that would soon be cast all over. The sun was so close to setting.

I turned over with the intention of doing exactly that when an arm wrapped around my waist and dragged me away from the peace I was hunting.

Screaming, I fought the hold, but he wouldn't let me go.

Earl's curses rang out in the night and with it, my anger as well. How dare he!

When we were back to shore, he threw me to the ground.

"What the fuck were you thinking?"

I didn't think. I got to my feet and attacked him. He grabbed my wrists, stopping me from clawing at his already scarred face.

I wanted to put a mark on him. So I knew there was something more to him than the asshole beast that kept me here.

He shoved me back, not hard, but enough for me to stumble.

"Why did you stop me?" I asked, screaming at the top of my lungs. My throat hurt. Tears spilled down my cheeks, and I made no move to bat them away. I wanted the tears, the anger, the aggression. It was all directed at him, and he deserved it.

"Do you really think I'd let you escape?"

"Is that what you think? I'm trying to escape you? I'm trying to get the hell away from this, from myself, from you, from everything. I don't want to escape. This isn't about freedom."

"You were trying to kill yourself?" he asked.

"Was this the torture you set out for me? To

break me down? To watch me lose every single part of myself?" I laughed. "Of course, it is. This isn't about my virginity. This is about you having complete control."

"You don't know what you're talking about."

"Yes, I do. If it was just sex, you'd have had me already."

"Get in the house."

"No!" I slammed my foot down. I wasn't going to be ordered around, not by him, not anymore. I wasn't in a position of power, but I did have something I could take away from him. Glaring at him, I stepped toward him. "Take it. Get it over with. Fuck me, Earl Valentine." I spoke his full name, and other than his nostrils flaring, it was like there was no reaction to him. He was a cold man.

"Get in the house before I make you."

"Then make me, Earl. But know this, if you don't fuck me tonight, your chance with a virgin will cease." I moved up toward him.

"There's nothing you can do."

"No. All I need is something round and deep. I can press it against my pussy and plunge it in, tearing away my virginity. That small piece of flesh you value so highly."

His fingers wrapped around my neck. He pressed down just a bit, giving the hint of what he could do, but he didn't go tighter. I could still breathe.

"You wouldn't."

"Test me. See what I do."

I screamed as I was suddenly thrown over his shoulder. I was drenched from the ocean. I didn't go willingly.

Hands clenched into fists once again, I pounded at his back. He slapped my ass, and I just continued to beat on his ass, screaming to make him put me down.

I didn't know what the hell was going on with me.

I was crazed. On the razor edge of oblivion. Hungry to make him react.

I was tired of being in this rut with him. I was even more tired of being left alone. The island was starting to get to me. I always considered myself a mentally strong person, but everyone had a breaking point. He was forcing mine.

We were in the house as I watched the floor come into view. His foot kicked the door closed, and then we were making our way upstairs. One step, then the other. He wasn't slowing, and the speed at which he was moving made me feel a little sick.

I didn't like hanging upside down. The desire to vomit was strong, and it immediately vanished as he dropped me onto the bed.

This time, I didn't run away. He stepped back and started to loosen his clothing, revealing the expanse of his heavily inked, muscular chest. The pants were next, but I didn't allow myself the pleasure of watching.

Getting to my feet, I removed the wet dress, followed by my underwear. With my gaze on his, I slid up the bed to lay against the sheets, open, exposed, ready for him. My legs spread for him to see.

My hands clenched against the blanket as he crawled onto the bed.

His cock was long and thick, slightly intimidating as he made his way toward me. He reached out, grabbed my neck, and pulled me in close. His lips slammed down on mine. Our teeth clashed together, and I groaned, gripping his shoulders for something to hold on to as he took full possession of my mouth.

All the other times, Earl had been holding back. This time, he gave me his all, and it was so fucking powerful. I couldn't stop the feelings swirling in my body.

The control he had was out of this world, and now, I was seeing the true man. The one he kept on a leash.

He held me in place as his other hand dived between my thighs, stroking me. His touch was gentle and rough at the same time.

His lips moved to my neck, and he sank his teeth against the pulse, sucking hard. "You're going to learn to be careful what you ask for."

Before I realized what was happening, he had my hands tied at bindings on each corner of the bed. They were soft, but he kept them tight. I couldn't pull them down. He was settled between my thighs.

He kissed down my body, taking time on each breast. His suction was too strong, verging on pain as he flicked his tongue across each bud, teeth biting down. I'd be marked tomorrow when he was done with me.

All the while, he fingered my pussy. Two, running either side of my clit, getting me nice and wet, ready to be fucked.

I'd started off dry, but now I was aroused. I liked what he was doing to my body. He was waking it up, as if I'd been in a long sleep and now it was time for me to know.

He moved up my body, and the length of him pressed to my core.

I couldn't touch him. My hands were tied above my head. There was no control. I was at his mercy.

His hand moved down between us. The touch of his cock at my slit. He rubbed himself through my arousal and then the tip of him was at my core.

His eyes were on me.

I couldn't look away. I didn't want to.

He'd captured me. Held me prisoner. I expected him to stop. To pull away. To leave me wanting.

Earl tensed up and slammed every single inch of his cock deep inside my pussy, tearing through the thin piece of flesh, fucking me to the core.

I couldn't stop the scream that left me or the way I arched. I knew why he had my hands trapped above my head. He didn't want me to fight him. I needed to push him off, making him stop.

Only, he wasn't moving.

His eyes were closed. His jaw clenched. Still.

Tears fell from my eyes. It hurt, really bad. I knew it would. Had no idea it would hurt *this* bad, but it was gone. My virginity was gone to a man I didn't even know if I liked half the time.

I held perfectly still. The pain started to ebb. Just the hard feel of his stiff prick inside me. He didn't go soft.

He cupped my cheek, swiping at the tears, and I stared into his eyes, wondering what the hell I was seeing.

We're not the same. There was no way we were compatible. He was an asshole of the highest order. I didn't like him.

And yet, he waited.

The kiss he gave me now wasn't rough, it didn't hint at punishment. This was gentle. It was sweet. It was lovemaking.

I didn't want lovemaking. I wanted fucking.

His hands moved down my body, stroking across each curve, coming to stop at my hips. I couldn't resist rocking my hips up toward him.

I swallowed down his groan.

Earl tensed up, and slowly, he started to move. Each movement so subtle to start with. A slight thrust.

Getting me used to the feel of him.

I moaned his name, and he didn't stop kissing me.

The pain was completely gone, and I couldn't keep myself still. So with each thrust inside me, he began to meet me until we were in a steady pace. He pulled out, and I thrust back, ass to the mattress. He pushed back in, I pushed up, meeting him.

Slowly at first, then it turned into a frenzy.

Earl sat up, put his hands on my arms, keeping me down, and then pounded inside me, the headboard hitting the wall.

"Fuck, so fucking tight, so fucking sweet." He sank his fingers into my hair, taking my mouth once again, and he came, slamming to the hilt within me.

Each pulse of his cock flooded my pussy as he finally spilled inside me.

It was over.

It was done.

I was a virgin no more.

I should be relieved.

Instead, I was terrified. What if he didn't want me anymore?

****

Earl

I hadn't left Ashley alone on purpose. My work didn't allow me the luxury of a lot of time away. I always had to be one step ahead of my enemies, and since fulfilling the dare to Ashley, I'd encountered several problems.

According to the cop I employed, three of the fifteen women had been reported missing again. Their last-known whereabouts put them outside of work. There was always the chance this could happen.

I wasn't the only trafficker in the industry.

There were a lot of men and even women who

used human flesh to make money.

The last shipment of girls had also been delayed because an attack at the docks had resulted in ten girls being taken, and three had been killed.

Not good.

I hadn't had to deal with this kind of disrespect since I had taken over from my grandfather and people were testing me. A show of strength was needed, and that meant less time on the island. So much so, I hadn't been back in days.

Upon coming home to find Ashley chin-deep in the ocean with the intention of swimming off, I lost it. With everything she'd caused, if she thought she was getting away from me, she had another thing coming.

I was shocked to see in the short time I'd been away, she'd lost weight. The sparkle in her eyes had dimmed a little. I didn't like the woman staring back at me. I had to make it stop.

The fire had come back with the threat of taking her own virginity. I wasn't entirely sure if she'd do it or if she was bluffing.

I hadn't intended to fuck her while I was so angry.

With her naked, spread, waiting, her pussy soaking wet, and the weeks apart, I'd needed her.

After taking her, I'd released her arms, and she'd wrapped them around me. Her words were unmistakable even as she muffled them against my chest. "Please don't leave me here. I don't want to be alone anymore."

I was a hard man. I didn't break easily. I was used to taking what I wanted. Of fucking women and moving onto the next.

She'd broken my heart.

I hadn't said a word. I picked her up, carried her through to the bathroom, and drew a soothing, salt-filled bath. Once she was inside, I'd returned to the bedroom. The sheets showed the evidence of her virgin state.

Blood mixed with my cum and her arousal.

I hadn't brought her to orgasm. Even afterward.

After stripping the bed, I kept the sheets, a token, changed them, and returned to the bathroom. I'd joined her in the bath.

All of Ashley's fight had left her. She'd collapsed against me, and I held her as I washed her body then my own. I'd put her to bed, and now I lay beside her.

I'd already slept for a couple of hours.

Watching her sleep was the pleasure I'd been after.

My marks had appeared on her body. Tiny bruises from my fingers digging into her flesh.

A stray curl lay across her face. Taking it with my finger, I moved it out of the way.

She looked so sweet. So sexy.

I couldn't help but touch her. Placing a hand on her shoulder, I pressed a kiss to her cheek.

Eyes opened, Ashley smiled at me, and as she did, she gave a little stretch, which then caused her to moan.

I waited for last night to come as a reminder to her. The moment it did, I saw it.

Her eyes went wide. Her teeth sank into her bottom lip. The blush coating her cheeks had me wanting me to give her a reason to be a little embarrassed.

"What happens now?" she asked.

It wasn't a question I expected. "I think it's time I took you back to the living. The island is getting to you." I didn't want to see her chin-deep in the water, or worse, not find her at all. I didn't expect her to ever try to escape. Her fear of sharks and the ocean kept her here.

I'd been unfair.

"Is this where you leave me?" she asked. "You got what you wanted."

"Don't. You freely offered it to me. In fact, you begged me to take it."

"I was tired of waiting."

"And do you think one fuck is going to satisfy me?" I pulled the blanket off her body and moved so I sat between her thighs. With her legs wrapped around my body, she couldn't close them or keep me away.

Pressing my thumbs to her lips, I spread them open and with a groan, looked at her wet cunt. She was turned on. I wondered if I was the cause of her arousal, or if it was something to go with another man? A dream perhaps.

Jealousy struck me hard and fast.

I was a full-grown man. I didn't feel this way. Not even about an imaginary friend. Pushing the thoughts to the back of my mind, I focused on her now.

I didn't have to hold back as I slid two fingers inside her pretty cunt. Newly broken in. My dick was the only one she'd ever feel.

Ashley still thought I was going to let her go. That there was a chance I'd leave her.

She was in for a rude awakening. One taste would never be enough.

Ashley was mine. I wasn't ever giving her back.

I'd never had someone that was just mine. All of her firsts, all of her memories. Ashley didn't even have a past boyfriend to compare me to.

She was all fucking mine and if I had to, I'd get it inked all over her skin, *property of Earl*.

"You only wanted one thing from me."

"And now I want more." With two fingers inside her, I pressed my thumb to her clit. She let out a cry, her cunt tightening around my fingers. She enjoyed it.

In and out, I worked her body.

She moaned my name. The sound I was becoming highly addicted to.

"That's right, Ashley."

Some of my cum would still be inside her. I cleaned her last night, but I had a lot to spill within her tight walls.

I gripped her ass and tugged her close. Now I used my mouth, tonguing her cunt, slamming inside her.

At first, Ashley started out tense, trying to fight against my touch. With each stroke of my tongue, the fight in her withered away until she was rubbing her pussy against my face, bringing her closer to orgasm.

I waited, leading her to the peak, holding her just there but not letting her go over. Finally, when I knew she couldn't handle another second, I thrust her over the edge.

Lowering her to the bed, I worked my fingers over her clit, eking out every ounce of her release. At the same time, cock in hand, tip at her entrance, I slammed inside her, feeling the aftershocks of her orgasm work their way up my dick.

She felt perfect. Closing my eyes, I allowed each ripple to surround my length until she couldn't take another moment.

I let go of her clit, gripped her hips, and started to fuck her. Slow strokes at first until they built, going harder and deeper.

She wrapped her legs around my waist, and I spun us around so she was the one on top. Running my hands up her body, I cupped her tits.

"I don't know what to do."

I fingered her nipples, loving the sight of her head tipping back, grinding on me as she lost a little control.

Such a highly addictive sight. I couldn't resist it.

Grabbing her hips, I showed her what I liked, guiding her over my dick, getting her to set a pace that would suit the two of us.

It didn't take her long to lead. Working her pussy, bouncing on my cock so I could marvel at the weight of her tits. So heavy.

I cupped them as I groaned, thrusting up to her pussy.

When I couldn't take it anymore, I held her ass and fucked up into her, making her take all of me. I came like that, filling her pussy.

Wrapping my arms around her, I took her back to the bed, stroking the hair out of her face.

"So, what do you think about fucking?" I asked.

The warmth in her cheeks made me question her.

"I love it," she said. "Can we do it again?"

"We're not ever going to stop doing it."

Chapter Thirteen
Ashley

"We're not ever going to stop doing it."

I released a scream. I'd been trying to hold it in, but the moment Earl touched me, all thoughts left my body. It didn't matter that we were in a fancy clothing boutique, or that I was naked, and he pounded into me from behind. His hands on my tits as he drove inside me. All the while, he made me watch him in the mirror.

It had been a week since he'd taken my virginity.

The next day, he'd packed us up, and I realized a few miles from the house, there was a small helipad. That was how he kept coming and going. We were away from his island in a matter of hours.

We stayed in the penthouse he owned in the city. Every day and night, we fucked.

I no longer felt sore, which was insane as all we did was have sex.

Each time I thought it would be the last, only the moment he touched me, I couldn't resist him.

He'd taken me to a restaurant yesterday, and he'd followed me to the bathroom. Even as people came and went, he had me pinned up against the stall, taking his length. Much like now, only this was far more intense.

The hand at my chest moved up to wrap around my neck.

He pulled me back so his lips were at my neck. "I fucking love how you take me. Your pretty pussy knows what it wants. I'm the only dick it craves."

I moaned.

"Say my name."

"Earl."

"What am I doing to you?"

"Fucking my pussy."

"That's right, and who owns this pussy?"

"You do."

He slammed in deep, and I felt wave upon wave of his cum as he came. The veins in his neck seemed to pop out with the restraint he showed.

With the last of his orgasm ebbing away, he laid gentle kisses across my shoulder.

"My cum is going to spill down your thighs the moment I let you go."

Sinking my teeth into my bottom lip, I nodded.

"You're not going to clean it up. I want it to stay there so you remember me."

As if I could forget him.

Ever since he found me chin-deep in the ocean, he'd been far more attentive. He'd pushed me to the breaking point.

I'd never been so relieved to hear cars and people. Even arguing. The first night back, we'd stood in the elevator as a couple screamed at each other.

I'd lapped it up. Loving the fact people were angry. I still lived.

Earl eased out of my pussy, and his cum spilled down my inner thighs. I pressed them together, thankful I had thighs that met in the middle so it couldn't go anywhere else.

I changed quickly into my clothes.

Earl grabbed my hand, and we left the stall. He'd picked up the clothes, and I left him to deal with the sales assistant.

He'd been determined to take me shopping. I hated shopping. Clothes were a necessity, but I never got any enjoyment out of it. The truth was, for me, my favorite kind of shopping was at the supermarket, buying food. Lame, I knew.

Within seconds, we were out of the shop. His

guards following in front and behind us as we moved along the street. People kept a wide berth, no one daring to come too close.

"Do you ever really get used to this?" I asked. I was so far out of my depth.

"What?"

"This? You know, people not wanting to be near you."

"It gets easier after a while. Don't worry, you'll get used to it."

I wasn't entirely sure I wanted to get used to it. I kept my mouth shut. Neither of us had spoken about our truth-or-dare game, or what happened after.

We found another restaurant to eat at.

I liked the food, but I missed cooking. The past week had been a lot of fun, but I wanted to eat my food.

His guards always took a separate table. If the place was fully booked, people lost their seats. I hated how powerful he was at times. How easy it was for him to move people along as if they didn't matter.

To Earl, they didn't. He rarely saw other people.

Sitting opposite him now, our first course already in front of us, I wondered how much of this life he truly enjoyed.

There was more to Earl than what met the eye. I got that. It was why I didn't fight my attraction to him.

"Do you still feel me?" he asked.

"Yes." I couldn't help but glance left and right.

"No one will say a word to you."

"It's not about that. I just, I don't want people to know what we get up to. You know?"

The smile on his lips was a combination of sin and dark secrets.

"You think they don't know that I've fucked you senseless? The mark on your neck and wrists, the plumpness of your lips? All of it is proof of a woman who has been taken."

I couldn't help but lick my lips.

I knew I'd been thoroughly fucked. My body was very much aware of it. The pleasure was intense.

Even when he took me in the changing room less than an hour ago, I felt an answering heat in my body.

"You're thinking about it now, aren't you?"

I simply nodded my head, not wanting to give this feeling any other kind of word.

The second and third courses came to us quite quickly.

Earl took care of the check, and I was in his arms. We were back on the street, only this time, we went to the car.

He gave the driver the instruction to take us back home.

As we drove through town, his hand rested on my knee. I wanted to move it up further. Even though we were in the car, so close, I craved his closeness. He didn't even move an inch.

Staring out of the window at the passing streets and scenery, I smiled to myself. I didn't think it was possible to be happy like this.

There was an easiness to it.

When I was around Earl, he was the one in control. He made me feel safe. The power he held came from sources I didn't like, but again, I had to question his feelings about it.

He'd gone through with the dare.

"Oh, fuck!" the driver yelled. "Impact!"

The car suddenly spun out of control, and we were shoved forward. I was wearing my seatbelt, as was Earl. The windows smashed. Just when I thought we were over the worst, something hit us from the side.

I cried out as my head slammed against the side of the car.

There was so much pain, and then everything went black.

****

Earl

Several hours later

I paced the bedroom. So close to calling the doctor and ordering him back to my place to check on Ashley again. She still lay on the bed. I'd changed her out of the clothes that were cut up and coated in blood.

We'd been ambushed today in the middle of the fucking street.

I'd been so distracted by Ashley, I hadn't noticed the guy tailing. I was angry that I was so careless. I never forgot how close I was to death, to my enemies. They were always watching.

I should have noticed we were being followed.

Now Ashley lay in bed. The doctor had promised she'd come to, but he'd gotten another call.

Just as I was about to lose my shit, Ashley started to moan.

We'd had such a good fucking day. I'd made the ultimate mistake of forgetting. I wouldn't make that mistake again.

"Earl?"

I was at her side, holding her hand. "I'm here."

She groaned, licking her dry lips.

I'd already gotten her some water, and I held out the glass, placing the straw against her lips. "Drink."

She did as I told her, swallowing large gulps of water.

I was so fucking relieved she was alive.

This wasn't what I had planned for the day.

Her face was heavily bruised. The doctor also had

185

to remove shards of glass from her hair.

After the car had slammed into Ashley's side, we'd been shot up. I'd gotten out free and took out two men. But I lost one of our own before I could help Ashley out of the car.

"What happened?" she asked.

"You were in a car accident."

She frowned, opening her eyes. "I feel like I'm going to be sick."

Grabbing the trash can, I held it beneath her, and she started to throw up. Gripping her hair, I kept one hand on her hair, the other on the trash can. Her hands shook. The doctor said she'd feel sick.

I held the water out to her as she finished with the bucket. Placing it on the floor but within easy reach.

"My head is killing me."

"You were knocked unconscious from the impact. The doctor will be back to assess you."

"I was out for a long time?"

"Yes."

She rubbed at her temple. "What happened to the other people? Are they okay?"

I frowned. She didn't even realize this was intentional.

"Ashley ... no, they aren't."

"What?" she asked. "We killed them?"

Cupping her face, I tilted her head back, but she covered her mouth. "They weren't good people, Ashley. They were my enemies."

"Enemies?"

"I've got them all over. I've told you this before, and today, they started a war."

It had been a long time since I'd been attacked this openly. With Ashley in the car, it guaranteed those behind it were going to suffer. I would never allow anything to happen to her.

I was known for my rage before, but this went beyond that. I was a cold-blooded killer. I struck without mercy.

With Ashley so close, the need to protect her overtook all other feelings. Those who had organized this hit would feel my wrath.

Tears filled her eyes. "Are you okay?" She put her hands on my body. "They didn't hurt you, did they?"

Even now, she was more worried about me than herself.

It made me want to kill even harder.

"Yes, I'm fine."

"Are you sure?"

"Yes. I'm not the one who banged my head." I placed my palm against her head. "How do you feel?"

"Fine."

"Don't lie to me."

Her lip wobbled as she smiled. "Like I've been run over time and time again."

"The doctor is coming back to check on you."

"I'll be fine. People end up in car accidents all the time."

Yes, but they didn't end up nearly dead because they were the enemies of one of the passengers.

"Earl, you're scaring me," she said.

I didn't mean to scare her. The truth was I was fucking enraged. Killing some of the men who'd been involved with the crash hadn't stopped my thirst for blood, for revenge. Now, I needed to fucking drown in it.

"Are you hungry?" I asked.

It wasn't like I could feed her. She was the best cook around. We both knew it.

She tried to pull the blanket off her body, but I took hold of her wrists and stopped her. "No. You've got to rest until the doctor gets back."

I wished I hadn't let him go now. Staring at Ashley, seeing how vulnerable and fragile she looked, it was hard for me to stay in control.

"Let me at least come and sit with you."

"I'm fine."

"And I feel fine. You can make me something to eat and this way it will at least taste good." She tried to wink at me, but it fell flat.

Stroking my thumb across her cheek, I skimmed across her lips. So plump. The way she'd looked in the car. I hadn't had time to panic as the bullets had been raining down on us. All I could do was react and deal with the problem at hand.

The minute it had all stopped, I hadn't wasted any time. The doctor had been pissed at me for moving her, but I had to get her out of there.

Anyone could have seen her.

I couldn't allow my enemies to know how I felt about her.

This went way beyond taking her virginity, as I knew it did back when I first took her.

"I'm right here," she said, pressing her face against my palm.

It still didn't help.

I felt I was on the edge of losing my mind. I needed distance. Getting to my feet, I eased off the blanket, and rather than allow her to walk, I slid my hands beneath her legs, supporting her back at the same time.

"Earl, what are you doing?" she asked, releasing a little giggle as I carried her all the way to the kitchen.

I made sure she sat in the most secured seat, high handles surrounding her, keeping her locked into place.

She touched my hand, and I kissed the top of her

head.

After going to the fridge, I stared at everything and just began to grab stuff. I wasn't paying attention. My only concern was the woman in front of me.

With all the food picked, I decided to chop everything up, throw it into a pan, and mix it around.

Ashley stayed silent.

I didn't know what I was doing. Onions, peppers, even potatoes chopped up went into the pan.

Giving everything a turn, I felt Ashley's eyes on me, but she made no comment as I seasoned it and then mounded a plate high, pushing it toward her.

Without question, she picked up a fork and took a bite. As she heaved, I realized I hadn't cooked the potatoes long enough.

"Shit. Fuck. Shit. Bastard. Cunts." The control I'd been going for ended.

I grabbed her plate, picked it up, and launched it across the room. It smashed against the wall. Some of the peppers stuck to the wall but eventually fell down to the floor.

The skillet. The glasses. I tore the kitchen apart even as Ashley let out a scream and flinched away.

Nothing got near her.

I wasn't going to hurt her. My anger was at how hurt she got.

Halfway through my rage, my kitchen was completely trashed, but the doorbell rang, alerting me that someone was joining us.

Running my hands down my chest, I smiled at Ashley before going to answer the door. The only way people could get to my apartment was through my men. They were all stationed at different points within the building. This way I knew, for the most part, everyone getting to my place had been vetted.

I expected the doctor. Emily came barreling into my apartment. I glared at the men who were supposed to be acting as guards.

Caleb, River, Gael, and Vadik were all with their woman.

This pissed me off.

"I'm waiting for the doctor to arrive."

"We heard about the accident," Caleb said.

"That's funny. I don't seem to recall making it to the news." These men needed to die. I didn't like them meddling.

I heard Emily and Ashley in the distance.

Stepping back from the door, I waited for them to enter before closing the door.

I wasn't in the best of moods. I didn't linger at the door. Heading back to the kitchen, Emily had Ashley's face in her hands.

"What the hell did you do to her?" Emily asked.

"Em, stop it. Nothing has been done to me." Ashley grabbed her friend's hands, pushing them off her face. "I'm fine. I'm good."

"For your own safety, I suggest you keep the suspicions to yourself." The last thing I wanted to put up with was her fucking meddling, poking at me.

"Look at the mess!"

Emily's four minions joined us as she put her hand on her waist. The heavy pregnancy was very clear.

"We're waiting to hear from the doctor. You're free to stay here until then. Afterward, you're going to have to leave."

"I'm not leaving her with you." Emily advanced toward me, and she was an easy target. I reacted. I wrapped my fingers around her neck. She was the cause of so much shit and trouble.

At my back, I heard Caleb, River, Gael, and

Vadik draw their weapons.

"We're all friends here," Ashley said, getting to her feet. She grabbed my arm. "I know you're angry. They didn't cause the crash. It was not their fault. Earl, please."

Her fingers sank even tighter, and she let out a groan. The moment she started to sway, I let Emily go and grabbed Ashley, holding her in my arms.

"I don't feel so good."

I pushed some hair from the back of her face.

Nothing could happen to her. She was too precious for this world. No one deserved her.

"You've done too much." Ignoring Emily and her men, I picked up Ashley in my arms and carried her back through to our bedroom.

I lowered her to the bed.

Ashley whimpered. "I'm sorry. I don't mean to look weak."

"Shut up. You're fine. You shouldn't have been doing so much. It's not good." I wanted to touch her, to surround myself in her to make sure she was fine.

All that kept going off in my head was how many people died from head injuries. Was it a lot? A little? People died for no good reason, and the thought of Ashley dying, well, it filled me with an anger unlike any other.

She couldn't die.

"Please, don't hurt my friend. She's been through enough."

"What about you?"

"I'm still alive to talk about it." She grabbed my hand where I held her cheek. Kisses filled my palm. "For me."

"You keep asking so much of me."

"And you do the same in my position. This isn't

Emily's fault. They came here to be friends."

The doorbell rang again, and I cursed. "That should be the doctor this time. I'll be right back."

I stood and found Emily in the doorway. "Stay with her."

Without another word, I left the bedroom to go kill anyone else who was at the door who wasn't a fucking doctor.

Chapter Fourteen
Ashley

I had a concussion.

Between Emily, Earl, Caleb, River, Gael, and Vadik, I was covered for company. I wasn't allowed to sleep for too long, and I needed rest. Just by going into the kitchen to supervise the mess Earl had tried to call dinner, I'd done too much.

For three days, I stayed in bed.

Earl helped me to shower.

Each person took turns in keeping me company. The men were the most awkward, apart from Earl.

I had no idea what to say to Caleb, River, Gael, and Vadik. It wasn't like we were ever really friends. I'd done what they asked of me. Seven years, I'd kept Emily safe and happy. Or as happy as I could.

When they sat with me, I ended up reading a book or taking a nap. I was allowed to nap, but had to be woken up every so many hours. It was exhausting.

After an entire weekend, the doctor returned and said I should be fine. I'd shown no other effects. Other than a few cuts and bruises, I was healthy.

This was good news.

"I was so worried," Emily said, throwing herself at me after I'd dressed Monday morning.

I didn't know where the men were.

Earl spent the nights with me, but he didn't sleep beside me.

"I'm starving. How about I make us breakfast?" Emily asked.

I wrinkled my nose. "I don't mean to be nasty, but you really can't cook."

Emily pouted. "That's no way to treat me after all I do for you."

I couldn't help but chuckle. "I do love you. Don't you want something you can eat?" I wasn't going to try to put anything else inedible in my mouth. The food Earl had served me a few days ago had looked … okay. The moment the potato crunched, I thought I was going to be sick.

My reaction shouldn't have pissed him off. Deep down, I knew it wasn't about me. He'd been angry at what happened.

There was nothing I could do about that. This went deeper for Earl.

Each time he woke me up, or we spent time together over the past few days, I got a really bad feeling.

I didn't completely understand it, but I felt like he was plotting something. Nothing too scary for me, I didn't think.

My thoughts were all over the place. Nothing made any sense to me, not really. All I could do was sit and think about what might be.

"I'd love to eat something."

I cupped Emily's cheeks, brought her head to mine, and kissed her. "Good. I wasn't going to allow you to cook."

Taking Emily's hand, I tugged her toward the kitchen, and I was so glad to see all the mess had been cleaned up. No remnants of Earl's temper.

After going to the fridge, I began to take out onions, peppers, and potatoes. Earl was totally onto something. I thought he might have been going for a potato hash. I wasn't completely sure since he'd appeared to be lost to his rage.

I hadn't stopped him.

He'd chopped and diced, thrown stuff into the pan.

I was going to attempt a similar version, just

cooked.

After grabbing a pan, I diced the potatoes. I'd already scrubbed them clean the other day and I hadn't needed them, so rather than throw them away, I'd placed them in the fridge, accidentally. I had a food storage bag somewhere, which I misplaced, where my potatoes should be stored.

I went to the sink and covered them with water, placing them on the stove to begin to boil. I'd keep an eye on them because I didn't want them mushy.

"I've missed this," Emily said.

I glanced up from dicing the pepper. "Missed what?"

"You cooking. All that is really missing is a cup of coffee or some wine."

Thinking back to the days in our apartment, I totally understand what she meant. After long days at work, Emily would rub her feet and pour us some cheap wine I rarely drank. I wasn't a big alcohol drinker. The most I'd consumed was at the nightclub celebrating her birthday, and with Earl.

We didn't have a lot of wine, just on rare occasions.

"I can make you a soda?"

Emily chuckled. "Isn't that what we usually drank?"

"Pretty much. Those pregnancy hormones must be affecting your memory. We rarely drank. Is that what you're craving, wine?"

"I think I'm craving everything I can't have. Wine. Lots of cheese. Raw eggs."

"Eww, gross. I wouldn't even make you runny scrambled eggs. They were so gross." I chuckled at the memory.

"I've grown partial to some burnt eggs," Emily

said. "The cook back home hates cooking for me."

"Well, if I ever need a job, I know where to come to." I winked at Emily and we both laughed.

This was good. This was getting back to where we were. Having a laugh. Enjoying each other's company. Just ... living.

I knew the reality would invade very soon. Earl and the men would come back. They'd gone out to handle business. I didn't know what kind, just something men had to do. Nothing I could understand.

"How has it been with Earl?" Emily asked. "Did he ... you know?"

Nibbling on my lip, I looked past Emily's shoulder, thinking about that night. I'd been pushed to the breaking point. Ever since we'd come back to the city, I felt much better. Noise helped.

"You want to know if he and I have, you know?"

"Don't mock me."

"I can't help it. You need to be mocked. I'm not going to tell you about my sex life," I teased her. I couldn't help it.

"So you totally have done it," Emily said.

With the peppers and onions chopped up, I stared at Emily. "Yes, we've done it, and it was the most painful and magical experience of my life. That first time, I'm never going to forget it. He was ... amazing." The way his hands touched me, the orgasm he drew from me, all of it played in my mind.

"Wow, I'm happy for you."

"It's just sex." Even saying the words hurt. I didn't want it to be just sex. There was a time limit on it. I got that. Each day I woke up, when he was gone, I wondered if this would be the day he'd toss me aside.

I was used to it.

My mom went through these phases all the time.

Good mom. Bored mom. Distant mom. Angry mom. Each one either showed me no attention, or treated me like I didn't exist.

"Don't say that," Emily said. "From the way he looked at you when we arrived, I don't think it's just sex."

This made me pause. Hope filled my chest. It was useless. I couldn't hope for something that didn't exist. "Please, don't do that."

"Ash, are you in love with this man?"

Tears filled my eyes as I looked at her. "No." The lie came out before I could stop it.

"You are. I can see it. You're in love with Earl Valentine."

I stopped chopping, putting down the knife. This wasn't good. I couldn't love a man who had no chance of loving me back. Shaking my head back and forth, I stepped back. "No, I don't love him."

"Ash, there's nothing wrong with it."

"Nothing wrong? This isn't a love relationship, Em. This is sex. All he wanted was my virginity, and he got that. I've got nothing else to give. I'm no longer special. He took the one thing that made me stand out in a crowd."

Once I started, there was no stopping me. "I'm no different than all of the other women he's screwed. Don't you see that? I do. I see that so clearly. I'm not special. I'm not unique. I can't fall for him. He traffics women."

I nodded and laughed. "So he has an entire slew of women at his disposal, who he sells to other men. Rich men. He makes money off of sex. He's a mon ... no, he's a beast. I can't fall for a guy like that."

"And yet, you have," Emily said.

I repeatedly shook my head as if that would stop all of this from being true. I couldn't love that man.

197

There was no chance. But as I fought against the feelings, I knew deep down they were right. I was in love with Earl Valentine.

Even as I hated what he stood for and what he did, the man himself was so loveable. He hid behind this façade of pain and misery, but little by little, I could see him.

He wasn't a complete beast.

Emily got to her feet and pulled me against her. "I've got you."

"I can't love him. He's not going to love me back."

"He loves you, Ash. You just don't see it."

"No one has ever loved me before."

"I love you."

I wrapped my arms around my best friend and sobbed against her neck. This was useless, and it accomplished nothing, but I needed a rock in my corner.

"I shouldn't be crying all over you." I pulled away, wiping away the tears and snot on a kitchen towel and then tossing it into the laundry basket in the far cupboard. "I need to finish the food."

The potatoes hadn't boiled over or gone mushy. After draining them, I allowed them to dry a little in the colander as I got to work on the onions and peppers.

My hands shook.

"Loving him is not a crime, Ash. You have the right to happiness."

"What about the other women?"

"There's nothing I can do about that, but, from my own experience with men who do bad things, you learn to deal with it."

"Do your men sell women?" I asked.

Emily's lips pressed together. "No."

"Then I don't think this is something I can learn

to love. Even though I love the man. I can't love what he does."

"It's not your place to do that. Maybe if he felt your love, he'd give up the business."

I wasn't that powerful. I wasn't worth giving up an empire of pain and suffering.

Emily didn't know that, but I sure did. I'd spent my life knowing how I didn't measure up. How I failed at everything.

Earl would never pick me over his power and his wealth.

****

Earl

Pissed off seemed to be an emotion I was feeling quite frequently these past few days. The only time it dissipated was when I was with Ashley. The way she joked and teased. Even when I was the one supposed to be taking care of her, she was the one who was constantly taking care of me.

"You ever heard of a guy named Knight?" Caleb asked, coming toward me.

"Yes."

"Word is, he's the one that put the hit on you." This came from River. Even though he had his woman, Emily, at his beck and call, he still had a fascination with knives.

I knew all their pasts and presents. I could also imagine their future, especially with how heavily pregnant Emily was. They were going to keep her bound to them and pregnant. It wasn't a hard future to imagine.

My thoughts went to Ashley.

Seeing Emily pregnant, I couldn't help but imagine Ashley full and ripe with my kid. I hadn't gotten her on the pill yet, and I'd been coming inside her every chance I got.

Running a hand down my face in an attempt to clear the distraction of knocking Ashley up, I focused my attention on the four men currently in front of me. We were in one of my legal offices.

This building had several floors, the Valentine name marked for the world to see. Advertising. Media. Cosmetics. Each floor dedicated to a segment of the company I'd built. With money came power. With power came control. This was how I was able to stay on top.

I was very much aware of who ordered the hit on me. It was the same man who had tried to take my city away from me, and had also tried to orchestrate a takeover merger. In my world, there was no such thing as clean business. Just dirty deals.

Money helped make the world go round, and my money helped to pay for all this shit to be kept silent and hidden.

Even now, men were out there conspiring to take me from the top.

Knight was one of many, but he was currently the most powerful. He didn't need to hide in the shadows.

Some bad men liked to keep to the night and the darkness. To allow others to fear them with tales of the bogeyman, and yeah, they were scary. The worst were the men who could walk day and night. Where there was nothing to keep the evil at bay.

This was my grandfather's doing. He started the company and built it on pain and death. I took it to the next level. There was a time my grandfather was a tiny shark in a tank full of them.

I became the fucking megalodon of them.

Now, my position was being challenged.

I wasn't afraid. It wasn't the first time this had happened, and I doubted it would be the last.

However, this was the first time one had gotten

close. The car crash was a clear message. My days were supposedly numbered.

"I don't need you boys here," I said.

Having the Monsters Crew on my turf didn't exactly help my cause. I didn't invite them. "I need you to leave."

"You think Emily's going to want to go?"

"Ashley's safe. I've given her time to visit her friend. Now you have to leave. This is going to get ugly."

Caleb laughed. "You know, we don't get along. To be honest, I think you're a fucking pervert, but that doesn't mean we can't help each other. You had our backs, so why don't you let us have yours?"

"Yes, because all people are saved when those around you think you're a pervert. I don't need, nor do I want your help. You're causing a problem for me." I got to my feet. I was done with this conversation. "I appreciate the offer, but I don't need you."

All four men stared at me as if I'd lost my mind.

"You know, we stay on top," River said. "Not just out of fear, but because we work together."

"I'm not about to join your little harem."

"You wouldn't be welcome to it," Gael said.

Caleb clapped his hands. "We will go collect Emily. The offer will always be open, even if you are too big of a fool to see it."

One by one, they filtered out of my office.

Sitting back behind my desk. I didn't do any work. I instead waited until I got the call to tell me they had all left.

Only when they were gone did I make the trek back to my apartment where I entered to some of the most delightful smells.

I found Ashley in the kitchen.

Just seeing her, in her leggings and one of my

shirts, made my dick hard. I went to her, wrapping my arms around her waist and pulling her close, and pressed my face against her neck.

She tugged out of my arms, whirled around, and slapped me across the face.

Not a reaction I expected, but now I was curious. When she went to hit me again, I captured her wrist, stopping her.

"Once was more than enough. Don't hit me again. I don't like it."

"You sent them away?"

I should have known they'd fucking tattle. They were nothing more than children.

"They're not needed here, and to be honest, they were getting in the way."

"In the way? They were helping you."

"I don't need help."

"Don't be an asshole, Earl. Everyone needs help every once and a while. There's no shame in it."

"No shame? I didn't tell you I had any shame. I don't fucking feel it." Sinking my fingers into her hair, I pulled her close to me. I wasn't angry. I didn't care that she hit me, or that her friends were gone. "They were getting in the way of this." Pulling her close, I slammed my lips down on hers.

At first, she struggled against me, but the moment I put my hand on her breast, she stopped fighting. The hands that had been pushing me away wrapped around my neck, pulling me closer.

There was no way I could let her go. No way that I wanted to.

Tearing my shirt off her, I got her naked. The bra took the longest time to get off her, but I succeeded, pressing those full tits together, running my thumb across each peak.

She released a moan.

"My bed, now," I said.

I couldn't wait.

Ashley turned off the stove and ran from the kitchen. I followed her. She had perched her ass on the edge of the bed as I entered the bedroom. Removing my tie, my shirt, I watched as she slid a hand between her thighs.

She knew how that turned me on. I loved to see her rubbing her fingers between her slit, getting herself close to arousal.

My dick was so fucking hard, it pressed to the front of my pants, begging to get out.

"Come and help me out of these," I said.

She got up from the bed and came toward me. As she was about to touch my dick, I captured her hand, stopping her.

Drawing her fingers to my lips, I sucked on each one. I couldn't get enough of her taste.

She moaned.

I let her go the moment her fingers were cleaned. She sank to her knees before me, and worked at the belt, releasing it before sliding the zip down. She worked my pants down, followed by my boxer briefs. I didn't give her another instruction, waiting to see what she'd do.

Her fingers curled around my dick. Starting from the base, she worked up to the tip and back down again, getting me nice and hard.

My balls ached to be inside her.

"You just want to play?"

I growled as her tongue flicked across the tip.

Staring down at her, I watched as she took me between her lips, the hard length of me disappearing between her plump red lips.

"Fuck!"

I wrapped my fingers in her hair, keeping hold of her head. I could fuck her face, but I let her explore my length instead.

When I hit the back of her throat, she released a little gagged moan that went straight to my balls, tightening them.

In and out. She bobbed her head, taking more of me.

Ashley would tease the tip of my cock at the back of her throat, trying to swallow me down, but she'd only get so far.

I couldn't stand it.

Using the grip I had in her hair, I pulled her off my dick, let go of her hair, and picked her up, taking her to the bed.

I didn't let her get far away from me before I had hold of her hips and spread her thighs open.

Cupping her ass, I drew her up to me, licking and sucking at her clit. She was already soaking wet. This was how I fucking loved her. Drenched in arousal and willingness. The way she rubbed her pussy over my face, I couldn't get enough. Using my teeth, I heard her cry out, and I soothed the bite with the flat of my tongue.

I slid down, going to her entrance, plunging in and out, taking her with my tongue.

"Yes, more. Please, more." The begs left her lips, and they only served to make me even more aroused. I wanted her so badly. She was going to come all over my cock this time.

I was a greedy bastard when it came to Ashley. Once was never enough. She set me aflame, and the only person to put it out was her.

I released her pussy, grabbed my cock, aligned the tip, and in one hard thrust, I was balls deep within her. I pounded her pussy, going harder and faster within her.

She screamed my name, the sound echoing off the walls.

I watched her take me. Her cunt widening to fit the length and width of my cock. She stretched for me and me alone.

My pussy.

My woman.

All fucking mine.

Each time we did this, it turned into a mantra of need.

I couldn't tell her exactly how I felt, only that I knew what she meant to me. How hungry she made me. There was no stopping it.

I loved this woman, and I hated myself for it. Love was a weakness I promised myself I'd never feel.

Ashley had gotten under my skin, and now there was no denying her. No looking back. I had to keep her all to myself.

I reached between her thighs, stroking her clit, drawing her orgasm back, and getting her close to the edge. I thrust to the hilt, feeling her release as she clamped around my dick. The pulses nearly set off my own release, but I kept it at bay.

I didn't wait for her to finish before I grabbed her hips and pounded inside her, fucking her harder than ever before. I wanted to fucking brand her. For every single part of her to be completely owned by me, so she would never doubt who owned her.

Ashley had already done the same to me.

She didn't know it yet, but I was hers.

So completely.

It was fucking hilarious. The beast finally was brought down by this woman. This unsuspecting beauty among so many. She was my weakness.

I slammed deep and closed my eyes, taking possession of her mouth as I came. Spilling every single drop of seed within her tight cunt, hoping it would get her pregnant. My desires were wrong, I knew that, but I couldn't stop it.

Getting Ashley pregnant was what I wanted. It would bind her to me indefinitely, giving her no chance to escape.

Chapter Fifteen
Ashley

"I don't care about the rules. This game is stupid."

"It's a sport."

"Not a very good one."

Earl laughed as I moved another pawn, and he tutted. To be honest, he'd written down the way the pieces were supposed to move, and I just played. I had no understanding of strategy or what piece needed to go where. All I remembered was the queen had to be kept safe. Every other player had a free-for-all.

"It's a skill. It's about knowledge and knowing what play to move and when."

I scrunched up my face. "It's boring."

We'd been playing for an hour now and the truth was I did find the game really boring, but I liked watching Earl.

Even though I had no doubt he could have easily taken me out with a few easy moves, he kept pretending I was some competition. It was all lies, but I couldn't help but find it cute.

Flicking my hair over my shoulder, I was drawn to his hands. They were so big, so creative. The need to reach out and touch him was strong, but I held myself back. I didn't have a choice. We were playing, and I wasn't going to initiate sex, which was so wrong.

It wasn't like we'd stopped doing it.

"You think I don't know what you want?" he asked.

His gaze was on me when I lifted mine up to look at him.

"I don't know."

"You've got a flush to your chest. Your nipples

are hard, and your hand is pressed near the juncture of your thighs, Ashley. Tell me I'm wrong, but you're thinking about how to get me to fuck you, aren't you?"

His dirty words heightened my arousal.

Licking my lips, I tried to moisten my already dry mouth. "I don't know what you mean."

"And you are a bad liar."

"It's your move."

He moved a piece. "Checkmate."

I had no idea what piece it was or how he did it. I didn't even care if what he did was legal or within the rules.

"Now, Ashley, it's your move."

Would it be so hard to close the distance between us? To fling the board to one side and have my way with him? I wanted to. My hands itched for me to be forward, to feel him inside me. To have his hands all over me, but at the last minute, I took the cowardly way out.

"I'm going to go make us another drink." I grabbed my glass.

Earl had settled for scotch. The smell made me feel sick, and there was no way I intended to drink anytime soon.

At the teapot, I filled it with water and placed it on the stove, turning the gas on to heat it. I gripped my neck, tilting my head left and right.

I was fine. I didn't need him. Sex was just an action. I was completely … fine. I lost count of how many times I thought about how fine I was, especially as I was the furthest thing from fine.

I was horny.

Why didn't they warn you about this in the science books?

I'd been aroused. A dirty film. Porn. I'd had moments, but nothing like this.

Earl and I had sex all the time. I shouldn't want it again. Just this morning, he'd woken me up to kisses down the spine. Then he'd turned me over and brought me to an orgasm before taking one of his own.

His cock was always ready to take what he wanted.

Earl cupped my hips, drawing me back. "Is it so hard for you to take what you want?" he asked, brushing his lips across my neck.

My nipples got even more painful. My body betrayed me while I tried to stay in complete control. I attempted to monitor my breaths, nothing.

All I cared about was his rock-hard cock filling me. Fucking me. Taking me.

"I'm not going to give you what you want until you ask me for it." His teeth bit down into my neck, and I moaned.

One of his hands went to my breast, cupping the mound. His palm skimmed across my breast. Just enough of a press to make me ache for more.

His touch set me on fire, and I was more than willing to burn.

Earl pulled away. His touch left me panting for more, but he refused.

I turned toward him, and he smiled at me. "What's it going to be, Ashley?"

Ignoring was one of my choices, but it also wasn't an option. I was tired of being stubborn. Of fighting what I truly wanted.

Even as I felt embarrassed, I closed the distance between us. I cupped his face and just stared. I didn't press my body against him. I waited. Time seemed to stand still for me, but I knew it was ticking, waiting for me to make a choice.

Did I cross this boundary or leave it to him?

I was tired of waiting.

Without another thought, I slammed my lips down on his, pressing my body flush against him, crying out as I felt his hard length against my stomach. So good.

His hands went to my hips, sliding down to my ass, and the other worked up into my hair.

I went for his shirt, tugging it off and throwing it across the room. Next, I went to the sweatpants he wore.

It was late, and he'd surprised me by wanting to play a game of chess and being in loungewear. At times, the man had the ability to surprise me.

He helped to kick them off but not before taking the negligee I wore.

"You've got me naked, Ashley. What are you going to do with me?"

Gripping his shoulders, I marched him back, going toward the sitting room. I pushed him down into his seat and followed him down, straddling his waist. The hard length of his cock pressed against my core, and I moaned as he seemed to bump against my clit.

His hands on my ass rocked me against him. Sinking my fingers into his hair, I kissed him, biting down onto his bottom lip. He opened up, and I plunged my tongue into his mouth. His nails sank into the flesh of my ass, and I relished the bite of pain.

The rush of pleasure took me by surprise.

I let go of his face and reached between us. My hands shook, but passion took over. I moved over him, and with his help, I got him to my entrance, and I sat down, taking him all the way inside me.

Tilting my head back, I released another moan and Earl took one of my nipples into my mouth. His hands moved down my body, then back up. He cupped my tits, pressing them together, his thumbs moving back and forth over the buds.

Rocking up and down his length, I fucked myself on his dick.

Earl grabbed my hips and showed me exactly what to do. He sped up my strokes, making me go harder as I claimed him.

With him deep inside me, I reached between and began to stroke my clit.

"Yeah, that's it, baby. Make yourself come all over my cock. I want to hear it. Come on."

I sank my fingers into his shoulder as I worked myself to orgasm. I came, and he didn't let up, pounding his way inside me, pulling me down one final time to flood my pussy with his cum.

We were both panting by the end of it.

My hair had fallen forward, and Earl pushed it back. He brought me in close and his lips on mine was the best feeling in the world.

The way he touched me made it harder for me to deny my feelings. I hated lying to him. Hated lying to myself.

This wasn't good.

Sex was amazing, but at no point Earl did promise more than this.

I didn't see a future for us. He'd never granted me the chance of having one.

"You're fucking amazing, you know that?" he asked.

"You're not so bad yourself."

The words he said. I easily forgot that he'd taken me as payment. All he'd ever wanted was my hymen, my firsts. The way he talked, it was like we were in a relationship, and each time, I kept on falling for it. I had to learn this meant nothing.

We were a business deal.

That was all.

****

Earl

I got a call from my yacht.

A plea for help.

I'd rounded up my men and went to where it was docked.

Blood covered the walls and floor. I'd discovered ten dead bodies. The three women who'd opted to work for me were slashed up.

To many, this sight was disgusting. With the life I lived, this was child's play. Wrong, but not unexpected.

This was a clear message, and Knight, the piece of shit, had sent it to me.

My men were already in the process of cleaning it up. Bodies would be destroyed and everything cleaned up as if there was no evidence. My cell phone rang, and I saw it was an unknown caller, but I wasn't a fool.

I ignored the call.

I wasn't going to give Knight the satisfaction of gloating.

With the mess being cleaned, I left the doc and found my right-hand man, Ford, waiting. He was the one person I trusted. He'd proven himself to me time and time again. I had no reason to doubt his intentions. He got off his cell phone.

"Security footage shows ten men entering the yacht at which point everything goes black. Within twenty minutes, it's all back on, and the yacht looks untouched," Ford said. "The clerk had to use the bathroom. It was the only time he wasn't manning the desk."

I could leave a trail of bodies up and down the city, but that was how amateurs played.

If I lost my temper now, Knight won. He'd been wanting my spot at the top for a long time.

My cell phone alerted me to an email.

Without a word to Ford, I opened it up. It was from an unknown sender. Most of these went to spam, so I was more than pissed I was being distracted.

However, I clicked on the wrong fucking thing and opened it to find a picture of Ashley in my apartment. It was taken outside of the building, but I saw her clearly. She stood a few feet away from the window, looking out over the city.

She was terrified of heights, and closing the curtains was a real challenge to her.

Who's watching her?

The words came with the attachment.

I pulled up my caller ID and started to make a call to the men I left in charge of her safety.

No one was picking up.

"Get me back to my apartment."

Ford had seen the email and already responded, putting a call out to his men, trying to get one of them to answer.

I ended up calling through to the apartment, but it rang and rang.

The dock was a good thirty minutes away from my apartment.

"Fucking put your foot down," I yelled at Ford.

I didn't care how this made me look. The only person who mattered was my woman.

Ashley. She was in danger, and it was all my fault.

I had to get to her. Save her. Protect her.

My heart raced as we made our way through the city. As he drove, Ford was still making calls, trying to find out what the hell was going on, and I was close to losing my mind.

I needed to get to her, to make her safe.

Ever since the accident, I'd put all the necessary precautions in place. More men in the building. I never took her out. I'd even resorted to playing games with her so she didn't get bored.

Whatever she even suggested, I got her.

I kept her safe.

There was no way Knight should have known about her, unless he had known about her and he'd used this as a distraction to get me out of the fucking house.

Ashley had been safer on my island, but her own mind had been working against her then.

Anger.

Panic.

Fear. I fucking hated the last one. There was no room for it in my life.

It was taking too long for us to get to the apartment. Ford broke every single speeding law known to man to get us as close to the building as possible.

On arrival, the car didn't even come to a stop before I got out. Charging my way through the building, I spotted the man working the reception desk, passed out, his hand flat on the surface.

I didn't take the elevator but went the stairs. It was long but my life depended on it.

I heard pants and grunts as I ran up the stairwell.

Not once did I slow down. Ford wasn't too far behind me. He had men already in the building, and I heard him barking orders. This was why he was my right-hand man, and why I left him in charge while I was on the island. He was the only person I could trust.

Like me, he worked his way from the ground up.

As I got closer to the sound, I held my gun, ready to fight. I passed one of the men who worked for me. He was dead, eyes staring out in shock.

The moment I saw my target, I shot, taking out

the attacker. I didn't linger to see if my man was okay. I broke through the door. I was panting, and it was a struggle to breathe, but I got to my door, which had been broken into.

The moment I entered, I heard her scream, followed by the sound of breaking glass.

Ashley put up a fight. I stepped over broken plates. Furniture was turned over.

The scream came from the bedroom, and I charged forward.

Ashely had been pressed over the bed, and the man was trying to work his pants down. She kept kicking and clawing.

With the gun at his temple, I'd already fired before he could stop me.

He fell to the ground and Ashley scrambled away. The impact sprayed her back and head with blood.

At the top of the bed, her wild eyes looked at me.

"It's me," I said.

I was still panting, but fuck me. I didn't know how it was possible. I got here before they raped her.

From the bruises forming, the cuts, she had taken a beating before they got to the bedroom.

"Ashley, it's me. It's Earl."

"You're here. You're really here." She threw herself into my arms, and I captured her, sitting on the bed, not caring about the mess.

Her entire body shook.

I was sick with it. Anger clawed deep into my pores.

Knight did this.

He wanted to play a game. He thought he could take on a beast, well, he was about to see what happened because he had just woken that beast up.

I held Ashley even as Ford entered the room.

One look was all it took, and he stepped back, giving me and my woman space.

She was stressed. Her body was shaking.

"I was making dinner, and the door, they broke it." She started to sob. I held her even tighter as she told me. "I threw food at him, and he hit me. I grabbed everything I could. I tried to fight back."

I kissed the top of her head. "You did good, baby. You did really good."

"He didn't ... he was going to. He told me he was going to kill me. That his boss wanted me dead."

I let her cry and just listened to what she had to say. All the while, I plotted.

This was the second time Ashley's life had been put in danger, but I knew it would be the last time.

Knight wanted to play. I was more than happy to join in.

We were enemies, and until now, he'd been quiet, but I knew things would only escalate. When you sat on the top of a throne, it was only a matter of time before someone felt they had a right to sit here.

It was time to get back in the game, and to do that, Ashley needed to go.

Chapter Sixteen
Ashley

One week later

Something was different.

Earl was different.

He didn't stay around anymore. Nor did he sleep in my bed. He was distant. Not exactly cold, but close enough.

I couldn't get through to him no matter what I said.

He moved me from the apartment to a hotel room. There was room service and multiple men at my door and inside it.

I'd been here for a week.

He only came at night.

Always sat in the chair, never coming to bed.

It was like being back at the island, only this was worse. I knew what to expect back there, but here, it was even harder.

The noises were an illusion.

I was scared. Someone had tried to kill me. An enemy of Earl tried to remove me from his life. In doing so, I saw the change in him. He wasn't the same man.

That night, when he entered the hotel room, I knew something was going to happen before he even opened his mouth.

"Come here, Ashley."

No hello. No asking how I was.

He'd sat through the doctor pulling out shards of glass that had been embedded in my body, tending to my bruises, and all he'd done was sit stoically as it happened.

No words.

No encouragement.

Just sat silently.

I'd hated every second of it.

Still did.

I had fallen for this man, and yet, I didn't recognize him. No smirk. No smile. He was dead inside. His eyes gave it all away. There was nothing there.

"Earl, what's going on?"

"Come here."

No room to talk. An order. A strict instruction. The desire to deny him was so strong, but I knew he wasn't ready for that. This was serious.

Getting to my feet, I walked closer to him.

I held myself perfectly still as he stroked his knuckles down my cheek. "This is for your own good."

The next thing I felt was a sting, and I glanced down to see he held a syringe.

Instantly, my body got heavy. I felt sick. The world began spinning.

He spoke the words again.

"This is for your own good."

Everything went black.

****

Everything felt heavy. My body wasn't my own. My arms were full of lead to lift up and wipe at my eyes. Even my eyes felt sore. My lips were numb.

"Ashley," Earl said.

Opening my eyes, I kept them open.

No blinding light. Darkness. It was night.

I tilted my head up and saw I was in a car, slumped in a seat but with the belt on. Slowly, my body began to work. I could move my arms but not quickly.

Everything around me seemed to be moving fast.

I reached up and rubbed at my eyes, looking out the car window. I knew this place. We were in the front yard of the Monsters' main house. This was where we stayed when they were hunting the fathers.

Why were we back here?

"Good. You're awake. I thought I'd given you too much of the sedative."

I turned my head to look at Earl. He sat in the back with me. I noticed his driver didn't turn to look.

"What is going on?" I asked.

"Simple. This is the end of the road. Our time together is finished. Your bags are already inside. Here is your passport and your purse."

With each word he said, I grew more alert. Panic seized me.

"What?"

"I told you our time would come to an end, and now it has. Your friends are expecting you."

I looked toward the door to see it open. Emily with her four men, and I turned back to Earl.

"You're getting rid of me?"

"I told you this day would come. I've had my fun. You're no longer a virgin. You hold no appeal, and to be honest, you're boring me. You're more trouble than you are worth."

His words cut me to the core. Each word tearing a layer of confidence, crushing my heart.

I'd known it all along, but there had always been a shard of hope. A glimmer of promise.

"You don't mean that."

"Ashley, please don't be a stupid woman now. I've enjoyed playing the hero and fucking you. You're nice and tight, but like so many times before, I'm bored. I've grown tired of you, and I don't intend to settle for one cunt. I'm not a one-woman man."

"Is this because of what happened? None of that is your fault."

"I knew I should have let you handle this, Ford,"

Earl said.

"Would you like me to remove her from the vehicle?"

"No, that won't be necessary."

"Ashley, you were good while you were what I wanted, but you're just so…"

"Flawed? Wrong? Irritating? Bad for you?"

"Whichever one you need to pick to help you get through this. I don't care, but I do need you to leave. I have work to do." He pulled out his cell phone, and as easily as that, I was dismissed.

He was done with me, no longer wanted me.

I wasn't surprised. This was a feeling I was so used to.

My mom did it. I'd felt it all my life.

A means to an end, and Earl had found the end of his use with me.

Pain shattered my heart. Tears filled my eyes, and a sob escaped.

"Don't be so dramatic. In time, many men will use your cunt and take what they want. It's the way of the world."

I tuned him out. I didn't want to hear him. I took my purse from him, as well as my passport. Gripping the handle of the door, I climbed out.

My body still hurt from the beating it took weeks ago. Ignoring the pain, I went to Emily. My best friend waited for me. She must have seen the despair in my face because she came out to me.

I'd known it would end like this.

Earl had never pretended to be a good man. He'd always been open, telling me right from the start what he'd wanted, and like a fool, I had thought I could make him want differently.

Emily wrapped her arms around me. I didn't want

Earl to see me collapse, so I held on to her. She was heavily pregnant and couldn't afford for me to lean on her.

To my surprise, Caleb, River, Gael, and Vadik surrounded me.

"We've got you," Emily said.

"You don't have to fight this anymore. We're the ones who have you. He's not going to hurt you anymore."

"He didn't beat me up," I said. I didn't know why I was defending him.

I had to be in shock. Everything hurt, and yet I felt completely numb. The pain was all over, and yet not one focal point could I pinpoint.

"We know what happened, and that's not what we're on about," Emily said. "I've got you."

In Emily's arms, I didn't fight it. I let it go. Pouring my heart and soul out to her, I broke down.

I had fallen in love with Earl Valentine, and in return, he'd shattered my entire world. Broken me down until there was nothing left.

****

Emily

I brought down the tray, and I wasn't happy.

Ashley had been with us a week, and she hadn't eaten. I'd already started to see the weight dropping off her, and I didn't like it.

Caleb, River, Gael, and Vadik were each in the kitchen when I returned. They stopped eating as I entered.

River was the closest, so I went into his arms, putting the tray down on the counter. "Still no change?" he asked.

"No change. She sits on the window ledge

looking out at the garden. I'm scared for her. She shouldn't be like this, should she?"

"You told us she'd fallen in love with the prick," Caleb said.

"Yeah, and this doesn't make any sense. Why did he get rid of her? We all saw the way he held her." I tucked some of my hair behind my ear.

Our baby was being a little pain today, not settling, and enjoyed kicking me in the ribs, winding me.

The base of my back was also giving me trouble, but I didn't tell any of my men. They'd only worry and put me on bed rest for the remainder of the day, and I had to take care of my friend.

Ashley needed me.

They all needed me, but I didn't have a problem with that.

I enjoyed being their everything.

When it came to my best friend, though, guilt clawed at my gut. Earl had gotten his hands on her because of a deal my men had made. If it hadn't been for me, or them, Ashley would have been safe.

No one would have gotten to her.

"We know he's been attacked. Ashley nearly got killed," Vadik said. "He's probably doing it to protect her."

"But once he's all done, he can come back for her. I don't get it. Why lose her in the process?" It was all getting a little confusing for me. "I hate seeing her like this. So broken. So lost. It's not fair. She's too good for him. For all of this."

"Do you want us to kill him for you?" Caleb asked.

"I'd be happy to," River said.

"I always hated that he got away with fucking lying to us. Breaking his bastard word," Gael said.

Earl Valentine was a sore subject for all of us. Even though I wanted him dead for the pain he currently caused my friend, deep down, I knew she'd hate me for killing him.

"No, we can't kill him. She loves him too much to put a bullet in his head." I stared at the counter, but it didn't offer any valuable alternatives. "We've got to be patient. Ashley's strong. She'll get through this."

Chapter Seventeen
Ashley

I'd always hated the movies where the girl was completely dependent on a man for happiness. I loved a good happy ending where there was love and romance. But doing absolutely nothing because of heartbreak pissed me off.

Now, I was the joke.

I was the person I hated most.

I sat on a window ledge, looking out at the garden. Crude Hill was an awful place. I fucking hated it, but it had lots of beauty surrounding it. My mom had loved this place. She'd been so happy to have finally gotten a place here. She hadn't held the pleasure for long.

Long enough for her to have gotten a taste.

Me, I liked it here, but it wasn't home.

Crude Hill had way too many memories and a lot of loss.

Each day, I woke up determined not to let it get to me. To get over the words Earl had said to me. I'd known it to be true even before he spoke them.

I'd been waiting for them. He'd helped to turn me into something I hate.

The phone wasn't going to ring because he'd made a mistake. Emily tried to help, she did. I'd turned into her, only seven years later. She was the happy one, and I was the miserable one. I hated myself. They were happy, and I put a downer on everything. It was why I stayed in my room.

I'd tried to eat dinner with them. The happiness and conversation emitted from the five of them had been too much. Emily had four men at her beck and call. I couldn't even keep one man interested in me.

Being surrounded by all that love made me feel

sick and full of failure.

What kind of man would want me?

I swiped at the tears threatening to keep falling. I wouldn't cry. I wouldn't give the tears the satisfaction of falling, but they did.

I'd gone through too many hankies and tissue because of my pain. I rubbed at my chest and still, it hurt so badly.

A knock pulled me out of my depression. I called for them to enter, expecting it to be Emily. It wasn't.

Drake stepped inside.

He walked toward me and plopped himself down opposite. "I heard you were back."

"Good for you," I said.

"I take it you're not good company." He didn't make any show of leaving.

Even as I glared at him, wanting to get him as far away from me as humanly possible, it didn't help.

"Why are you here?"

"You don't call or write, and you don't eat anymore. I came to see if you were dead."

"You're not funny."

"I'm not intending to be funny. I don't know any jokes or anything." He folded his arms across his chest.

I wasn't in the mood to talk to him. "Can you please just leave me alone?" I asked. I didn't even know why I was attempting to be polite. This man was an asshole in school. I didn't care what Emily said, it wouldn't change who he was. The man was just a bigger one now than ever before.

"Does everyone do what you ask them to do?" he asked.

My thoughts went to Earl, and I shook my head. "No."

"You know, I don't know why you're angry.

225

Shouldn't you be happy about being let go?"

"Drake, please, go away."

"Not happening, doll. I just don't understand it. This guy only ever wanted your virginity, and I'm guessing because you're sitting up here moping, not eating, and scaring Emily half to death, there has to be another reason."

Tears filled my eyes, and with each word he spoke, my heart began to shatter.

"Right from the start, you knew this was a done deal. You weren't anything special to him, and a woman's hymen isn't going to last long. One good fuck, and it's gone."

"Enough!" I screamed the word, hoping he'd shut up. "I get that I wasn't important to him. Okay? I understand that all I was to him was a piece of virginal flesh. A cherry for him to pop. I'm so sorry I can't be a mechanical asshole and not have feelings. He was doing what he wanted to do, and I fell in love with the fucking bastard. There, will that make you happy? Will that get you to leave me the fuck alone so I can be miserable in peace?" Each word got louder as my rage took over. I was so upset, I just couldn't stop it, and saying how I loved him out loud only served to make it worse.

Covering my face with my hands, I sobbed.

I couldn't stop.

The truth was I was so fucking heartbroken. Even though I'd spent all of my time with Earl knowing I was going to be let go of and tossed aside, the actual fact of it hurt. I'd tried to protect myself, but it didn't work. I'd fallen in love with a man who would never, not in a million years, love me back.

I jerked back as Drake wrapped his arms around me. It was so unexpected, and I tried to pull away.

"I'm not going to hurt you. Just holding you. Let

it out."

I didn't trust this. Drake wasn't a good man, at least not the last time I met him, and yet, he held me as I sobbed out my pain.

It hurt so badly. I couldn't control it. I'd never experienced this kind of hurt. Even my mother's selfishness couldn't compare to the pain I felt right now.

Drake stroked my hair, and I don't know how much time had passed, but eventually, the tears stopped coming. The pain didn't.

My chest was hollow. I was so unhappy.

"Are you okay?" he asked.

"No, I'm really not okay."

"Look. I know this isn't my place to say, but locking yourself up here, not eating, you won't heal this way."

I tucked some hair behind my ear. "What makes you such an expert?" I asked. It wasn't spiteful or mean, just fact.

"Easy, I understand it."

"You've been heartbroken?"

"No, but I've been hurt. It's not the same kind of level, but I understand you, Ashley. We all do on some level. Even Emily. It's breaking her heart to see you like this."

"I can leave," I said. "I don't want to hurt or upset anyone. I'm trying to get through it. I even promised myself I wouldn't feel anything for him. He's a horrible person, and he does horrible things."

Drake got up and grabbed a few tissues, handing them back to me, and I blew my nose on them.

"You're up and walking again," I said.

"Don't turn this on to me. I'm fine and I heal fast. Just because he did horrible things doesn't mean you can't love the person. He hasn't been horrible to you."

"No, because fucking me and dumping me is a way of life."

"Then don't give him chance to think he won," Drake said. "You've got your life. He didn't dump you at one of his auctions. You ever thought that maybe Earl did love you?"

"No, he didn't."

Drake sighed. "He loved you enough to let you go. To start a life for yourself. He didn't kill you, nor did he sell you. That's a pretty big step forward from the shit I've heard about him."

He had a point.

Still, if Earl had loved me, would he have really let me go?

I couldn't believe it. I didn't believe it. He wasn't the kind of man to let a woman go just because he felt like it.

"Thank you," I said.

Drake's cell phone began to buzz. "I've got to deal with this. We'll talk again, right?"

"Of course. Unless you turn into a creepy guy between now and then."

"Try to eat something. Try to do something other than sit here crying." He surprised me even more as he stood up, cupped my face, and pressed a kiss to my forehead. I watched this man have a temper tantrum in high school. This cool, calm, collected person in his place didn't seem real to me.

I watched him go and went back to staring out of the window.

As I watched the garden, I couldn't help but acknowledge he had a point. If Earl didn't feel a single thing for me, then he would've sold me to the next bidder. I didn't know what good I would've been, seeing as I was used goods and all.

I had to look at the positives, even though they made me want to burst into tears at a moment's notice.

I was alive. Earl didn't love me, but he had cared. It meant something just to know he cared, even if it was just a smidge. It was something.

Getting to my feet, I decided against staying in my bedroom.

My heartache had been so acute, but it hadn't stopped me from showering, so I didn't stink or anything. Leaving my bedroom, I didn't encounter Emily or her men. I nodded at the guards they had on different exits and entrances. No one stopped me as I got to the doorway into the garden.

It was nice weather. A slight chill in the air, but the sunshine glowed down.

Stepping out, I wrapped my arms around myself and walked toward the grassy area. I had a pair of sneakers on, and I took them off, allowing myself to feel the cool chill of the ground beneath my toes.

So good. Everything was different now.

My chest still felt hollow, and I didn't know if I'd ever feel any kind of happiness, but getting up, moving forward, and accepting what it was were all parts of the process.

I was going to get through this.

One day, I'd forget about Earl, and I hoped I'd fall out of love with the bastard as well.

After spending a long time out in the garden, I made my way into the kitchen and became reacquainted with all the ingredients on offer. There were so many, and my mouth salivated at the thought of cooking.

Once I'd rolled up the sleeves of my shirt, I got to chopping. I was thinking a chickpea spiced stew with couscous.

I started with an onion, going through the

mechanics of chopping and dumping them into the large cast-iron casserole pot I had.

It didn't take long for the smells to bring guests.

Emily arrived first. Her mouth fell open as she looked at me. "Ashley, what are you doing?"

"Do you not want me to cook?"

"No, of course not. It's good to see you cooking."

I smiled at her.

She took a seat at the counter, putting her chin on her hands. "It has been too long since you cooked."

To help me get through it, I vowed not to think of him. It was how I was going to survive.

With the bell peppers chopped, the onions sweating down, I got to work on the garlic. I hated the smell of raw garlic, but it was a necessity in cooking and couldn't be overlooked. With the garlic smashed, I ran my knife through it, and that was when Gael and Vadik joined.

"I wondered what smelled so good," Gael said.

"Just some home cooking. Nothing special." I put the garlic off to the side and then grabbed the necessary spices. I looked through the collection they had and made a few selections.

I didn't know what kind of meal I was going for and just started to add an array of them, starting with a small cinnamon stick. That went into the pot, followed by some paprika, cumin, and a couple more spices.

When I next looked up, Caleb and River had joined.

"Is it so odd for someone to be cooking in your kitchen?" I asked.

Emily chuckled. "It's odd for you to be out of your room. You know, after everything."

I smiled. It didn't feel quite as forced, but it also wasn't as happy either. I wasn't over what happened.

"Does Drake do some counseling in between his work for you guys?" I asked.

"Not that I'm aware of, why?"

"Let's just say he helped to draw me out."

"Drake did?" Gael asked.

I nodded.

"Well, fuck me. That guy is pretty useful after all." He let out a snort.

"A man of many talents," Caleb said.

"Yeah, and I know you've guys have been really nice putting up with me and all, but I was wondering if it would be at all possible to go back to England?" I'd been thinking about this all afternoon, and it was where I wanted to go.

"England?" Emily asked.

"Yeah." I looked between all five of them, and they seemed a little surprised. "Is everything okay?"

"England's not your home," Gael said.

"Actually, it is. Crude Hill isn't my home. I don't belong here."

"Ashley, this is your home."

"No, it wasn't. My mom lived here to fuck your dad easily. She wanted a good life, and she got it. I totally understand what she wanted, but I'm not her. This life isn't mine. There is nothing here for me, and I don't want to stay here, waiting to see if you'll marry me off or something."

"That would never happen," Emily said, slamming her hand on the counter.

The last thing I wanted to do in the world was upset her. She was heavily pregnant.

"I don't mean it like that. You've all got a job around here, and I cook. That's it. I'm not designed for this life with you all. My mom dragged me into your world, and with the threat now gone, don't you see? I should be able to survive without any of you, right? I can go back to England, but as myself. I don't even have to go to London. I can go anywhere. I just, that place felt more like home than this one. It's time for me to move forward, not look back. Earl made his choice."

Emily got to her feet and came toward me. I'd already added some tomatoes to the pot as well as some good vegetable stock. It smelled amazing, and I was hungry.

My best friend pulled me into her arms.

"I don't want you to go. I don't think it's fair."

I wrapped my arms around her. "I know, but this isn't about you. It's about me, and I know I can't truly heal being here. He's not coming back, Em. I need to do this for myself. Please."

Emily pulled away enough to cup my face. Tears glistened in her eyes, but I wasn't going to back down. I'd made my decision. Crude Hill had offered me nothing but pain, from my mom, Emily's dad, and now Earl. I needed to leave. To find my own roots, to find my own way of life.

"Fine. We'll help every single step of the way. You're always going to be family to me, Ash. Blood or not, I'll help you."

****

Earl

"What do you want me to do?" Caleb asked.

I didn't want him to talk. He'd already said enough, and now I was pissed off. Sitting in my office, in my kingdom with the Knight threat close at hand, this wasn't the news I wanted to hear.

"This is what she wants?" I asked.

"This was all Ashley's suggestion. Nothing Emily or we say is going to change that. She wants a clean break."

Against the Monsters' Crew liking, I'd found a way to get regular updates about my woman. I'd asked them first, but they'd refused. Then I'd gone to Emily. After that, I'd reached out to Drake.

They were all loyal to the Monsters' Crew and to Ashley. So I'd had no choice but to hire someone to find out how my woman was doing.

Ashley had struggled.

No, she was downright fucking in pain. I didn't know how they managed to get close to her, but I'd been sent a video of the noises coming from her room. The man I'd hired had turned up dead with the Monsters telling me not to send anyone else or they'd all end up the same way.

We were all kings in our world, and working together proved difficult. The fact Caleb was even giving me this call was a giant fucking leap.

"Why are you calling me now?" I asked.

"I didn't have to call you," he said.

I wanted to drag his ass right in front of me so I could pound it. Then he'd be done with his smartass answers.

"I know what you didn't have to do, fucking prick. I want to know why you're contacting me now when you told me to stay the hell away."

I'd dropped Ashley off, and once I returned to my penthouse, I had given in and called to see how she was doing.

I got nothing.

The truth was, I shouldn't be calling Caleb. I shouldn't even care what Ashley was doing. I'd made my decision clear. She and I were over. I'd gotten what I wanted, and there was no going back.

Only, staying away from her was proving to be

difficult. This wasn't a decision I'd taken lightly. I hadn't wanted to get rid of her. Ashley was mine. I still fucking saw her as mine, and one day, she'd be mine again, but until I sorted out the fucked-up problem that was my life, I couldn't risk her.

People would kill her to spite me. I was the enemy, not her, but she was an easy target. A weakness of mine. One I had to keep protected at all costs.

By severing ties, any connection people had made for her meaning something to me was severed.

"She can't leave the country," I said. There was no way I'd be able to fucking survive with her in another country.

I'd lost count of the number of times I'd tried to get to her, only to stop myself when I was so close. I was doing this to protect her. Not because I wanted to.

My apartment was fucking lonely. My bed even more unwelcome. I slept in my office or a hotel room. Women made attempts to come on to me, and I took them back to my hotel room. Not to do anything with. I paid them to shut up. They stayed for an hour, and then I kicked them out.

Whores liked to embellish the truth. They got paid for their silence. I helped to create the image of Ashley meaning nothing to me. The women were nothing. Even having them in my apartment or my office felt like a fucking betrayal. If my grandfather could see me now. He'd consider me a disgrace to him, to men. Women were nothing more than ornaments or toys. To be used and put back until you needed them again.

They were a product. A commodity.

And right now, I was fucking falling apart because the one I wanted now wished to leave the country. To start a life elsewhere, and it was all my fault.

"Hello, Earl? Are you even listening?"

"Shut the fuck up, Caleb."

The line went dead. The bastard had hung up on me.

Running a hand down my face, I dialed his number and waited for it to ring. It went to voicemail.

"You piece of vile fucking shit." I called again. If he didn't answer, I was going to make him pay. I'd drive down there and tear out his balls. I'd make him pay in every single way possible.

Rage rushed to the surface.

I was tired of people getting in my way.

Just as I was about to hang up myself, Caleb answered.

"Now, do you want to use nice words?"

"Listen here, don't test me."

"Don't start."

"You want to play this game? Hang up on me again, and I'll make the call that can guarantee Emily's life is in the fucking balance." It was a low blow. I could do it. I had the power.

"You wouldn't do that to Ashley."

"I think it's safe to say I will do anything for my woman. Think of what you did to get Emily back. You sold her to me without fucking blinking. No wonder my woman wants to be far away from you. She doesn't trust any of you."

"I'm not going to stop Ashley from leaving."

Damn it. Deep down, I knew he couldn't stop Ashley. My woman wanted a clean break. From the video I heard, she'd never said the words to me, but in some way, she loved me. Ashley fucking loved me. What she didn't know was she owned me. All of me, she had me in the palm of her hand. The moment I cleared this shit up, I was coming to get her.

I wasn't going to be held back.

I loved her so fucking much, and being apart from her, well, the beast within me boiled with a rage unlike anything I'd ever felt. I had to wonder if I should feel sorry for my enemies. The moment I finally got the chance to let loose, they were all going to suffer.

"Everything she wants is hers. I'm paying for it. Guards are to be with her at all times, but she's not going to know about it. I want to know when she leaves and where she's going. I'll have men stationed at each point. Money is all hers. If she needs a job."

"Earl, you don't have to tell me any of this. We'll take care of it. She's one of ours."

"No, she's not yours. She will never be yours. You sold that right to me."

"And Earl, you gave it back when she landed her ass right back here. This is done. I won't call again."

He hung up, and I threw my phone across the room.

I'd find a way to protect Ashley.

She was mine. She didn't know it yet, but the moment it was right, I was coming for her.

Chapter Eighteen
Ashley

Two weeks later

I was leaving tomorrow. Excitement filled every single part of my body. My hands shook a little. I'd be alone, but there was already a job lined up for me at a restaurant on the other side of London. I wasn't going back to the place that knew me as my other name. I'd be free to be myself, and I couldn't wait.

My bags were already packed.

Rather than check on absolutely everything for the sixth time, I'd decided to head to the kitchen to cook one last meal.

A cake was already cooling. I'd made the frosting, and that was waiting to be spread all over. Now I was baking an entire head of cauliflower, crazy but also fun. I'd been trying out a bunch of new recipes the past few weeks after seeing some experiments online. This one I was baking in a tomato roasted sauce.

It sounded so good. My mouth watered for a taste, and the scents coming from the sauce made me hungry.

"I'm going to miss you," Drake said, coming into the kitchen.

I smiled at him, keeping my hands busy as I made a salad.

Amelia, River's sister, was also around. I'd rarely seen her. She either kept to her room or ate in the kitchen. She wasn't mean, but I'd come to realize she was incredibly shy and had a way of sneaking around the house undetected. Three days ago, I'd managed to meet her. She'd been eating breakfast when I entered. For a good ten minutes, she didn't say anything until she finally spoke hello softly to me.

That was all she said.

I'd kept on talking to help fill the silence. I didn't know if it helped, but I liked to think it did.

She was … different.

"You're going to miss my cooking," I said.

"You can't cook well. Honestly, it's disgusting."

I laughed as he wrinkled his nose. "You're cute when you lie."

"Damn, woman, I'm clearly losing my touch."

"No, you're not. I get it. You don't want me to feel bad for leaving and then you're going to have to find another cook."

The cook who had been here before I turned up quit. Everyone had asked for me to cook instead. I didn't even know their name, and I never saw them in the kitchen. At first, I thought they were happy to not have to do any work. Now they lost their job, and I did like cooking a lot.

Emily told me not to worry about it, and so I didn't. Tomorrow would be the start of a whole new life for me. One I intended to grasp with both hands.

I couldn't wait.

Earl Valentine.

His name was like a whisper in my ear.

Even as the days were filled with excitement where I held control over what I could think about. If he so much as came close to the surface, I got busy. I made sure I was distracted. He couldn't invade my thoughts, at least not for too long.

At night, that was a whole different game.

I couldn't stop him from invading them.

He did so all the time. The nights were always the worst. When memories flooded and desires rushed through my body as if they had a right to. They didn't.

I hated it.

Even though I was carving an entire life out for myself away from all of this, he still filled my mind.

I wondered all the time if he was okay.

Did he think about me?

"Earth to Ashley," Drake said, snapping his fingers.

I swatted at his hand but smiled, not letting him see where my thoughts had drifted. "Don't go snapping your fingers in my face. It's so rude."

"I've got a call. You were way too off in your own little world. We'll talk when I get back."

I laughed. "You don't have to keep trying to make me feel better."

"I can see it, Ash. You're not a very good liar."

Pressing my lips together, I tried to gain focus once again and forced a smile to my lips. "I'm fine."

"Are you saying that because you believe it or to make me believe it?"

"Does it even matter which one?" I asked.

I didn't know what I was doing, why I was even talking to him. He was right, though. I was a bad liar.

Once he left, I looked at the salad in front of me and tuned Earl Valentine out of my head. Thinking of him didn't help.

With my focus back on food, I went to the fridge. This was going to be a fully loaded salad, with everything on it. Olives, artichokes, salad leaves, avocado, and so much more. I even grabbed some feta.

"Just keep working, Ashley. It's all you can do. Just keep working."

The salad was done. The cauliflower was finishing in the oven, and I glanced around, seeing the cake. I tested to see if it was cool enough. My hands shook a little, but I ignored them and began frosting the cake.

This was what I was still doing when Caleb entered the kitchen.

"Hey, Ashley."

"Hey."

"How are you doing?" he asked.

"Fine. You?"

"I'm great."

"Good."

Silence.

I was happy with the silence. He'd moved behind me. I heard the coffee pot being taken out of his holder, poured, and then pushed back in.

I ignored his presence. My attention was on the cake in front of me.

I could never get smooth sides. It sucked. I continued to do so though, using it as a way of not having to talk to Caleb.

I should have known my life wouldn't be that easy, though.

"Can we talk?" Caleb asked.

I paused and stared across the kitchen at the doorway, looking at the potential escape. I could just leave. "No, we can't talk."

"I know you're angry and you're hurting."

"Stop it," I said.

"Ash, you're Emily's best friend."

Holding the palette knife, I whirled around and glared at him. "Exactly. I'm Emily's best friend. You don't get to call me Ash."

"Everyone calls you Ash."

"Not you."

Caleb frowned. He lowered his cup and placed it on the counter. "And why don't I get to call you Ash?"

"This is all your fault." I had promised myself I wouldn't say anything.

"You're clearly tired. We'll talk another time."

"I'm tired. That's what you're putting this down to. You don't even see what you did, did you?"

"I saved you."

"And then you fucking sold me," I said. "I get that you saved me, but it wasn't because of me. You saved me for Emily, and I am grateful for that. I spent seven amazing years with her. She's a wonderful friend. I don't have a problem with you until you negotiated her return."

He continued to glare at me. "I did what I had to do."

"You sold me as if you had a right to. My body. Every single part of me."

"Look, you fell in love with him, didn't you?"

"And you think it makes it okay?" I asked. "You sold me for my piece of flesh that was supposed to be my choice. It's my body, but to save my best friend, I didn't put up a fight. I never expected to fall in love, and I certainly didn't want to feel this way. I hold you responsible for all of it. You being the big, bad monster that you are, you should have found another way. I don't like you. I will never like you. Emily could do so much better than the four of you. So no, I'm not okay with any of you. Nothing you say will ever make any of this okay. You think I forgave you? You think I really wanted to be sold?"

The tears I hadn't spilled for two weeks came to the surface. I didn't even realize how much I hated the Monsters' Crew until this moment.

Analyzing my life, I knew they were the ones who put this crap in motion. Their desire for Emily had set me on a course of pain.

I loved my best friend, and I'd do anything for her.

These men, however, I didn't owe them a damn thing.

Caleb didn't say anything. I turned my back on him, and he stormed out of the kitchen. If he thought we were cool, well, I'd just proven we weren't even on the same page.

"That was a little cold," Amelia said, appearing around the corner.

"You were there the whole time?"

"Enough to hear." She spoke so softly as she stepped into the room. She wore a large shirt and sweatpants. Her body was always covered, even when it was warm. Her hair was down, long blonde lengths, almost white in color, and she had shockingly blue eyes.

She was stunning, breathtaking to look at.

"Do you want to have a seat?" I asked.

She lowered herself into the chair. Her hands clasped together as she looked at me.

"Are you okay?"

She always looked ready to bolt at a moment's notice.

"I'm fine. Everyone is sad that you're leaving."

"I thought you'd be glad. I'll be one less person to avoid," I said.

"I don't intend to avoid anyone. It's a habit."

I noticed how white her knuckles were. "A habit?"

"You only get hit so many times before you start to learn to avoid them."

"Oh."

Amelia winced. "Sorry. That was an overshare."

"You got hit a lot?"

"I was a girl. I was unwanted, and as I grew, I was told I was an ugly baby. Always a disappointment. Compared to River, I didn't walk as early as him. Nor did I get out of diapers until I was like three, I think. I don't know." She shrugged. "I've always been a disappointment. I'm not as clever as he is." Amelia tucked her chin against her body.

"Who hit you?" I asked.

"My dad. My mom. My nanny. Anyone who felt I needed to be hit just hit me. It was easy for them." She whipped out her arm. "So easy. At school, girls do it, so do guys. I'm a punching bag." She shrugged.

"Amelia, you need to tell your brother."

She shook her head. "He's busy with running everything. At least I'm not traveling the world anymore, being left in places and having to wait to be picked up. It's nice just having a room to myself." She smiled, and it was so sweet, almost wistful. "My life isn't so bad anymore."

I didn't know what else to say to that.

"I am going to miss you. I hope you find whatever it is you're looking for. You deserve some happiness."

I wasn't sure what to make of that. How much had Amelia heard? What did she know? She didn't stick around. She gave me a quick hug, which I reciprocated, and then she was gone.

I stood alone in the kitchen. Time passed. The scents of the food filled the air.

Gripping my neck, I tried to massage the kinks that had worked into my body. Nothing eased the tension.

"I can't believe it's your last night," Emily said. "And of course you won't let us cook for you."

"I don't mind cooking."

"I know." Emily chuckled. "You always have a way of making us feel better, and I don't have the first clue what to do to help you."

"Don't make this hard, or about you."

"I'm not that selfish, am I?"

I smiled. "You can be when there's something you want."

She released a sigh, putting a hand on her swollen stomach. "I don't want you to go."

"Well, I want to."

"Is it so awful here?"

"Not too much, but this isn't my home. I'm not happy here, and it's time I started to live my own life, you know?"

Emily groaned. "What about when I give birth? I don't want you to miss it."

"I won't. You call me, and I'll be on the first plane back. I promise." I moved around the counter and went to her side, pulling her in against me and pressing a kiss to her head. "Nothing is going to change. You're going to see that. You were doing fine when I wasn't here." I couldn't bring myself to say his name.

This was a clean slate. A new beginning. One I intended to take full control of.

She tried to stand up, but I wouldn't let her. "You need to rest," I said.

"You're so bossy. When did you get to be that way?"

"I learned from the best." I gave her a wink and she groaned.

"You make me sound so awful."

"Not awful. You always knew what you wanted. There's no harm in that." I pulled the casserole pot out of the oven, resting it on top of the stove, and removed the lid. A nice wave of steam came out, and along with it, the delicious smells of dinner.

"I can't believe you're going to get us to eat an entire head of cauliflower. I'm expecting my guys to moan."

"It's going to taste good." My mouth salivated. "I'm going to set the table." I made to pass Emily, but she captured me, pulling me into my arms.

"I'm so sorry he did what he did."

I held on to her. "It's not your fault."

"It is. I should have done something to protect you."

"It's no one else's fault I fell in love. This is all on me." I rubbed at her back. "I love you."

"I'm going to miss you."

I gave her a squeeze. I was going to miss her too.

****

Earl

"Fuck you. You fucking piece of shit."

I listened as Knight spat out the words. I cleaned off my blade from the blood I'd gotten on it. Ashley was out of the country. Landed safely at Heathrow airport, arrived at her apartment without a hitch, and had finished her first day at work. Then her second day. For a week, she'd gotten into a routine, and I knew because I'd been the one to closely monitor her.

As I used her as my distraction, Knight made his move, just as I knew he would.

The shipment of girls he intended to take were fakes. I'd arranged for mannequins to be placed within the cargo hold, and when his men had come to get them, we'd been ready.

I'd sunk the ship with some of his men still alive. There had been cameras on the ship, and I'd made Knight watch as his men drowned.

Some would call me cruel. This was simple payback.

Knight's attacks had grown in severity and

frequency. His patience being tested to the limit and along with it, my own.

I won. Like I always did.

I'd been waiting for Knight at his secure location, which happened to be a beautiful country estate. For the women who had been slaves here, I'd already made the necessary calls to be set free. Their stories would make the news, and Knight's entire kingdom would fall. Along with it and all stocks and shares, people would be begging for a way out, and they wouldn't get it. Every single investor would suffer, and just the thought made me smile. Also, I had him tied to the pool table, completely naked as he spewed out his curses.

His body dripped blood. I'd already taken my blade to him, cut him up really bad.

I'd gotten a text alert while I'd been about to take care of his cock. Ashley came first. She'd arrived at her apartment for the evening. I got to watch her for a few short minutes. No sound. Just the way she toed off her shoes, tilted her neck left to right. She'd been struggling with a knot in her shoulders ever since she got to England.

I wanted to help her ease out the tension, to help her relax, but I was miles away. An ocean away.

Closing temptation, I pocketed my cell phone, moved toward the pool table, and clicked my tongue at the man on top. "This isn't a good look for you."

"What the fuck do you want? Huh? You want money? You can have it. I've got enough to go around."

"This isn't about the money, and I'm really disappointed you'd think that." I ran the tip of my blade across his nipple. One of them was already gone, removed with the single swipe of my blade.

"It's about the whore!"

I drew my knife back and slammed it into his gut,

twisting the handle as I watched him scream.

"No one talks about her like that."

Knight groaned. "I'm fucking dead anyway. I can say what I want." He kept on coughing in between each word. I ignored him and looked at his body, thinking about what I could do to him. The kind of damage I wanted to inflict. Part of me wanted to keep him alive. To have him as my own personal toy to torture at will, but once this was taken care of, I had other business to attend to.

Ashley. She was my business.

"You think you can keep her safe? Men like us kill women like her," Knight said.

I looked at him, and I knew. My grandfather destroyed women, as did my father, and I'd picked up the game because it was what I was meant to do. I'd fought to be different to the men who called me son and grandson, but I wasn't. I was just like them.

Without another word, I thrust the knife into his neck and stood, watching the life ebb away.

Knight was a good-looking man. A competition for power.

Not anymore. He was useless. Lifeless. A dead waste of space.

And now, no longer my problem.

By the time the press learned of his demise, he'd have been lost in a house fire to which he set himself as he knew the past would catch up to him. The women who'd been used by him would get the chance to tell their story, and no one would care about the billionaire businessman who lost his life.

He was a monster. Killed by me, a beast.

I cleaned off the knife and took a step back. My men were already pouring gas around the building, preparing to start the blaze.

My cell phone beeped again, and I got the single text to say the news headline had started. The knowledge of what he had done would be seen far and wide.

I'd been playing this game in life according to my grandfather's rules.

It was time to change it up. Time to be the man Ashley needed me to be.

Stepping out of Knight's mansion, I smiled. I was about to cause an entire shitstorm of trouble for a lot of people, and I didn't care.

Chapter Nineteen
Ashley

My life sucked.

Really fucking sucked.

Like, I couldn't even think of a worse time in my life than right now, not after I stared down at the stick again, read the instructions, and groaned.

"No. No. No. No. No." I screamed the last *no* as I reached into the box for another one. The first stick had to be wrong.

Forcing myself to pee again was hard, but I managed to do it, and of course, that test lied as well.

"I'm not pregnant. I refuse to be pregnant." I couldn't be. I knew I had a cycle. Life had been crappy, which was why I couldn't remember exactly when I had a cycle.

Melinda, the woman I worked with during lunch shifts, had asked if I was pregnant. I'd mentioned the sickness bug I kept getting in the morning. Woman must have thought I was crazy or something because I didn't even put the two together. Morning sickness and pregnancy.

It wasn't like Earl and I had been cautious. He hadn't wanted anything between us.

Now, I was on edge. I was pregnant.

It didn't matter how many tests I tried to use to tell me something different, it wasn't going to change the fact I was pregnant.

My hand rested on my stomach. A baby. Earl's baby.

I had to call Emily, but I stopped myself.

I couldn't tell her. At least not yet. I'd need to see a doctor. It was too late to call to arrange an appointment today. Sitting on my bathroom floor, I rested my head against the wall.

"Why did this have to happen, huh? It's not that I don't want you, I do. I'm not sure I know how to take care of myself," I said. I kept rubbing my stomach. Would I have a boy or girl? "I always imagined your daddy being with us. You know. I had my entire life mapped out. I'd go to college, get a great education, a job. I always wanted to be a television cook. Not a chef. I like creating my own meals and all that stuff. I'd meet a really great guy. We'd fall in love, get married, and then you'd be born. Look at me, talking to myself."

Tears filled my eyes, and I groaned at the unfairness of the tears.

"I'm sorry. I shouldn't cry."

Getting to my feet, I grabbed the boxes and the used tests, then threw them in my trash. I washed my hands, splashed my face with water, and gave a deep breath.

"I'm fine."

I wasn't fine.

Life in England wasn't doing what I wanted it to do.

The truth was I missed Earl no matter where I was, and with each day that passed, the more I hated myself for my feelings for him. It wasn't right. I shouldn't love a man who sold women.

I'd even made myself a pros and cons chart. First with the cons. He was a human trafficker, he killed people, he wasn't a nice man, bossy, took too long in the bathroom, and he enjoyed eating frozen garden peas. Again, peas weren't something I enjoyed, especially not frozen garden ones. Yuck. For the pros, and I hated this. An excellent kisser, great in bed, kind, sweet, considerate, loving, protective, and I felt safe with him. The list went on and on, and I hated that I could think of anything nice to say about this man.

I released a growl and went to my kitchen, pouring myself a glass of water.

"I'm not doing it anymore." Raising my hands in the air as if to ward off whatever being was haunting me, I grabbed my keys and let myself out of my apartment.

I left the building, not thinking where I was going until I found a pub. It wasn't too busy when I took a seat at the bar. While there, I ordered a beer. The guy behind the counter asked me what kind and listed off a whole load of ales and lagers and bitters, to which I told him I didn't care, to just pick one.

So many options.

With a pint of beer in front of me, I stared at the glass.

I wasn't a drinker and certainly not a beer drinker.

I was pregnant. Beer was bad for the baby. I wasn't a bad person, and I couldn't harm this baby.

With my hands flat on the counter, I rested my chin on my hands and stared at the drink. I wasn't going to drink it. I wasn't going to touch any alcohol, and first thing in the morning, I'd get an appointment and confirm I was indeed pregnant.

Time ticked slowly by.

I stared at the glass.

People came and went.

Tiredness consumed me. I'd already paid for my beer. When I couldn't take it anymore, I got to my feet, and left the pub, going back to my apartment. I stepped over the threshold, feeling all the fight leave my body. I turned and felt something tear beneath my feet.

Flicking on the light, I caught sight of a large brown envelope. It had been slid beneath my door.

I quickly closed and locked the door before

bending down to pick up the envelope. I didn't recognize it, and there was no stamp or sign on it to show it had been delivered by a postman or courier.

After tearing into the envelope, I reached in and found a single newspaper clipping.

At first, I didn't focus on it. I looked back into the envelope and was surprised at the waste, seeing as there was only a single piece of paper, and it wasn't even the size of the envelope, it was tiny.

Whoever had posted this through my letterbox, they didn't want me to miss it.

On the back, I couldn't make out the story as half of it had been chopped off. I turned it over and saw the headline: *Cargo of missing girls found. Families are in the process of being contacted.*

With the paper in my hand, I walked back to my seat and sat down.

I read the short piece. The story was taken a few days ago. A cargo of kidnapped girls had been found. The girls had been badly beaten and suspected of being sold to the slave trade.

Human trafficking.

Who would send me this?

"You weren't home."

I released a scream and fell off the edge of the sofa where I'd crawled over.

That voice.

I knew it. Gripping the edge of the sofa, I peered over the top to find Earl sitting in the corner of my sitting room. His boots only appeared in the light of the lamp I'd switched on.

"You scared me."

"I didn't mean to. This was posted first, and then I let myself in when you didn't respond."

"You've got a key to my apartment?"

"I arranged for you to be here," he said.

"Of course you did." It should have been good to see him, but at that moment, I was so angry. He'd broken into my apartment, was sitting on my furniture, and I was supposed to be grateful for that?

I wasn't.

I was angry. Totally angry.

He was alive, which also made me really happy, but this man had abandoned me. Had told me he was done with me. He'd gotten bored with me, and now I was supposed to what? Be happy to see him?

"What is this?" I asked.

He leaned forward, and I saw parts of his hands were bandaged. "This is me turning over a new leaf."

I groaned. "I'm not going to have this conversation with you in the dark." There was no reason to be afraid. I stood, went to the light, and flicked it on.

Still, he sat here. He blinked a few times, adjusting to the light.

He was here, in my living room. Talking to me.

My mouth went dry.

"Where were you?" he asked.

"You don't get to ask me any questions." I wanted him to stay silent so for a short time, I could just look at him and try to understand what was happening right now.

Tonight, I'd found out I was pregnant with this man's baby, sat in a pub, didn't drink a single drop of beer, came home, and discovered him here.

"Why are you here?" I asked.

"I came back for you."

I shook my head. "No, you let me go, remember? You'd grown bored. You had enough of me."

"Why is it so easy for you to believe the lies I fed you but you can't accept the truth?"

I ran fingers through my hair. "You wanted me gone."

"I had to have you gone." He got to his feet and took a few steps toward me.

I held my hand up. "No! You don't get to come here to my carefully organized world and be a part of it. You made your choice. You had your fun. I'm not a virgin anymore, Earl."

"You think I give a fuck about your virginity?"

"You cared enough to want to take it!" I slammed my foot down. I didn't care how childish I might look. He wasn't going to get away with this. I refused to let him.

"Ashley, this isn't about your virginity. You read the article."

"So you're trying to be a hero now?"

"I had to let you go. Your life was in danger. I wasn't going to let you die because of me."

"And what, now my life isn't in danger?"

"The man who was going to hurt you is gone."

"Gone?"

"Dead."

"I can't be hearing this stuff." I turned on my heel, about to walk away. I released a scream as his arms wrapped around me. His face pressed against my neck.

I wanted to hate his touch.

The moment I felt him against me, I melted. Even as I screamed and tried to fight, my body submitted.

For a few blissful seconds, I allowed myself the chance to enjoy him. But it was only a few blissful seconds before the pain returned and there was no way I was going to let him get over this.

I yanked myself away from his arms, taking him by surprise with my fight. Spinning around, I slapped him hard across the face. I only did it once, and he looked at me in shock.

"You don't get to come in here after what you did and pretend everything is okay. You hurt me, Earl."

"I know. I'm going to do everything in my power to make it right, Ashley. I'm not going to leave. I won't hurt you. I'll give you your space, but I'm not going away. I'm here to stay, to be the man you deserve. The man you can fall in love with."

He opened his jacket, and I watched as he removed a single red rose.

So beautiful.

I wanted to tell him to stay. To hold me. I needed to tell him I was pregnant.

I said nothing as he left my apartment.

The silence was deafening. I was alone.

The newspaper clipping was still in my hand.

I didn't know what the fuck was going on anymore.

****

Earl

During the days, Ashley worked at a café. It was a small greasy spoon. Offered good old-fashioned traditional English breakfast, chips, and all the good stuff people seemed to enjoy. There was no smoking allowed on the premises, and signs were displayed for people to see.

I listened to a few grumbles, but no one complained.

Tea was served by the gallon in silver teapots, with little plastic tubs of milk and sachets of sugar for people to make their own drink.

It was charming.

Ashley came in around ten. She wore a pastel-pink uniform, no apron, and her was hair tied back. The women who were cooking had on hairnets. I sat in the corner. There were no booths, no privacy, and the tables were quite close together.

She spotted me immediately.

I watched her close her eyes and she appeared to be counting to ten before she came toward me, a small notepad and pen in her hand. "What can I get you?"

Her accent was cute. A little twang of English softened her tone.

"I'll have the full English," I said. I had no idea what I was ordering. I'd never done breakfast in London before.

"With or without black pudding and mushrooms?" she asked.

"The full works."

"Okay. I'll do you a tea refill."

"Ashley, I want to talk to you."

"Then make an appointment," she said. "I'm busy. I work."

I wanted to reach out and grab her. I gave her space.

She went to a few other tables before taking my order up to the counter. One of the women took it and then started to point at a few tables and gave her hand a shake. Ashley smiled, and then I watched her go start cleaning the tables of the plates that had been left. By the counter, along the opposite wall, were stands where the trays needed to be taken. Clearly, people had left their trays for others to clean up the mess.

I couldn't tear my gaze away from Ashley. She worked efficiently, but I noticed her gaze kept straying to mine. I didn't know if she was annoyed with my presence or just couldn't seem to help it. She was as drawn to me as I was to her.

Being apart these several weeks had been long

enough. I wasn't going to allow her to get away again.

Ashley came back with my pot of tea and my breakfast. The plate was huge. A couple of slices of toast, bacon, sausage, hash browns, fried eggs, beans, tomatoes, mushrooms, and what I assumed was black pudding. All on one plate.

"Enjoy." She turned on her heel and left.

I'd ordered the food. I was going to eat it.

I started on it, and Ashley kept on looking at me.

She didn't work at the café for long. Only a few short hours until after the lunch rush. I finished my breakfast and ordered tea.

The lunch rush came, and when she disappeared, I waited by the staffroom door for her to exit.

She'd been hoping to sneak out before I caught her. She had a tight grip on her bag as she looked at me. "What do you want?"

"To talk. To spend some time with you."

"I've got a doctor's appointment," she said. "Maybe some other time."

She tried to brush past me, but I captured her arm. "Are you sick?"

"No. I'm not sick."

I checked her over, not trusting her opinion. She'd lie to me, and I needed to know if she was okay.

"Damn it, Earl. I'm fine. Clearly, I'm more than fine." She pushed at my arm, and I let her go but got into step beside her.

"Then I'll come to the doctor's with you. I can drive you."

Ashley stopped and turned toward me in the doorway of the café. "No. I can do this on my own."

"Either you get in my car willingly, or I force you."

"You can't do that."

"I can do whatever the hell I want to. Push me. Try me."

She glared at me, stormed out of the café, and stopped on the street. "Tell me then, which one is your car?"

With her arms folded, she looked up and down the street. "I don't see anything."

"I parked around the back." I took her hand, and she didn't fight me.

Pressing the button, I unlocked the car then held the door for her to climb in. She did so, muttering under her breath.

I went to the driver's side, climbed in, and started the ignition.

She gave me directions to her doctor's, but I didn't need them. I'd gotten a thorough background check done on her while she'd been working. I might not had been back in the States, but I still had men at my fingertips, willing to do whatever I needed.

The doctor's surgery was full. I struggled to find a parking space. Ashley kept saying she'd jump out of the car, but I found a spot, and then once I was parked, I followed her into the surgery. She booked herself in, and we took a seat.

"You're not coming in with me," she said.

"I am. I need to make sure you're okay."

I wasn't going to be left alone. I'd fucked up once, and Ashley needed to understand I wasn't going anymore.

People coughed. Some had one leg crossed over the other. Many people were on their cell phones. Others were reading a magazine. The crinkling of the paper offered a distraction.

Ashley's name flashed above the screen.

As much as she hated me right now, she wouldn't

cause a scene, and getting me out of the surgery would require a scene. One I was more than happy to partake in to get what I wanted.

The female doctor was waiting, and the moment we sat down, she asked what seemed to be the problem today.

I waited.

Ashley kept offering me glances.

"I ... er ... I took a couple of tests last night, and I wanted to see if they were accurate."

Tests?

"Pregnancy tests?" the doctor asked.

"Yes."

Everything fucking faded.

I looked at Ashley, and she wouldn't meet my eyes.

Was that where she'd disappeared to? A pharmacy? I only snuck into her apartment, I didn't snoop.

The appointment was a blur. Ashley talked and the doctor took some blood, promising to have the results back very soon.

I was a little dazed. I shook the doctor's hand on the way out.

Neither of us spoke as I got into the car.

Pregnant. It wasn't like I'd attempted to be safe. Every chance I got, I fucked her pussy raw. There was nothing between us, and now there was a chance she could be pregnant.

"Say something," she said.

"Why didn't you tell me last night?"

"I'd just found out myself, and I wasn't exactly in the right frame of mind." Her hands shook, and I watched as she clenched them into fists. "It ... surprised me."

"Do you want to get rid of it?" I asked.

"What? No, of course not."

"Some women do."

"I don't. Okay. I … I'm not sure how I feel right now, but it could be a couple of false positives. I'm sure it has happened before." She shrugged her shoulder. "Can you take me home, please? I need some space."

"I can't give you space."

"Earl, don't do this."

"I just found out that you could be pregnant."

"And you think I wasn't freaking out? I found out before you turned up back in my life. I got to see the stick change, believing my baby's daddy wanted nothing to do with me."

"You should have told me last night. You weren't even going to tell today."

Ashley groaned. "You're right. I didn't know when I was going to tell you, or if I was even going to. The way you dumped me back in Crude Hill, you hurt me, Earl. I … damn it, I was fucking falling in love with you, and you just threw me away because you were done with me, and it hurt. I struggled and I couldn't be back in that place. So I left. I'm trying to make a life here, but I can't stop this feeling. I love you and you hurt me, and it's not going away. Now you're back and I might be pregnant and everything is all so confusing. So please, don't look at me as if you're accusing me of something because right now, I will fucking flip out. I didn't do anything wrong. I'm just surviving."

She sounded like she was falling apart, and I understood her so much. I knew what she was going through.

Sinking my fingers into her hair, I pulled her close and locked my lips against hers, kissing her.

It had been too long since I'd kissed her.

As I slid my tongue across her lips, she opened up for me, and I plunged inside.

She moaned my name. Her hand came to my cheek, and I knew she felt it too. She loved me. She fucking loved *me*. I didn't deserve her love. I wasn't a good man. I relished in others' pain, but hearing her say the words, now that was a sweet victory. One I couldn't deny loving.

Ashley had no idea how fucking obsessed I was with her. The lengths I would go to ensure her safety.

She was my soul mate. The other half of me.

The age gap could go and get fucked.

This woman was mine.

Ashley put her hands on my shoulders. "No," she said. "We have to be sensible. We don't know what's going to happen."

"I don't care, Ashley. Pregnant or not, you will be soon. I'm not letting you go."

"Until when, Earl? When you get bored? When you decide?"

"Never." I stroked my thumb across her cheek. "You need to understand, I'm not going anywhere because this is the only place I want to be." There was nothing anywhere else.

Ashley was my family. My future. My path.

Wherever she went, I would follow.

Chapter Twenty
Ashley

The doctor confirmed the news within a few hours.

I was pregnant with Earl Valentine's baby. We both sat in my apartment, and neither of us had spoken. I'd put the call on speakerphone.

There was so much to be said, and yet, neither of us seemed to be able to get a word out.

After pushing out my chair, I went to the kettle and flicked it back on. Was I even allowed tea?

This all seemed so out of place.

"Marry me," Earl said, taking me by surprise.

I whirled around and saw he stood there, hands clenched at his sides.

"You don't need to propose to me."

"Ashley, you need to understand, this is not me being forced into any kind of situation. I want to marry you. It's why I came back."

"If you were going to propose to me, you would have done it already," I said. I couldn't stop thinking that the only reason he was proposing to me was for the baby. Deep down, I should have been happy he'd be willing to take responsibility, but I wasn't. When I married, I wanted it to be with someone who loved me. Who couldn't imagine another day without me.

Not with someone who felt obligated.

"I know I've fucked up big time with you. I can't take a lot of the shit back that I've done, and I'm sorry. So fucking sorry for everything. You're pregnant with my child, Ashley. That's not going to change, and I don't have time to prove to you how I feel."

Licking my lips, I shook my head. "No."

"Ashley?"

Tears filled my eyes, and I was getting so frustrated with crying. This wasn't fair at all. Being emotional was turning into a curse.

"Look, we've got history. I get that. We're pregnant, but I'm not going to forget you walking away."

"I did that for your own good."

"And because you're back, you expect me to be happy about that?" I asked. "There are a lot of things going on right now. I can't process all of this. You're going to need to give me time."

"I'm raising this kid with you," he said.

"Of course. That's not in question. I want to raise this child with you, and that wasn't a lie. But you've just come back into my life. I don't know if this is even the right thing to say. I'm … having to get used to you, okay? I'm not going to fall into a trap with you."

He stepped close to me, and I held my hand up, but he didn't stop.

My palm touched his chest, and he grabbed my arms, placing a kiss against my head. "I'm not going to let you down. I'm going to prove to you that I'm in love with you, Ashley, and you will be mine."

I got another kiss to the forehead, and then he was gone.

My apartment suddenly felt so empty.

He'd been in my life for a matter of hours, and he'd managed to make my life seem hollow.

Sitting down at the table, I reached for my cell phone and pulled up Emily's number.

I swiped at the tears falling down my cheeks. They had no place.

With a deep breath, I put the cell phone against my ear, and my hands shook slightly.

It was late here, so it had to be slightly earlier there.

The phone kept on ringing, but I didn't hang up.

I waited.

Patiently.

Waiting.

"Ash, hi, is everything okay?" Emily asked.

With my palm flat to the table, I took a deep breath. "Emily, hi," I said.

"What's wrong?"

Silence. I didn't know what to say.

"Ashley, you're scaring me. Is someone there?"

"Earl's here," I said. "He, er, he arrived yesterday. He was waiting for me in my apartment."

"Fuck. I had no idea he was even coming to see you."

"I don't imagine he really cares about giving people the heads-up, you know? He's always been the kind of guy who just does what he wants to and to hell with the consequences." I ran my palm across my table. It was so clean. No roughed-up dry pieces of food.

"What's wrong?"

"Oh, you know, it has been a long couple of days. Earl told me he loved me, and to add to that, I'm pregnant. It has been a pretty hectic couple of days."

"Pregnant?"

"Ah, you heard that part." I rubbed the back of my head. There was so much to take in.

Earl being back was messing with my head. With everything.

Emily let out a squeal. "How far along are you? Is it Earl's, or did you find yourself a hot Brit? Come on, I want details."

I laughed. "I'll try not to be offended, but this is Earl's baby. I've been so busy working. I've got two jobs."

"Ashley, you've been working yourself to the

bone because you've got a broken heart."

"It worked for you."

"Damn it, I don't want you to cry, but I can hear it," Emily said. "Now I'm crying and I can't give you a hug."

"I know you would if you were here." I wrapped an arm across my body, trying to give myself a hug. It didn't exactly work, but just hearing Emily's voice was enough to calm me down. "I can't believe I'm pregnant."

"Wait, a minute, Earl told you he loved you?"

"Yes, and he asked me to marry."

"So why do you sound so sad? Isn't this good news? He's going to do the right thing?"

I sighed. "I don't want him to marry me because of the baby. It doesn't seem right, nor fair."

"Ashley, babe, it's his baby, and you love him, and he told you he loved you."

"I get all of that, I do, but ... if he wanted to marry me, wouldn't he have asked before the baby?" I couldn't help but feel he only asked because of the baby.

Part of me wanted to be happy he'd asked at all, but I didn't want to get married because of a child.

I loved Earl, so damn much. It hurt to be around him. My emotions were all over the place, loving and hating him with equal measure.

It was good to be in his arms. At the same time, I also hated it. This was my time to get over him, and now he was back and I was pregnant. Everything seemed so ... hard.

"Do you realize our kids are going to be close in age?" Emily asked, changing the subject.

This, I could handle.

I released a laugh.

"I know, right."

"Ashley, I know it doesn't seem it right now, but

everything is going to be okay. I've got a feeling."

At this time, I had nothing but the knowledge the only man I'd ever loved was back, and this wasn't over. I was pregnant, and everything was so chaotic, I couldn't trust a single thing.

****

For a week, Earl didn't show up.

Not at my work.

Not at my apartment.

Nor did he appear randomly on the street.

I had him for approximately twenty-four hours, tops, and he was gone. I'd already booked my appointment at the maternity ward at the local hospital. The doctor had called back the following day to give me all the details of what I needed to do next.

My appointment wasn't for another couple of days. I had no way of reaching Earl to let him know. He was the dad and had a right to be there at each appointment.

After a long shift at the restaurant and trying not to throw up, I was more than happy to get back to my apartment. I'd removed my jacket and toed off my boots, heading into the kitchen when my door was knocked.

I removed the band at the back of my neck, loosening my hair. I needed a bath, food, and some sleep.

Opening the door, I stopped when I caught sight of Earl. He looked good. A pristine suit, his hair slicked back, but it didn't appear to have any gel in it.

"Earl," I said. "What are you doing here?"

I should have been screaming at him for abandoning me again. For leaving me alone to deal with everything. The truth was, I wasn't the kind of woman to hold a grudge for long. I'd already sent Caleb and the rest of the Monsters a gift basket. A personal card to Caleb, apologizing for blaming him for everything that had gone wrong.

I'd been angry, hurt, and heartbroken. When he'd been trying to talk to me, I'd wanted someone to blame, and it was so easy to put it on him. He'd put me in Earl's path, but I was the one to fall in love with him.

"I want you to come with me. There's something I need to show you."

"Can it wait?"

"No. Once this is over, I'll have to wait for the next one." He held out his hand.

Something in his voice told me to follow him. I quickly put my shoes back on, even as my feet cried at the injustice of it all, and I went with him to his car.

I had no idea where we were going until we ended up at a dock near the south. Earl tapped his fingers on the steering wheel as he looked ahead.

Following his gaze, I saw a whole load of cop cars.

"What's going on, Earl?" I asked.

He climbed out of the car and rounded the vehicle, opening my door and holding out his hand.

I placed mine within his and climbed out of the car.

Earl wrapped his arm around my shoulder, and the cops allowed him to go past. I didn't like this. My heart raced.

We came to a stop near several containers, and that was when I saw it. A cargo hold had been open. Women were spread out. Ambulances were close by, and six men were on the ground, in handcuffs.

"Should you be here?" I asked.

This was part of Earl's life. Why would he bring me here? He was going to get arrested. He'd pissed me off. Made me angry and hate him, but the last thing I wanted was for him to be arrested.

Fear worked its way up my spine as each police officer passed. This was too much. I fisted his jacket.

"Let's go before they arrest you," I said.

I couldn't have him thrown in jail. I loved him so fucking much, and it hurt being around him and knowing there was a chance he was only saying all the right things for the baby. But I just couldn't do it.

There was no way I was going to be able to survive without him.

One of the officers seemed like a serious-looking man, high up in the ranking.

I felt sick to my stomach as he approached and held out his hand. "Thank you, Mr. Valentine, for your full cooperation."

I was still tense as they shook hands. The officer nodded at me, and then we were alone.

I let Earl go and looked toward the officer. This wasn't ... why weren't they arresting Earl?

"I think you've seen enough." Earl took my hand and led me back to the car. I sat inside, staring out at the chaos before me.

All this time, a little taken aback.

Was this real?

They weren't going to arrest Earl.

He pulled out of the docks, and we drove for a short time, coming to a stop near a rundown side-road café.

He didn't turn the engine off.

The sounds of the engine filled the air.

What had I just witnessed?

I licked my dry lips and glanced toward Earl.

He stared right at me.

"Do you want to tell me what is going on?" I asked. "They didn't arrest you. Those girls were yours."

"No, they weren't mine. In fact..." He reached

into his pocket. "I don't deal in women anymore. I've removed all parts of human trafficking from my life, and I've got a lot to make up for." He held out a file.

I took it and flicked through it, not understanding any of it. "What is this?"

"This is a document. A legally binding agreement that I signed. I'm going to help stop human trafficking. I don't imagine we'll ever truly stop it, but with my contacts, I'm going to be working undercover as a buyer to expose the men responsible."

"This is crazy. What about all of your other businesses? Your way of life?"

"I've been working to get out of it, Ashley."

"I don't believe you." This was a lot to take in.

"You will be the last woman I ever take. I hope in time you can learn to forgive me. I love you so damn much, and it wasn't just your virginity I wanted. Seven years ago, I saw you at a party. You stood out. So sweet. You had an easy smile. No matter that people were avoiding you or ignoring you. You gave them all a smile. I watched you. Not Emily. She was a business agreement, but you, you were like a fucking beacon calling to me. I had to have you."

"You did?"

"Yes, I did. Then of course there was a great deal of unsavory business. Work needed to be handled, and I had to make sure you were safe. The threat on Emily's and your life, it wasn't one I couldn't handle. I had to keep you all safe. First, I needed to guarantee a plan that would make you mine."

"You planned all of this?" I asked.

"I didn't plan everything. I wanted you, Ashley. I never thought I'd fall so deeply in love with you that I'd change my entire existence. My goal had always been for me to prove to my grandfather that I was better. To take his business into the next level, and I did that, with ease." He ran a hand down his face. "I was crueler than he was, but I changed the way he did business. You already knew that there were ... he didn't believe in an age restriction when taking and selling people."

I remembered him telling me.

"You deserve a man you can love. A man you can look at every single day and be so fucking proud to have known him. I can't promise you I'm going to always be a good man. I will still kill people who get in my way, but I'm changing to be the man you deserve. I love you, Ashley."

I reached across the car, put my hand to his cheek, and kissed him. I couldn't not.

He loved me.

The words didn't matter at this point, but what he'd done couldn't be questioned. A lifetime of hurting others, and he'd turned it all around for me. The tears on my cheeks were those of happiness.

"Earl, I loved you even before tonight. It's why I had to leave Crude Hill. I was so in love with you, and everywhere I looked, you were there. It hurt too much to have fallen for you. You didn't need to change who you were. I was learning to accept that part of you."

"I'm not going back. I will make amends for all the women I've hurt." He stroked my cheek. "And I'll do it for you and our baby."

I laughed.

"Ask me again," I said.

He smiled at me and ran his thumb across my lip. "Marry me."

No hesitation. No wondering.

"Yes," I said.

How could I turn down a man who'd changed his entire life for me? He loved me and I loved him. We were going to make this work.

He kissed me, and I submitted to him.

"Just so you know, I consider your yes a legally binding contract, and if you so much as try to back out, I'll keep Emily and all the Monsters."

I burst out laughing. "Yeah, right. That would have worked if I hadn't already known the beast had been tamed."

"Only for you and our family. I will not stand by and let anything bad happen to you, or to us."

"I know."

Earl was the tamed beast for me, but if anyone tried to hurt me, they would have to deal with the true evil lurking beneath the surface.

For everyone's sake, I hoped they left us in peace.

Epilogue
Earl

Five years later

"I hate boats."

"It's a yacht, babe," I said.

"It's a very large boat."

Even as Ashley held on to my arm, I couldn't help but smile. Five years we'd been married. Our anniversary was tomorrow. Our two children were currently in the care of Emily and the Monsters at Crude Hill. I didn't like leaving them behind, neither did Ashley, but I wanted to spend some time with my woman when we weren't invaded by the patter of little feet and screams for Mommy and Daddy to wake up.

Our first child, Corey, was such a sweetheart, and had come into this world causing a few problems.

Ashley's first pregnancy had held a whole host of complications. She had ended up bed-bound for the last few months of pregnancy, on doctor's orders. It had made her incredibly cranky and such a fucking pain to be around. Still, I loved her, and our son was a shining light in our life.

Two years later, Athena had been born. Our precious little baby girl. Her pregnancy had been easy.

We'd settled in England. Ashley wanted us to have a fresh start, and I'd already been in the process of buying us a house. Emily and her men visited us regularly, and we went to Crude Hill a couple of times a year.

I never thought I'd fall in love or feel this way about anyone, but Ashley was different.

She was all mine, and I was hers.

I continued to run my empire. Building it from strength to strength. I didn't need any of the other businesses, and I worked alongside law enforcement whenever they needed me. Going fully legal hadn't come without risks. I had enemies, and I made sure my wife and children were protected at all costs. The Monsters back in Crude Hill were also protected. Their lives were not up for questioning within relation to me or what I do.

Life was a balancing act, but Ashley was worth it.

Some people believed I'd become a pussy with a wife.

I hadn't.

I was far deadlier than ever before, and there were at least three people who were now dead who could have told everyone. During the first year, my wife received death threats, and one day, I came home to find someone in our house. I'd killed them without Ashley ever finding out, and I'd buried what was left of the body.

Each time people thought to take me on, they were fools to try.

My professional life had taken a turn, but that didn't mean the beast lurking beneath me was gone.

Only Ashley and my babies got to see a good man. Everyone else got to see the real me, the man they all deserved to see.

Once I was in position, I removed Ashley's blindfold. She blinked against the full beam of light. We were out on the ocean. There were several clear days scheduled. I wanted my wife, naked, waiting for me, and with no chance of kids asking what their daddy was doing to their mommy.

A few mornings that had happened, and a couple of nights. I'd been so fucking close, and my kids were cock blockers, but I loved them.

"Hello, Mrs. Valentine." I pressed a kiss to her neck.

She tilted her head back and moaned. "Yes."

"I want you to get completely naked and spread those legs for me. I'm totally taking you right here, right now."

"Anyone could see," she said.

I growled against her flesh. "Haven't I proven to you that no one but me will see you? No one will look at you or know. They will have to answer to me."

She groaned as I cupped her pussy. She was already so wet. "I love you, Earl."

"I love you too."

By the end of this anniversary, I intended to knock her up. It was time she had another kid. Each baby we had bound her more firmly to me.

I was an obsessive guy, and when I knew what I wanted, I went for it. Ashley was mine, and no one else was ever going to know what fucking treasure they all gave up.

Mine.

The End

BESTSELLING BBW ROMANCE
SPICY ROMANCE FOR REAL WOMEN

SAM CRESCENT

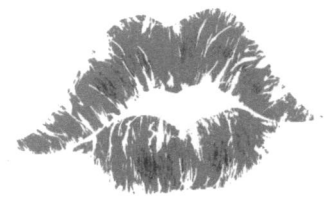

EVERNIGHT PUBLISHING ®

www.evernightpublishing.com